Secrets Ever Green

The Everlight Series

Book One

Sara Knightly

Portal Publishing, LLC. Boise, ID.

Cover design Krafig Designs

Paperback ISBN: 979-8-9894891-0-7

Library of Congress control number: 2023921295

To learn more about the author please visit saraknightlybooks.com and join the newsletter.

For Kennedy Rae—
My drop of golden sun

ONE

The worst part of my life was pretending to be something I wasn't.

I sighed, nudging Loon deeper through the ferns and farther into the forest. She neighed softly, brushing her nose against the foliage in search of something to nibble on. As we moved beneath webs of branches, I lifted my eyes to search for what I needed to go home.

If I was who everyone thought I was, we would already be gone. But we had been wandering now for hours, and were much deeper into the woods than I'd intended.

I was just glad no one could see me.

Because no one, not even my instructor Mr. Everett, knew how little I understood the trade I was working to inherit. As the daughter of the town's leading Arborist, I should know the differences between species and possess the instinct to help plants grow, but I couldn't and I didn't. And Adeline Rose was the only reason no one knew.

Adeline should have been my father's daughter. His protégé.

When we were first partnered in class, she assumed, like everybody else did, that my father had already taught me everything. Adeline spent the entire class blurting out answers before I could and asking me if she was right. I nodded, gratefully hiding my ignorance while agreeing with all her solutions. Because of her, our wilted plants bloomed and our pruned trees grew stronger than anyone else's. We fell into a pattern of Adeline suggesting and me approving. To this day, I couldn't believe she didn't realize how little I contributed.

But today I was on my own. For part of our final test, we each had to forage for a truly rare plant. In a few days, everyone would present their specimen to the class. If I didn't find something spectacular, everyone would finally see I had been faking it all along. I would fail the test.

I would be eliminated from my father's trade.

I would lose everything he left me.

His shop Forest and Fern, his research, our home. It would all be given to another Arborist.

And I would have nothing.

My stomach dropped at the thought.

As the afternoon light softened between the leaves, I imagined myself continuing down this path and never returning to the small town behind me. The town I had been born in, but never truly fit into.

I had Loon with me; I could leave the pressure of walking in my father's footsteps behind. Footsteps that could never be filled, especially not by me. I could find a place where I could be myself. Discover if there were people like me, who hoped for something to happen that would disrupt their mundane days. Something extraordinary.

I stamped that dangerous thinking out immediately. I wasn't a person who left others. I wasn't like *her*. Besides, York would never forgive me if I left him behind. Even if I felt discontent with my life, I was grateful to my best friend, who made it better. I could live this life. I just needed to find one rare plant in this endless forest. If I couldn't do that, then I truly didn't deserve to become an Arborist.

I slipped off Loon and walked down the path a little further, hoping nature would be kind and reveal something to me. Then, that same prickle rose on my neck and the feeling that I wasn't alone stole over me.

My heartbeat quickened as I glanced around. Loon continued nibbling at the grass, unconcerned. I didn't see anything besides birds fluttering above, or hear anything more than the scampering of small feet, so I tried to brush the feeling away. I wasn't usually nervous in the forest, but this was the second time I'd sensed an unseen presence. It was why I'd brought Loon with me today.

We reached a place where the branches overhead curled away, leaving a sunny patch of grass beneath a stretch of sky. It was so unexpected that I forgot my nerves and stared around me. A tall leafy plant with tiny yellow flowers was growing in the sunlight. The flowers burst apart in a wide bouquet that was unlike any flower pattern I'd seen. Hope fluttered through me as I walked up to it. Surely this plant was something special. I reached forward to pluck a yellow flower—

"Don't touch that!"

I gasped, my heart slamming into my chest. Loon whirled around with me and reared at the man standing behind us.

"Don't let your horse touch it either," he warned. "Unless you both want a rash that eats away at your skin and blisters and scars. That sap can blind you too."

"What is it?" My voice shook.

"It's wild parsnip. Did you touch it?"

I looked down at my trembling hands. "Almost, but no."

"Good," he said, after a long pause.

I studied him as my ragged breathing slowed and tried to assess the situation. He stared back with serious blue eyes. His silver hair was pulled back at the base of his neck. Not exactly threatening, but definitely different from anyone in town. He seemed part of the woods in a way I had only felt about my father. My chest constricted at the thought, but I brushed the feeling away.

"You're sure that's what it was?" I risked looking away from him to ensure Loon hadn't stepped into the plant either. Maybe Mr. Everett would be impressed with something like this.

"Yes." He studied me for a moment before a look passed over his face. "But you should have known that, I think."

I bristled. His words felt accusatory even though I knew he couldn't have meant it like that. He didn't know me, after all. "Why? Is it common?" I asked.

"Common enough." There was another long pause, like he wasn't used to the filling silence with words. "But you look like someone I know."

"Oh?"

"An old friend. Philip Rune."

I startled. "He was my father."

He nodded as if he had already come to that conclusion. "Your eyes are the same."

I frowned. That wasn't true. My eyes were green; my father's were dark brown. In fact, the only time anyone mentioned my mother was to say I looked like her, not my father.

"I meant their intensity is the same," he said, seeing my reaction. "His were brown."

I nodded, relaxing slightly. "Yes."

"Then, you are . . . Ivy?" he said as if he were reaching very far back into his memory.

Goosebumps prickled my skin. "Did my father tell you that?"

He inclined his head in response. The only sound was the leaves shimmering gently as the wind blew through them. I shifted uncomfortably. Why would he remember my name after all these years? We had never met.

"How did you know him?" I finally asked.

His expression sharpened. "You said *did* . . . Something happened to him after all, then?"

My breath caught. No one had asked me about my father in years, but it was the *way* he asked . . . Like he had expected something to happen.

I gripped Loon's reins tighter. "He died."

He shook his head. "You mean disappeared?"

I shook my head right back. "No, he died."

"Was his body found?"

My mouth dropped open. "No."

"Did they look?"

"Of course. For weeks."

"If you didn't find his remains, how do you know he died?"

"There was a bad storm. They told me there was no possibility of anyone surviving . . ." I hadn't spoken those words out loud in years. The blood seemed to drain from my body, leaving me cold all over as I imagined my father dying in the woods he loved.

The man studied the forest around us before he said, "Except Rune wasn't anyone. He knew the woods better than even I do."

I stared, stunned and unsure of what to say. Part of me doubted that this man really didn't know my father had died. Things like this traveled easily in Windermere. But he also didn't look like someone who came to town often. Before I could respond, his next question shocked me again.

"So you believed them?"

"I was *seven*." My voice was cold as I drew out the word, warning him that he was going too far. "A child. So yes, I believed them."

"Seven." He rubbed his chin as if *this* was the worst news of all. "I didn't realize how much time had passed. It's been a while since I've seen Rune." He squinted back at me. "Then you are . . . what? Sixteen?"

"Seventeen." My voice shook slightly. He didn't seem upset to know my father had died. If anything, he seemed more worried about the ten years that had passed.

York would tell me to leave if he were here, but part of me wanted to know everything this man knew about my father. Something about how he spoke my father's name felt like he did know him. And there was so much about my father that *I* still didn't know.

"Sometimes, a year would go by and your father was the only one I had talked to," he said in his slow way.

That was not what I expected him to say. A sliver of sympathy thawed me. "What's your name?" I asked.

He hesitated before answering. "Nicholas."

"I've never heard of you. Do you live in Windermere?"

He shook his head. "I live out here. Alone."

My brow rose. "In the forest?"

He nodded.

"Don't you get lonely?" I asked, curiosity overtaking my fear.

His blue eyes bore into me. "You live in town, among people at all times. Don't *you* ever get lonely?"

I froze, wondering if he saw the truth in my face. Except for my friendship with York, I had always felt lonely.

He nodded, lifting his eyes to the trees around us. "I did too. But being out here changed that. There is no *should do, should be.* Out here, I just am."

I absorbed his words, thinking they sounded like something my father would have said.

As if he read my mind again, he said, "I met your father out here. He researched so often he practically lived out here too."

I nodded. That was true enough. "What did you talk about?"

"First, the forest. The trees, of course. Then, slowly, our lives. Our families. We'd each lost people along the way. It leaves a mark."

I swallowed. "It does."

Nicholas's eyes looked haunted by memories. He didn't speak for a long time.

"Did he ever talk about me?" I finally asked, breaking the silence.

Nicholas rubbed his neck. He looked unsure of how to phrase what he wanted to say. After another long pause, he said, "Yes. And of this moment."

A feeling of alarm slid down my back. "Which moment?"

He hesitated, before saying, "You're old enough now, I suppose."

"Old enough for what?" I inched closer to Loon.

"For something your father gave me. To keep safe."

I frowned, unable to believe my father had anything he needed to keep safe. And if he did, why would he give it to someone I had never heard of?

"He made me promise to keep it. And make sure you got it if he ever went missing."

"He thought he might go missing?" My voice was just above a whisper. This was becoming too strange. "What is it?"

"I'm sorry I didn't know sooner. But maybe it's best this way. You would have been too young before now."

"What is it?" I repeated through clenched teeth.

Nicholas looked down at his hands, rubbing a spot of dirt off his palm with his thumb. "He also said you need to bring me something."

"Right. I'm leaving now." I turned and hoisted myself up into the saddle before he could blink. "Goodbye, Nicholas."

"A knobby owl? Your mother's owl? I think that's what he said. Seemed so odd to me at the time. Still is, I guess."

The breath knocked out of me as I steadied Loon's restless stamping. She could feel my fear and wanted to leave too. "What did you say?"

Nicholas peered up at me. "Rune said, have *Ivy bring the owl and then give her what I left*. The owl doesn't mean a thing to me, but maybe you'll understand."

"You couldn't know about that owl unless my father really told you."

Nicholas held my gaze before his eyes shifted back to the trees. Was he lying or was he just uncomfortable talking this long?

"I'll go get what he gave me. Meet me back here tomorrow and it's yours. Same time."

My mother's owl. There was no one else who knew about it. No one.

"I'll think about it." My voice didn't sound as strong as I hoped.

Nicholas nodded. "I'll be here regardless." Without waiting for me to respond, he turned back into the forest. I watched him silently as he vanished within the trees.

Shaking, I turned Loon around and we flew back through the woods. I didn't want to think about anything until I was safe at home.

But if there was one part of being an Arborist I did understand, it was seeds.

Seeds wanted to grow.

So by the time I reached the edge of town, Nicholas's words had planted a seed in my mind that had burrowed and grown roots.

Now I couldn't think of anything else except what my father had needed to keep secret.

From everyone.

Including me.

Two

L oon raced out of the woods and slowed to a walk as we came upon the crossroads.

Continuing south would take us right into the heart of Windermere, and west would take us out to the Taylor's land, where I'd lived since my father died.

I could see the lights of the small town twinkling against the navy sky, the brown cluster of rooftops, and beyond that, the white sails of ships on the sea. To the east were the grey spindly towers of the Count's castle, buried in the tops of trees. It was the most anyone saw of his property.

The owl. It had been years since I saw it. There was a chance it was still in my father's old shop, Forest and Fern. But that place had been locked since the night my father died, and no one had been allowed back inside. In a surprisingly generous move, the Count had ordered the shop—and my childhood home above it —to remain untouched until I took my Arborist test. If I passed, Forest and Fern would be mine.

I had spent years thinking about it, and now my final test was just two weeks away.

Anxiety tightened my chest. I'd never worked harder for anything. I didn't want to move to another trade or lose my childhood home, but I never thought it would be so hard to make plants grow. Worry kept me awake most nights as I imagined losing everything that should easily be mine.

I shook myself out of those fears. It was too late for me to check Forest and Fern now. It was growing darker and I would need to break in. Someone would see the light inside. And the thought of doing anything more today was exhausting, so I turned down the path towards the Taylor's.

I didn't know anything about breaking into buildings. I would need York's help. I'd find him tomorrow. Tonight, my head was too full of Nicholas's words.

Now that I was safely on my familiar path back home, Nicholas's claims seemed less ominous and more crazy. Was I really going to believe him, and go back tomorrow to see if he had something? That was foolish. Reckless. Especially when the biggest test of my life—the *one* thing that decided my future—was looming over me. All I should be doing was finding my plant and studying.

For years, nothing else consumed me, but now I couldn't seem to shake what Nicholas had said. If he did have something from my father, I wanted it. And why would he assume my father wasn't dead? Why had my father thought something might happen to him? And why was I allowing myself to think something had?

My father was dead.

But . . .

It wouldn't be so unbelievable to think that he might have left something behind, like a last wish. My father lived a well-organized, planned-out existence. Everything about his life and death had been neatly tied up. There were no loose ends.

Unless . . .

No. I flicked that thought away quickly before it could bloom. Still, it snaked around my head like an unrelenting weed.

I had to admit, it was possible that whatever had happened with *her* caused my father to worry about himself. To be even more cautious about my future. I could imagine him in the woods, nurturing the trees and plants, but being distracted by my mother. She was the one thing that no amount of research could help him understand.

She was the loose end.

So, maybe out of his frustration, he had asked Nicholas to keep something, should he die, so I would have no questions about him. He would not allow himself to be a mystery to me too.

Yes, that made some sense. If my father did give something to Nicholas for me, it was only out of extra planning and thoughtfulness, nothing strange. So I should find out what Nicholas had. If there was something my father wanted in his death, I would do it. Just like I was preserving his legacy and working to follow in his footsteps as an Arborist.

I wouldn't let him down. Not like she had.

Up ahead, tucked deep within the purple lavender fields, the Taylor's stone house glowed against the twilight. I stopped at the stables and settled Loon in for the night, with extra carrots, before I began the long walk up to the house.

Ignoring the winding dirt path around the field, I made my way straight through the neat rows of purple flowers, inhaling the deep scent of florals and earth. My hand brushed over the rough stems as I pushed all other thoughts from my mind and allowed the walk to calm me.

I'd done this many times in the last ten years and it always helped me, even on my hardest days. This, and riding Loon. I was grateful that I had been placed here with close friends of my father. This wasn't my real home, but it had become a peaceful refuge.

As I stepped out onto the grass of the front lawn, every light from the house greeted me. To my dismay, the two front rooms were full of people. My hand instinctively reached up to smooth my hair and clothes. I knew I didn't look the way Mrs. Taylor would want me to in front of guests, so I quickly slid into the shadows and moved around to the back of the house.

But when I walked through the back door, the smell of roasting meat and spices made my stomach grumble. Unable to resist, I grabbed a roll from the empty kitchen and hurried up the back stairs before anyone spotted me.

I passed four empty rooms that had once belonged to the Taylor's children, who were now grown and lived in town with families of their own. They each helped run Taylor's Mercantile, which sold food from the family farm. My room was at the end of the hall, the smallest in the house, but I didn't mind. I was grateful not to live alone, and I loved the simplicity of the white walls, cozy bed, dresser, and best of all, the large window that overlooked Loon's field from my bedside. I'd filled my room with items I collected, just like my old home had been full of all the things my father collected.

His things were still in the apartment above Forest and Fern. In a few weeks, I would either move back in or lose it completely. What would happen if I failed? Would the Taylors keep me, or would I be out on my own?

I crossed the room, unable to worry about any of that now. I pulled my father's old leather satchel out from under the bed. The leather was cracked and fading, but the handles still gleamed—maybe from the oils on his hand, I thought. I swallowed, remembering him using this satchel my entire life.

It had been years since I'd opened this satchel. Inside were all the things that were truly important to me. Things that belonged in our old house, not in this temporary room. Not that I wasn't grateful, but I'd always known this wasn't my home and was never intended to be. When I moved back into our family home, I would finally take these items out of the satchel and put them back in the spots I had taken them from the night my world imploded.

I sat on the bed and opened the bag. On top were three old books bound together with twine. I unwrapped the twine and flipped one open, even though I knew the pages were blank. That was the only reason I was allowed to have them—they contained no important Arborist research. My father's other books, crammed with notes, were still in his office. As I flipped through the thin pages, something fluttered out and swirled to the ground.

The petals of a white orchid, now pressed flat and wilted.

If I closed my eyes, I could still recall the way the earthy, vanilla smell clung to our furniture and walls. My father kept orchids all over our house and his study. His Arborist work focused mainly on trees, but his passion was white orchids. They didn't grow naturally around Windermere, so every summer he sourced seeds from the visiting merchants that flooded into town. The pots in Forest and Fern now sat empty.

Waiting to see if they would be filled again. Just like me.

I picked up the pressed flower gently and laid it back in the pages, closing the books. I dug into the bag again and pulled out a brown paper sack holding a dozen orchid seeds that I had taken from my father's shop—well, stolen really, but no one noticed. They were all carefully separated into their own paper bags, so they would last until I could plant them. I knew nothing about orchids, but maybe someday, I would know enough to fill those pots again.

I put the seeds next to the books.

Next out was a tiny, white jewelry box carved by Mr. Gable, Windermere's most prestigious Carver, and my friend, Percy's, father. He'd generously gifted it to me on my last birthday. It was so delicate and lovely that I kept it wrapped in the box. I set that to the side too as I reached in again for the oval-shaped lump of wood that might be at the bottom.

It wasn't there.

Frowning, I rummaged around more but still didn't find it.

It must be in Forest and Fern, then. I truly never realized I'd left it.

I sighed and rubbed my forehead. If I decided to bring that owl to Nicholas, I would have to break in sometime after class tomorrow and before the afternoon.

I sat back and looked out the large window to the distant

mountains and forests, lost in thought as I mindlessly picked at my roll. I imagined walking into my old house again, being among my father's belongings, and getting the owl.

I wasn't sure how long I sat there lost in the past until I realized I should be studying. I couldn't let myself be distracted now. Too much hung on the next few days and time was running out. But here I was thinking about a stranger and plotting to break into the Count's property. I didn't even want to think what would happen to me if I was caught. Was I going to risk everything I'd worked for?

I rose, getting undressed for bed. Then I settled beneath the covers, hoping to fall asleep quickly. But as the moonlight streamed in through my window, creating familiar shadows on the walls, I couldn't help but feel something else. A small part of me imagined that tomorrow something extraordinary would happen. That another path would open up for me. Something that would make sense of why I didn't fit in with any trade, or, really, with anything else here.

I closed my eyes and imagined the sea that touched the shores of Windermere. I couldn't hear the relentless pounding of waves here on the farm, but they had always filled the background of my life when I lived in town. Now, I couldn't help but feel that the waves of my life were crashing onto some unknown shore.

Where a new future might lay.

THREE

The smell of bacon and freshly baked bread greeted me as I made my way down the sunlit stairs.

Mrs. Taylor was in the kitchen, standing by the big iron stove. Her white hair was swept into an elegant bun and her dress was crisp as always beneath her checkered blue apron.

"There you are. I thought you snuck in sometime last night." She turned and wiped her hands on her apron, inspecting my uniform.

I straightened, even though I knew she wouldn't find fault with my appearance today. My white button-up shirt, brown skirt, and wool tweed vest were each clean and pressed. And my tall brown boots gleamed. She nodded once and turned her attention back to the stove.

"Sorry I didn't say good night," I apologized. "It was such a long day and I didn't look presentable after walking through the woods."

She waved a spoon at me. "Nothing to apologize for. You're not required to check in with us, you know that. Besides, the men's meeting went long and we women had enough to gossip about with all the new ships docking this week without bothering you for news." She looked back at me. "Would you like breakfast before class?"

"Yes, please." My mouth was already watering at the smell wafting towards me.

"Here. You must be starving after skipping dinner."

I took the full plate to the table and sat, fanning a napkin over my lap. I bit into a piece of bacon and savored the way it melted and crunched in my mouth. It tasted even better than it smelled.

Mrs. Taylor set a cup of coffee in front of me, already a beautiful caramel color with cream. "I assume you found your plant yesterday, then?"

The bacon turned to sawdust in my mouth. I swallowed quickly. "Um, actually I didn't."

"Isn't this the last week? And you haven't found anything?" Her tone was light, but a frown creased her face.

Fresh panic filled me at the thought of another day slipping by. Why was I even entertaining the idea of breaking into my old house and meeting Nicholas?

"Nothing is unique enough," I said, carefully.

Her brow cleared. "Ah. Well, that's to be expected. You have high standards, of course, being raised by your father. Don't be too picky though."

I nodded. "I'll try not to be."

"Then you'll go out again after class today?"

I paused between bites, thinking that maybe I could search for a plant and meet Nicholas at the same time. Two birds, one stone. "Yes. And I plan on asking York to come too. In case I need help carrying it back."

"Speaking of him, that reminds me. Look what I found." She reached into her pocket and pulled out a small wooden statue of a horse. Not just any horse—Loon. Carved by York, years ago.

"I thought I lost that!" I plucked the smooth figure from her hand.

It was one of York's first carvings, so it wasn't perfect, but it was special all the same. "See how he nearly cut off the tail?" I grinned, remembering how York had nearly jumped out of his skin, thinking his father was about to catch him whittling when he should have been working. That wiped the smile from my face.

Mrs. Taylor watched the emotions play across my face. "I'm glad you two have each other. I know you feel strongly about him."

I turned the figure over in my hands. "York's my best friend. Of course I care about him."

Mrs. Taylor hesitated. Then, as if she couldn't hold it in any longer, said, "Are you sure there couldn't be something more between you two?"

Apparently, I wasn't the only one wondering about my future. "York and I are only friends. As I've said before."

"Mm-hmm." She walked back to the stove. The room quieted to the sound of her spoon stirring eggs and me gulping my cooling coffee. Now I couldn't get through this breakfast fast enough.

I ate faster. "I'll probably be in late tonight too. I can't be the last one to bring in a plant."

"You're not. I passed others in your class in town yesterday. Nearly half are still looking too."

"But everyone expects more from me." I clamped my lips shut, surprised that I'd admitted this out loud. *I must be more stressed than I realized*, I thought.

Mrs. Taylor stopped stirring and looked at me thoughtfully. "Becoming an Arborist is one path, Ivy. One your father certainly wanted for you, but it is not the only one. Most girls marry and don't need to worry about a trade at all. Family becomes their purpose."

I nodded, my heart sinking a little at the thought of giving up so easily. "I know, but I want to do this. If I don't, everything my father accomplished ends with me."

"You've grown into a respectable young person. Any parent would be proud of that in their child, even if that was all they accomplished."

I flushed at the rare compliment, unsure how to respond. I knew that Mrs. Taylor valued her place as a wife and mother over everything, and if I didn't accomplish that too, I would also disappoint her. Even if she would never say it.

"Is this all that's worrying you?" she asked. "You seem unsettled."

"Yes, that's all." I stood as my cheeks burned with guilt. I wouldn't tell her about my encounter with Nicholas. Or that I was considering meeting him again. Or that I planned on breaking into my father's shop.

Maybe I was wrong to keep it to myself. Maybe I should get an adult perspective on this, but I didn't want to risk her telling me I shouldn't go. This was my decision.

Since it had to do with my family, it was something only I could decide.

———

The smell of sugar and rising dough from Wilder's Bakery, mixed with the salt from the sea, brought back every good memory of living in town when I was a child.

I could hear the crashing of water from the fountain before I turned the corner. It sat in the middle of the town square, the stone ship high in the air, spilling water down into the basin below. The symbol of the Count's trade with other lands. But even with its impressive size, it did not hold anyone's eye for long.

For lined around the town square were what the merchants braved the summer sea for. The prestigious shops of Windermere. These wooden shops were works of art themselves; intricately carved fronts, ornate shutters, spindled columns, and charming steps leading up to wide porches. Each building stretched two stories up and leaned snugly against its neighbor as if they were all exhaling. The Count's silver crest was carved deeply into every door, and flower baskets hung from the second-floor windows above.

A few assistants were outside sweeping and dusting off signs. The buildings gleamed, their wood shining from fresh coats of sealant. Soon, merchants would begin pouring in from the single road that led down to the harbor and the inn. It was easy to spot them. We locals wore the colored vests of our trades, but merchants decorated themselves in rich fabrics of vibrant colors. Sometimes I thought we looked like plain ducks mingling with colorful peacocks.

Only merchants invited by the Count were able to visit Windermere in the summer. They sought items handmade by our Carvers. Fine wood combs; beads and jewelry; buttons; broaches; boxes; all kinds of furniture; and, of course; statues. The Carving trade was not only the backbone of our economy, but many considered it the soul of Windermere. It was Carving that breathed new life into the town every summer and put bread on the tables of every family for the following year. Items here were unique, hard to acquire, and considered heirlooms and treasures to all other lands.

I turned down one of the narrow alleys that extended like the spokes of a wheel to the other parts of town. My old home, Forest and Fern, was just a few streets further, but I turned and headed to The Hidden Thorn, the only Arborist teaching shop in Windermere.

It sat at the end of the street. This building was painted a deep Arborist green and had more windows than any other shop in town. I stepped into the wide vaulted room that smelled more of moss, dirt, and pine than the real forest did. Curving branches of trees pushed against the high ceiling and vines snaked between pillars. Our teacher, Mr. Everett, encouraged the plants to abandon their pots and grow out into the room.

Most of the stools in the room were already taken. It seemed that all of my classmates had come early to claim a seat that had not yet been overtaken by a newly potted plant. I picked my way through living green walls and managed to find a small table not yet claimed in the back.

After setting my things down, I glanced over at the newest wall of plants. I was shocked to find that over half the class had already found their specimen. My heart sank as I realized that many of the pots were filled with plants I couldn't identify. I didn't even think I would have looked twice at any of them in the woods. I was doomed.

I looked to the front of the room, where Mr. Everett's wooden desk sat. It was overrun with books about herbs and mushrooms, but his chair was empty.

"Don't you just love the smell of fresh loam in new pots?" Adeline asked, setting her books on the only open space beside me.

My eyes returned to where the plants were. "Not really."

When she didn't answer, I looked back at her. Adeline was staring at me, her brown eyes wide and confused.

I shrugged and quickly said, "I guess I prefer the forest where everything grows as it should."

Her expression turned to understanding. "Oh, I get it. You're a purist. Like your father, you think nature should grow where it is and we should go to it, not bring it here."

I ducked my head so she wouldn't see me flush. *No,* I thought. *I just like that I don't have to take care of them, because they take care of themselves.*

"We match today," Adeline said, sounding pleased.

I couldn't help but laugh. "We always match." I gestured around the room. All of us were in our trade uniforms. Our student vests were brown tweed, the color of bark. But those who became Arborists would wear a beautiful hunter-green vest.

Trade positions usually stayed in families, but that didn't mean someone was guaranteed a position. If a student failed, they were dismissed and given a white vest, void of color so everyone would know they needed a position. Another trade could offer a position, but only if one was available. (It usually wasn't.) If a student didn't get a new trade, then they had no way to make an income except by doing work beneath a trade. Work for people without talent. Sometimes merchants offered positions, but that meant leaving Windermere and family behind, so such offers were rarely accepted.

"No, our hair," Adeline was saying. "I wore mine down too."

"Oh. It looks nice." I said, noticing her hair wasn't pulled up like usual.

"Thanks." She brushed her shiny brown hair off her shoulder and sat. "Where's your specimen? I put mine over there yesterday." She pointed to the wall where a plant taller than any other stood proudly in the largest pot. "My dad had to help me carry it, it was so heavy."

I stared at her plant dumbly, imagining her father helping her. Of them doing it together.

I didn't have anyone to help me.

I didn't even have a plant.

"So, where's yours?" Adeline asked again.

My throat closed up. I didn't know what her plant was, and I couldn't ask her. Suddenly, I felt overwhelmed and alone. This feeling of failure was just a taste of what I would feel if I didn't pass my test. I'd be viewed as a liar. And a failure. I would lose everything and have no future. My eyes burned. I blinked furiously, overcome with an intense need to visit my father's shop before I lost it forever.

I wanted to run from the room.

"Ivy?" Adeline asked again, but her voice sounded very far away.

Before I could answer, Mr. Everett stopped at our desk. "Wonderful specimen, Adeline. Most impressive. Ivy, have you brought yours in yet? I don't see your name on anything."

Adeline's brow raised in surprise. There was a trace of confusion on her face as if she couldn't understand why I hadn't beaten everyone—her included—at this part.

I cringed as I imagined her face if I failed my test and I blurted out, "I wanted to talk to you first. I found something, but it's dangerous and I didn't want anyone to get hurt."

Mr. Everett looked surprised. Adeline looked impressed.

"How dangerous?" he asked, curiously.

"It causes a rash that eats away skin and blisters. And the sap can cause blindness." As I recited what Nicholas told me, the noise around us quieted. Everyone was listening.

"Fascinating. I won't spoil the surprise and make you say what it is out loud. So, yes, bring it in. And if someone in this class touches it, well, it just proves they shouldn't be an Arborist, doesn't it?" He chuckled, before adding, "well done, Ivy. I enjoy the unexpected."

I looked back at my books, avoiding the questions and envy in people's eyes. Class began, but I barely heard what was being said.

All I could think about was now that I had to get that wild parsnip, I might as well discover if Nicholas was telling the truth.

FOUR

s soon as Mr. Everett dismissed us for lunch, I was through the door and onto the street.

Adeline called my name, but I didn't stop. I had to get the owl, meet with Nicholas, and dig up the wild parsnip before the sun went down. But first, I needed to find York.

There were two places he would be this time of day: down at the harbor helping his father, or in a Carving shop. Most Carving students usually came from Carving families, so they didn't need to split their time between two trades. But with the number of merchants visiting this time of year, York's father always needed help inspecting the ships. I would pass the Carving shop on the way down to the harbor, so I ducked in there first.

When I pulled open the door to Whittling Wood, the scent of my childhood washed over me. The smell of warm wood and fresh sawdust reminded me of the days I'd spent trying to master this trade. In Windermere, every five-year-old started in these workshops building up their skill. But as we grew older, those who were less talented were redirected back to their family's trade, or to another trade that suited them. Only a select few were invited by the Count to enter his upcoming Woodworking Tournament and showcase their skills as a Carver.

I had trained for two years as a Carver before I was reassigned to the Arborist trade. Now all I smelled was the scent of the forest and dirt mingled with the living herbs growing inside The Hidden Thorn. But I missed this scent of sawdust and newly carved wood and felt a tug in my chest whenever I entered a wood shop.

I breathed in deeply as I made my way past the rows of wooden statues for sale and headed to the back part of the shop used as a teaching workshop. An unfamiliar young girl stood outside the door of the carving class, peeking in. Tassels on the arms and ankles of her turquoise silk dress swayed with her movements. Definitely a merchant's daughter. When she saw me approaching, her face lit up hopefully.

I smiled at her, watching her wide chocolate eyes inspect my clothing.

"Excuse me, are you a Carver?" she asked.

My smile faded. "No, I'm not."

"Oh." She paused, her black curls swung around her head as she looked back to the room and then up at me. "Is the Count in there?"

I shook my head, sorry to disappoint her again. "No. He never comes to town."

"Not even for his Tournament?"

I shrugged. "That I'm not sure. The contestants are not allowed to speak about what happens inside."

"Have you ever seen him?"

Again, I shook my head. Her face fell and I realized she was probably hoping for a story to tell when she returned home. About sailing to Windermere and meeting a Carver, or better yet, the mysterious, reclusive Count.

"You won't find anyone important hanging around this shop." I bent down and lowered my voice. "These are just Dusters. Do you know what that is?"

She shook her head and leaned in closer. Her eyes lit up at sharing a secret with me.

"Before Carvers become Carvers, they're called Dusters. It's because they almost always whittle their carvings with so many mistakes they turn to dust at their feet. That's why their vests are the color of sawdust. It takes many years to earn the title of Carver."

"Oh." She smiled at me, revealing two dimples and straight white teeth that gleamed against her dark skin.

I lowered my voice even more. "If you want to see something truly remarkable, something so unique and special that you can talk about it your whole life, go to Gable's Emporium. Mr. Gable has a technique for putting his pieces together without anything but the notches he carves. Merchants come from all over to debate if he actually uses bones and how they are joined. But Mr. Gable never reveals his secret. Maybe you can uncover it?"

She smiled wider now and nodded. I stood as she ran off, pleading with her father to take her to the bone shop.

I grinned and stepped through the doorway into the teaching room.

A lowered stage faced three tiers of U-shape benches fanning around it. The seats were filled with students in tan vests watching a white-haired teacher carve into a tall tree stump. He wore a navy vest over a white shirt with the sleeves rolled up to his elbows. Rough bark still covered the lower half of the stump, but it was falling steadily to the ground.

I spotted York sitting with Percy. York's tousled brown hair and dusting of freckles contrasted with Percy's black hair and olive skin. Percy wore his usual serious scowl as he absorbed the lesson before him. Beside him, York watched too, but looked much more relaxed.

Something eased in me when I saw York. I wanted to tell him everything.

My boots crunched over layers of wood shavings scattered on the ground as I made my way down to sit next to them, but then someone stepped in front of me.

I looked up and groaned. Bryn Bryer's narrow-set, pale eyes

stared back at me. She looked even more annoyed than usual (if that was possible).

"Well, if it isn't Ivy Rune, the *best* Arborist in her whole class. You must be lost. This class is for Carvers, not second-rate trades."

"It's for anyone who wants to watch," I said, moving to duck around her.

Bryn moved swiftly too. "No, it's not. It's for Carvers. You know, people who actually have talent and will become something more than a forest gnome."

I rolled my eyes. "No one here is a Carver besides the teacher. Not till the Count's Tournament. Or did you already get your invitation, Bryn?"

Her eyes flashed. "You could at least sit in the back row and leave the front seats to people who need to see."

Her eyes darted down to the empty seat next to Percy, and then I knew she didn't care about seeing what was on stage. She cared about who sat in that chair.

"Relax, I'm here for York." I pushed past her again.

"Right. Your only friend," Bryn hissed, behind me. "And it's just because he just feels sorry for you . . ."

I tensed, but I didn't stop moving until I sank into the open seat next to Percy.

York leaned over and smiled at me. Then he saw my face and his brown eyes narrowed as his gaze shot back up to where Bryn was watching us. I could feel her eyes boring into my back. "You OK?"

I forced a casual shrug. "Fine."

York frowned, not so easily fooled. "You know, Percy, you could say something to your *girlfriend* and she'd leave Ivy alone. Or give her more attention so she's not so angry and jealous all the time."

My eyes flew to Percy. He never talked about Bryn or treated her differently, but we all thought there might be something between them. I was shocked that York would tease him about this.

Percy's eyes never left the teacher. "She's *not* my girlfriend."

York winked at me. "I forgot. Carving is. Poor Bryn."

I smiled, and York grinned at me. Percy ignored us. He was determined to win the Count's Tournament this year. I thought he might, too, but York also had a good chance.

I leaned back and looked up at the stage. The teacher muttered through a technique as his hands moved slowly and evenly over the log, his expression full of concentration. Over and over his chisel thinned the stump, sending tiny spirals of wood shavings to the floor.

A calmness settled over me as I watched the slow methodical movements of the teacher. Specks of sawdust swirled in the air and I breathed them in along with the sweet scent of wood. I always thought the aroma of wood soaked a room like warm sunlight being freed from the insides of trees. When I was younger, I imagined Carvers releasing that trapped sunlight through the careful cuts of their knives. The chisel never stopped removing the wood effortlessly from the stump. Soon, the shape of an owl slowly emerged from the block; its large wings poised to fly as soon as the rest of the wood was stripped away.

Eventually, I glanced back at York. I thought the class would have stopped for lunch by now, but the teacher looked like he had forgotten. I couldn't stay much longer, but I didn't want to rush York out either. He was already invited to the Woodworking Tournament. I didn't want to take him away from his learning a minute too soon.

"When is lunch?" I whispered to Percy.

"Who cares," he answered, his eyes still fixed on the owl.

"How long are you going to stay?"

Percy scowled. "Till it's *over*."

York caught my eye and nodded. "Let's go."

We got up quietly, ignoring the huff Percy emitted as York briefly blocked his view, and made our way up the stairs.

"It's about time you left, *poison ivy*. Before you poison us, too," Bryn whispered as we passed. A few people snickered.

York leaned down and said calmly, "Call her that again, and I'll make sure you have a nickname you never get rid of."

The laughter stopped immediately.

Bryn's eyes narrowed, but she wouldn't challenge York. Not only was he Percy's closest friend, but York wasn't someone anyone bothered. No one wanted to deal with his unpredictable father.

York didn't wait for a response. He grabbed my hand and steered me out of the shop. I tried not to let Bryn get to me, but her words bothered me more than I wanted to admit.

Out on the street, I dropped my calm demeanor. "Why is she so awful to me? I've never done anything to her."

"She's jealous."

"What would she have to be jealous of me about? She's a good Carver."

"Well, you did sit right next to Percy."

"So? I'd never *ever* like Percy."

"Really?" York sounded curious, like he'd wanted to know before, but hadn't wanted to ask.

"What? No!" I said, shocked.

"He used to like you."

I stared at him, sure he was just teasing me like he did Percy. But I was surprised by the incredulous look on his face.

"You didn't know?" he asked.

"Of course not!" I crossed my arms defensively. "How could I ever think that? Most of the time Percy ignores me. He only talks to me because I'm friends with you."

"That doesn't mean he didn't like you."

I shook my head. "I don't care. And I don't believe it."

"He's not the only one."

Something in his tone made me glance up, but York was looking at his shoe. Mrs. Taylor's prying questions ran through my head, making me flush for even thinking about them. An awkward silence stretched between us. Then York began to drag his toe through the dirt, leaving lines on the street.

I struggled to find the words that would ease the tension between us. But why wasn't *he* saying something to let me know that wasn't what he meant? I felt like the ground was shifting beneath us and I was determined not to let that happen. York was my best friend and the only person who felt like family. I didn't have anyone else. I couldn't lose him too.

"I have to tell you something," I blurted out.

His toe stilled. "Go ahead."

"I need you to look out for me while I break into my old house."

York looked up at me and I could tell that was not what he expected me to say. A smile tugged his lips as if now *I* was teasing *him*. "What?"

I took a deep breath. "Then, I need you to come into the forest with me to meet a man who says he knew my father."

He stopped smiling. "*What*?"

"I'm serious," I said, holding his gaze.

York studied me for a minute, before frowning. "Who is it?"

Suddenly, I felt silly saying it out loud. It sounded unbelievable. "I don't know. He lives in the woods. But he claims my father gave him something to keep safe before he died. And now I need to bring him something before he'll give it to me."

"What does he want?"

"An owl."

York's brows lifted. "We have to catch an owl?"

"No, my old wooden one. Look, I know how it sounds, but I have to do this now. And I still have to dig up a plant today. So if you're in, I'll tell you on the way."

York rolled his eyes. "Ivy, you know I'm in."

I smiled, relieved the air between us felt normal again. "Then let's go."

Five

I leaned on the window that displayed sewing supplies and bolts of fabric while keeping an eye on the street.

If anyone glanced at me, it would look like I was just waiting for someone shopping inside Threads.

York suggested he go to Forest and Fern alone to pick the lock while I waited here, a street away, so I wouldn't be noticed. York would use the alley and hopefully, he wouldn't be seen either. It was overly cautious, maybe even paranoid, but I didn't want to risk either of our futures more than I already was.

I wasn't sure what the punishment would be for breaking into Forest and Fern, or if the Count would care, but breaking into one of his shops didn't seem wise. And who would I ask for permission to go inside? Mr. Mallon, the Count's Regent, was the only citizen of Windermere who spoke with the Count and I had no connection to him. I'd only seen him from afar and I didn't dare approach him. He was a man who rarely smiled and I'd seen him clear a path through a crowded street with a single look.

I stamped my feet to keep warm. The chill in the air was slowly dissipating as the sun rose in the sky. In an hour, the sun would be its warmest, but I would be in the forest then and miss it. New merchants were surprised by our cold, foggy summers, and they came to Threads to buy wool shawls.

My stomach growled. York and I had both missed lunch. I glanced around, thinking it was strange to be here. I had avoided this part of town since moving to the Taylor's farm. It had been too hard to visit at first, and adults advised me to wait until I was older. Still, I could have come back anytime in the last few years. I stayed away to protect myself from this uncomfortable feeling burrowing its way through my chest.

A part of me that had died, something young and innocent, was waking. Memories of when life was perfect and simple began to resurface in my mind as I stared at the street. I had walked here with both of my parents. I couldn't remember my mother's face, but I did remember the feeling of her. Of happiness and warmth, the feeling of light rainbows on a wall, or eating freshly baked bread. I remembered walking here with my father, just the two of us. He would hold my hand as he took me to carving class, and later, to check on trees and plants around town.

Now I stood here alone.

I realized I only remembered my father as an Arborist when I thought of him. But now, I was pushed to remember him as a father. How many times had I looked up at him and wondered what he was thinking? How many of our walks had I spent wishing he would talk to me? I still wondered about who he was, but now I would never know.

"*Boo.*"

I shrieked and whirled around. "What are you doing!" I hissed at York.

He laughed. "*Shhh.* We're trying to go unnoticed, right?"

"Then walk up properly so I can see you," I snapped.

"Couldn't help it." He grinned. "And the back door is open for you."

"Was the front locked?"

"Maybe from inside. I didn't notice one on the outside as I

walked past and I didn't want to stop and look. But it's not like anyone would break in."

"It's weird it's locked at all," I said.

"The shop next door has its back door wide open, but no one is outside. Go around this side to the alley and slip in quickly."

My heart began to skip faster. "And you'll wait here?"

York nodded. "You'll be fine. No one is watching, everyone is eating lunch. We don't have anything to worry about. Right?"

I stared up and down the street.

"Right?" York repeated.

I steadied myself. "Of course not. It's Windermere."

"So get in and out. Then we head into the forest to meet this Nick guy."

"Nicholas."

"What a proper name for someone who lives in the woods. Well, are you going?"

I squared my shoulders and took a deep breath. "I'll see you in a few," I said as I made my way down the alley.

———

It was the first time I walked into a shop to steal something. It was just ironic the shop was my own home.

The back door opened without a sound as I slipped inside. It clicked shut behind me and for the first time in ten years, I stood in our small kitchen. One window over the sink let in dim light. Wooden cabinets lined the wall, and our small table and two chairs sat with a layer of dust on them. My eyes traveled to the short hallway that led to the stairs. Above that were our bedrooms.

I swallowed and crossed the kitchen to the front room, at the edge of the official space of Forest and Fern. I peered into my father's office and library, staying in the hallway so I wouldn't be noticed through the wall of windows that looked onto the street.

Everything in the room was frozen in time, transporting me to that day ten years ago when my life changed. Only, I'd never realized until now that I'd been frozen inside ever since too.

In this room, the sun shone brightly through the wide windows, making the wood glow warmly. Shelves still held all my father's leather-bound books. His desk sat beneath a wall of countless frames holding species of leaves he found in the forest surrounding Windermere. On the opposite wall hung the framed plants my father had collected from other lands that he never visited.

If I closed my eyes, I could imagine the way this room used to smell of him. Of the cinnamon he put in his tea, the sage and herbs he smoked, the decay of dead branches and leaves he brought back from the forest. Now the air smelled stale, thick with dust and ghosts.

His desk sent me reeling back in time. Books always in the center, pens on the right standing in a carved wooden holder. Slender glass jars of colored pollen and seeds lining the back.

A possessive feeling struck me. These things were part of my childhood, my history, but I had no claim to them unless I proved I was worthy of his legacy. My father's work and research belonged to the Arborist trade. Even though I was his only child, unless I became an Arborist, I would lose it all. That wasn't fair. The Count could have all the books and all of my father's research back—I just wanted the things that reminded me of him.

And I wanted my childhood home.

I'd always known I wanted it—I just hadn't realized I *needed* it just as badly.

The thought of someone else moving in, using my father's things ... was unbearable. Everything here still had his touch on it. In a way, it was a link to him. There was nothing he loved more than his work. Not even me.

But what if Nicholas did have something important? Something no one could take from me? I didn't want my hopes to get up too much, but deep down that was what I wanted.

I sighed and forced myself to turn away from the front room

and go upstairs.

I'd forgotten how the stairs creaked under the slightest weight. The noise filled the quiet house. A memory of me at six running up and down the stairs to get my father's attention sprung to mind. The stairs creaked then too, and I hadn't stopped until my father came over to see what I was doing. He hadn't been amused. He had been consumed with his research for months. I'd just wanted him to stop and talk to me. I remembered how instead of laughing, he told me to stop and went back to his desk. I stood on the stairs awhile, waiting, but he never came back.

A new ache filled my chest as I continued up the creaking stairs. I passed by my father's neat and orderly room and went into mine. I found what I was looking for in the top drawer of my dresser.

The owl.

I lifted it out slowly, dredging up memories with it. It was small enough to fit in my palm and it looked just as I remembered it. Its back and wings were covered in bark that looked like feathers. Its face and pointed ears were round and smooth, with rings marking the age of the tree used to make it.

Looking at it now, I realized it didn't look much like an owl. No one would look at this and think it was anything but a lump from a tree or a knot that fell out of a piece of wood. No one would think to call this an owl. Except for my father and I.

The first time I saw this owl, I couldn't have been much older than three. That day, instead of my mother, it was my father who came to get me from school. The owl was tucked in his arms. I played with it as we walked down the street toward home. I loved how unbreakable it was, so unlike the delicately carved statues that filled the houses and shops in Windermere. I remember saying it looked like an owl. My father said that was my mother's.

Then he announced quietly that she was gone and would not be returning home. His face is still engrained in my mind. Every question died on my lips as I saw the sadness and despair hiding in his eyes.

Later that night, I found him at his desk, staring at the owl as if it held all his answers, but wouldn't reveal them. He never said more about the owl, beyond promising to tell me its story when I was older. He died before that time came. Now I wondered why he would want me to bring it to Nicholas and not keep it for myself.

If it was really my mother's, it was all I had of her. My father had kept no photographs, clothes, or anything. He didn't even speak of her.

But when I got older, I heard him tell others that she had left on a ship suddenly and was gone.

There were many times I wanted to insist I was old enough to hear her story, but I didn't want to push him into silence, as he was often prone to. I thought if I held the space as gently as he held his orchids, he would open up. But he never did. Sometimes when he saw the owl, his eyes would glaze over as if he was remembering the last time he saw her. To spare him further pain, I tucked it away in my room and kept it hidden. It had been in this drawer for ten years.

I turned the owl over and over in my hands. I'd resigned myself to never knowing its story, but I never thought I would have to give it away.

I left the room, pausing by my father's door. It felt too sad to go inside. The stairs creaked again as I started down them. Then I heard a sound downstairs, towards the front door. A knob rattled.

I froze on the creaky stair, startled, as I heard a click. I didn't move or breathe as the front door opened.

Was it York? I must have been in here too long and he was worried. Just before I moved or called out, I realized that York would have announced himself. My heart hammered as the sound of footsteps filled the house.

It wasn't York.

Someone else was in Forest and Fern.

And I was trapped on the stairs.

Six

Footsteps echoed across the room.

Heavy and slow. Footsteps of someone who had no fear of getting caught.

My heart sputtered when they stopped. I held my breath, thinking whoever it was must be near my father's desk ... or just around the corner from me.

I was scared to move or make a sound. I couldn't go up or down. One shift and the creak would give me away.

A drawer slid open. They were by the desk. Things were being rifled through. Then I heard the scrape of a chair. More footsteps. Closer to where I was in the hallway.

If they walked around the corner, they would see me. I clenched my fists, praying they wouldn't. My chest burned from holding my breath.

They stopped at the shelf on the other side of the wall. Books were being picked up, fluttered through, and slid back in. The quickness of these movements made it seem like whoever it was knew what they were searching for.

Who was going through my father's things? And why? Was this the first time someone had been in here? The layer of dust in the rooms made me think so.

I was terrified of being caught, of the punishment I would receive. But even so, a flare of anger welled up in my chest. This place was supposed to be sealed for me. The Count promised it. Had something changed? If it had, I should have been told.

Nicholas's words came back to me.

Your father gave me something to keep safe.

For *you.*

You're old enough now.

Did that have something to do with this intruder?

It was quiet. Too quiet. I strained to hear anything, but the silence was a roar in my ears. Every muscle in my body strained from holding still. What were they doing now?

A book slammed shut, and I nearly jumped out of my skin. The footsteps began again, but now they were quicker. Fading. To my relief, they were walking away from me. Then the front door swung open and closed. The lock turned.

I was alone again.

Slowly, I exhaled, not daring to move until I was sure they were gone. Then I lifted a foot and descended the stairs. Creaks filled the air until I cleared the last step.

Heart pounding, I peered into the office. Nothing looked out of place. Or missing. Somehow, even the dust looked as if it hadn't been disturbed.

But someone had been here.

Someone had touched everything and changed my father's last day in this room. They had erased some small part of him. Now instead of his fingers being the last to put everything in its place, a stranger had touched it all. Before I had the chance.

They had stolen a part of me reconnecting with my father.

But why?

I put the owl in my bag. I needed to hurry back to York. I had been here too long.

With one last frustrated look at the room, I crossed into the kitchen and eased out the back door. The sound of laughter from the shop next door jolted me from the quietness of Forest and Fern. I hurried away before I was spotted.

I couldn't help but think that this time as I walked through the back alley, I was not a dutiful daughter, but a thief.

Except now, I wasn't the only one.

———

YORK WAS WAITING ON THE CORNER WHEN I GRABBED his arm, breathless.

"Did you see them?" I whispered as I began to pull him along with me.

York pulled back, surprised. "Who?"

I shot him a pointed look. "The person who came through the *front* door while I was inside!"

"What?"

I folded my arms over my chest and glared at him. "Some lookout you are."

York tugged the bag off my shoulder and put it onto his, looking sheepish. "I was starving. I really didn't think something would happen. Here, I was thinking about you too."

He held out something wrapped in brown paper.

A sandwich from Wilder's Bakery. My stomach reacted instantly just seeing it. I took it and unwrapped the paper. The fragrance of the soft rosemary bread nearly overwhelmed me. The bread was still warm, its inside stuffed with roasted turkey and smoked cheese. My favorite.

I bit into it and groaned. "Fine. You're forgiven."

"Good. Now tell me what happened."

Between the bites I inhaled, I explained what happened. There wasn't much to tell since I didn't see the person, but I couldn't shake the uneasiness of someone being in my home.

"Whoever it was had a key," I finished, sad to find I was also done with my sandwich. I crumpled up the paper and threw it into the garbage we passed. "But they took something, I know it."

"You don't know that," York commented.

"But I *feel* it. And now I'm wondering if there is really something to Nicholas's claims. Maybe my father did have something to keep safe. Why else would someone be searching in his shop?"

"Well, they had a key," York said.

"I know."

"No, that's my point. They had a key. They didn't break in. *You* did."

That startled me enough that I stopped walking. Then I felt incredibly silly. "Right."

"Whoever it was had permission to be there. So maybe it's not as bad as you think."

I saw the truth in what he was saying, but I couldn't shake the feeling that there was more to it. Maybe it was because I had been the one alone in the house. Maybe I was imagining the situation as worse than it was. If they had a key, they were probably just getting something they needed. Something for our trade. Maybe something to do with our upcoming test.

I began walking again. "I see your point," I admitted, reluctantly. "Who has access to the shop's keys?"

"I'm not sure, but we can find out. Hey, where are you going?" York asked when I turned down a street that didn't lead us to the outside of town.

"The Hidden Thorn. I need tools to dig up my plant."

We passed through another narrow alley to the back of The Hidden Thorn. Mr. Everett kept extra supplies in a trunk by the back door so students could come as they needed. I opened the top and grabbed one of the backpacks. I checked inside to make sure it had two pairs of gloves, a wide piece of burlap, a rope, and a small field shovel.

York held out his hand. "I'll carry it."

"Thanks," I said, handing it over to him. "We can switch off."

"I got it."

"It'll get heavy on the way back with the plant," I warned.

York rolled his eyes at me. "I'll manage, Ivy. I *am* about twice as big as you."

"Why do you think I asked you to come?" I joked.

"Not for my company, then?"

He meant it as a joke, but our conversation from this morning came rushing back and I froze, unsure what to say back. Before it turned truly awkward, the back door opened and Mr. Everett stepped into the alley. The interruption flooded me with relief.

"I thought I heard something." He looked at me with interest, his thumbs hooking into his hunter-green vest. "Going after your mysterious plant now, Ivy?"

"Yes. Would you mind if I left it out here tonight? I'll wrap it so no one touches it."

"That's fine. Good luck, then." He moved to go back inside.

"Mr. Everett?" I called.

He turned. "Yes?"

"Um. I was wondering..." I paused, unsure how to phrase what I needed to ask and not raise suspicion.

"Yes?"

"I was wondering if someone in our trade has been to Forest and Fern lately? You know, for research?"

Mr. Everett looked surprised. "No. Even I have not been inside since your father's passing. No one has. I thought you understood it is being kept for you. Until you pass the test, that is."

"I do. But if I wanted something inside ... could I get permission?"

He frowned, his bushy white eyebrows pushing down into his glasses. "I don't think that would be wise, considering how close the test is. And the fact that the current assignment is to find a unique species. People might think you had help."

"Oh, I don't need help," I said, quickly. "I just wanted to see it again. It's been years. Not from an Arborist viewpoint, but a family one." I stumbled over my words as I saw the uneasiness on Mr. Everett's face. I wasn't sure how to ask about a key now.

"Who could give permission to get inside?" York asked, behind me. "Who keeps the keys?"

"Why? Do you plan on going inside too, Mr. Pembroke?"

"There are sentimental things inside," I cut in. "I'm worried about the test and I just wanted to know if I could have them no matter what the outcome is."

"Ah." His expression cleared. "I'm sure that won't be a problem. The Count only specified your father's shop, trade tools, notes, and supplies be passed to another Arborist if you do not enter our trade. After all, everything is the Count's property too, given that he supplies our education. But don't worry, I have no fear you will pass. You and Adeline have been my top students for years."

I nodded. "Thanks."

"You should go if you want to get back before dark. Good luck, Ivy." Mr. Everett hesitated before saying, "And I wouldn't mention anything about this to others. I do understand your position, but others may only be able to think of your request from a trade standpoint. After the test would be a better time to revisit this topic."

When the door shut behind him, York looked at me.

"You just got your answer."

"I did?"

He nodded. "No one but the Count could have given permission to go inside."

SEVEN

Those words stuck in my mind as we walked through the forest.

No one but the Count.

Well. Then I was plain out of luck finding out who went through my father's things. If the Count had allowed it, there was nothing I could do. It was his shop, not mine. It hadn't even been my father's, not really. Every building in Windermere was built by the Count or his ancestors.

But why he would want or allow someone else in Forest and Fern was beyond me. The Count's interest lay in Carving, not other trades. He didn't even seem to be interested in Windermere anymore, beyond hosting his annual Woodworking Tournament.

We still referred to him as our generous patron, especially to the merchants. But in truth, the Count had become more of a myth to us than a real person. Most locals had never even seen him. The longer he was absent, the stranger and more embellished the stories about him grew. Parents warned he left his tower only at night to collect the bad children and take them back to his castle. And that he bred enormous guard dogs to roam his property and tear apart anyone who trespassed.

Of course, this was only whispered behind closed doors, and

only among the locals. No one dared be caught gossiping by Mr. Mallon. As Regent, Mr. Mallon enforced the Count's orders with an iron fist. He was also the only one allowed to travel the deserted road that led to the Count's gate, to give his reports.

"Does that mean only Mr. Mallon would have been able to ask for the keys?" I wondered out loud. "Or give out keys?"

It had been too long since I'd spoken, and my voice startled York. I grinned when he jumped.

"What! I'm not comfortable out here like you are." York frowned. "Honestly, I don't know how you can stand it after..."

His voice faded, but I knew what he meant to say. After my father had died in the forest.

I shrugged. "I guess I'm just used to it."

Those in higher trades, like Carvers, rarely left their shops. Or the town border. After my father died, fear spread through Windermere: If someone as knowledgeable as him could get lost and die in the woods, how was anyone else safe? The Arborist trade was considered risky and was filled with those whose talents did not lie in higher trades or those who broke town rules. But, as years passed after my father's death and no one else died or went missing in the woods, the fear faded a little.

Strangely, I didn't mind being in the forest. I liked the solitude and the peace of it. Whenever I needed to escape the expectations placed on me, I took Loon riding. I felt more connected to myself when I was surrounded by trees. It was just ironic that I was terrible at caring for them.

"Mr. Mallon would be the person to ask," York said. This time, it was his turn to laugh when I jumped. "What are you thinking about?"

I sighed. "How terrible I am at being an Arborist."

York frowned. "You're too hard on yourself."

"You know I'm not. You're the only one who knows that I'm not good at this. And soon, everyone else will know."

"They will not, because you *are* going to pass your test, Ivy. You're smart and you will figure it out. Just because it doesn't come naturally to you doesn't mean you can't be good at it. We'll find your plant and I'll help you study when we get back. All week, if that's what it takes."

I smiled. "How will you practice Carving if you're helping me?"

"I'll manage somehow."

"Percy will love that. It will make you easier to beat."

York grinned at me. I grinned back, until I looked away, blushing. Our earlier conversation just wouldn't let me be.

I guess that was the thing with words. They never stayed in the place where they were spoken. Once freed, they followed along, their implied meaning haunting all other conversations.

"Is it much farther?" York asked, his eyes now focused ahead of us.

"Um, just a little bit, I think. I was riding Loon yesterday, so it's hard to gauge."

We walked in silence. The birds had more to say to each other than us. For the first time, I was worried about what he was thinking.

Had York meant *he* felt that way about me? Or was he just saying others had felt that way?

Could York even view *me* like that? Could *I* see him like that?

I chewed my lip, wondering if it would be so hard to think of him as more than my best friend. He was kind and good, and he had unwavering faith in me. He made me laugh and feel safe. I trusted him. Wasn't that how I should feel about someone I liked?

When did feelings of friendship change into stronger feelings?

I glanced at him out of the corner of my eye, carefully, so he wouldn't notice. I tried to see him differently. I could admit he was nice to look at. Tall, and growing more into himself every day. I liked the dusting of freckles across his cheeks. He had nice hair. But shouldn't I feel something stronger than appreciation? Something more desperate or flustered? Shouldn't I feel the same knife-sharp jealousy Bryn flashed at anyone who went near Percy?

I tried to gauge the depth of my feelings, but all I felt was grateful and happy that York was in my life. I didn't want things to change. And I wasn't even sure he did either.

Maybe *I* was the one misreading what he was saying. As soon as I thought that, I realized it must be true. I needed to stop reading into this so much.

"We're close!" Relief flooded me as I began to recognize the place where I had met Nicholas. "Be careful you don't touch anything that looks like lace. Or with yellow flowers. Actually, we should probably put on the gloves now."

York pulled off the backpack and opened it. He took the bigger pair of gloves and gave me the other pair. "Do you want this too?" He asked, pulling out the folded-up field shovel.

"Not yet. But hand me the burlap."

York gave me the burlap but kept the shovel in his hand. "Should I keep this handy just in case I need to use it against your new friend?"

"Shhh!" I warned. "He might hear you. But he's harmless, I think. If he wanted to hurt me, he could have done it yesterday when I was alone. Ready?"

York nodded and gestured to me to go first. "After you, Arborist."

I rolled my eyes. "Thanks, Carver. But seriously, don't touch a plant with stems that look like they're bursting apart. Nicholas said it can eat away your skin and maybe cause blindness."

"Didn't you look it up?" York asked, tossing the shovel back and forth between his hands.

"Um, no. I haven't had a chance yet."

"But you told Mr. Everett that it was special enough to bring back?" His voice was carefully neutral, without judgment.

Still, I stopped and stared at him. "Oh my gosh. What if it's nothing at all? What if I just told the whole class that I found a rare, dangerous plant, and it's not?" My fears began to spiral and tears sprung to my eyes. "What if it's not wild parsnip at all? Everyone heard me. *Everyone.* I'm going to look like a fool now. Worse than that. I'm going to *fail.*"

York opened his mouth to answer, but a deeper voice spoke first.

"Don't worry, Ivy. I wouldn't lie to you."

York's eyes widened, and I spun around.

Nicholas stood on the path behind us. In his gloved hand was a long stem of wild parsnip. "This sap *can* cause blindness and make the skin blister." He looked away from me to glare at York. "So I'd appreciate it if you'd tell that boy to drop his weapon."

EIGHT

Nicholas wore the same dark clothes as yesterday, his silver hair pulled back from his face.

I was struck again by how different he was. Wild, not in an unkempt way—in an ungoverned way. As if rules and social expectations meant nothing to him. He stood like he had nothing to lose and nothing to fear. He continued to stare at us, his blue eyes like ice.

Tension crackled in the air between us.

I shifted closer to York, thinking Nicholas had a knack for saying the wrong thing to strangers. He'd even hit a nerve with me when he implied I should have known about wild parsnip. And now he'd called York *that boy*. He managed to sound just like York's father, dismissive and annoyed. No wonder York was still bristling.

I don't think I'd ever heard Mr. Pembroke call York by his name. York could hide that pain when he was around his father, but with anyone else, the word triggered him. No one called him that. We all knew better.

"York." I touched his arm. He looked at me, a scowl clouding his face. I didn't say anything, but I knew he'd understand what I meant. *He's not your father. He didn't mean it.*

A second passed before York's face cleared and he nodded. His grip loosened on the shovel as he looked back at Nicholas, now calm. Emotionless. "I wasn't planning on using it as a weapon."

Nicholas's eyes shifted between us. "I heard you. Through the trees."

"I was joking."

"Hmm." Nicholas's gaze fell on me. "No one is completely harmless, but I don't mean you harm, Ivy. I wasn't expecting you to bring someone."

He studied York again, but he didn't seem upset anymore. He looked interested.

"You didn't ask me to come alone," I said, drawing the attention back to me.

He looked back at me, curiously. "Would you have?"

I shifted, uncertain of why he was asking. Was he trying to gauge how naive or foolish I was?

"I wondered about your claims. So if York couldn't have come with me today, then yes. I probably would have come anyway to see if they were true."

Nicholas didn't comment on what he thought of that. He looked out into the trees as if he was gathering his thoughts. For a while, we listened to the snapping of twigs, the fluttering and chatter of birds, and the leaves rustling above us before Nicholas finally spoke again.

"Your father was not a nervous man. But the last time I saw him, he acted strange. Spooked. Paranoid, even."

A shiver went down my spine. "Why?" I asked, my voice catching.

Nicholas looked down as if he didn't hear me. I remembered the slow way he talked yesterday. It dawned on me how much he had already spoken today. I tried to be patient, but the silence was suffocating. All I wanted were answers.

Nicholas finally stirred. "I tried to reassure him that all was well," he continued. "But Rune wouldn't calm. Not until I promised to keep something safe. In case something happened to him."

I glanced at York. He was watching Nicholas, frowning.

"Did he say what?" I asked.

"No. I don't know what happened to make him like that. But he wasn't himself." A pause. "He was ... full of fear."

"About what? He was an Arborist!" I exclaimed.

Nicholas's eyes snapped to mine. He looked uneasy at my outburst. "Yes."

Worried I might spook him before he told me everything, I took a deep breath and calmed myself just like I had told York to do. "So he was fearful about ... that?"

"His research, I think."

"His ... *research*?" I faltered. This didn't make any sense. Worried about trees and plants? Paranoid over them? I looked at York, but he shrugged. He looked as lost as I did.

"I kept my promise," Nicholas said. "It's been longer than it should have been. But time runs differently for me. Here is what he gave me." Nicholas lifted a wooden cube. It fit in his palm perfectly. "Did you bring the owl?"

I hesitated. Was I going to give up my mother's owl for my father's research? Research I might have to give to the Count if it was important. A flash of anger shot through me. I was sick of my entire life being about this trade and my father's research.

I wanted a family. I wanted my parents back. I stupidly thought that my father might have left me something personal. Something to give me closure or to bring me closer to his memory. But this didn't feel like it.

Still, I couldn't walk away without knowing what the cube was.

I reached into my bag and pulled out the owl. I tried to believe that my father had a reason for mentioning it to Nicholas. I stepped forward, and York shadowed me.

"Here." I held the owl out to Nicholas, who looked uneasy with me so close.

But to my surprise, Nicholas handed me the cube and stepped back without taking the owl. "No, that's yours."

I frowned. "Then why did you ask for it?"

"Rune wanted you to know that is important. He said it's a key."

I stared down at the owl in my hand. "A key to what?"

"I don't know. Maybe that will explain more." He gestured to the cube. "I never tried to open it."

Open it? Then something was inside? I studied the cube closer but there didn't seem to be a place to open it.

"Well, good luck, then, Ivy Rune."

I looked up, surprised by his abrupt goodbye. This man had kept a promise to my father for ten years. And I hadn't even known he existed.

What else had my father hidden from me?

"Thank you," I said, but the words felt hollow, like I should say more, or feel more. But all I felt was confused. And unsettled about my father's state of mind. And what I was supposed to do with the owl and cube now?

But I didn't get a chance to ask him anything more.

Nicholas had already turned and vanished into the trees.

———

I slipped the owl back into my bag and studied the cube again.

Dark rings of woodgrain ran in diagonals across the polished surface. No matter how I turned it, I couldn't find a keyhole or a way to open it. After a moment of fiddling, I handed it to York.

He inspected it just as I did. Then a look of surprise crossed his face. "This was made by a Carver, but not a Windermere Carver. It's not like ours."

"Then why do you think it was made by a Carver?"

"It reminds me of something Carl used to do a few years back. Remember him?"

I nodded. Of course I remembered the only other person to leave town like my mother. Carl was three years older than us but he kept to himself, so I hadn't talked to him much—if ever. He left Windermere to work for a merchant and no one knew why he chose that instead of becoming a Carver. After a while, people stopped asking about him. Even his parents continued with their lives and didn't seem worried or upset over it.

"Carl was better than Percy, even." York turned the cube carefully, the polished wood gleamed in the sunlight. "He should have won the Tournament that year, but he quit during the competition. Or maybe it was right after—"

"I remember all that. But why does *this* remind you of him?" I cut in, confused.

"Carl used to make things like this. Things that couldn't be opened with anything but a sliver of wood he whittled as a key. This is much more refined, though. But maybe it's the same idea."

York pulled out the small carving knife he carried. The blade was thin and flat.

"Want me to try and open it?"

I nodded.

York made his way around the cube, trying to fit the blade gently into any paper-thin seam. "If I can't get it, I bet Mr. Gable can figure it out."

I frowned. "I'm not sure I want anyone else to know."

York's brown eyes flashed to mine. "We don't have to tell him where you got it."

"But he'll be interested to know if it's from another Carver. He'll ask a lot of questions."

"True." His concentration returned to the cube. Then I heard a tiny click.

"Got it." He slid his blade out of the smallest joint between the wood pieces as I watched, amazed. I wouldn't have known an opening was there. York carefully pushed his thumb along the top of the cube until the top flipped open.

"That is a neat trick," York said admiringly as he held it out to me.

I took it, eagerly peering inside at a raw wood compartment. It was hollowed out more than I expected and there was a slip of aging paper that looked like it had been folded over and over. I imagined my father making each crease, trying to make sure the paper would fit and remain safe for me. His worry was folded into each crease.

Suddenly, I was worried whatever was on the paper wasn't written for me at all. That it was meant for the Arborist trade, not his only child. All my feelings, the ones I thought I buried deep or made peace with long ago, grew up within me like sprouts in the earth.

This must be for the trade.

I wasn't important enough for my father to leave me something.

I closed my eyes and took a deep breath so my voice wouldn't betray how devastated I felt. "Will this lock if I close it again?"

"You don't want to read it?" York sounded surprised.

I shook my head. "Not now."

York took the cube back and shut it. Then he slipped his knife inside the seam again and pushed gently. It clicked and the top opened again. York looked at me to make sure I'd watched. When I nodded, he shut it again and handed it back without another word. That was the best thing about York. He didn't push or try to give opinions if I wasn't ready.

"Thanks." I put it in my bag. I would read it later when I was alone. And more prepared than I was now.

I looked around us. The forest was turning that magical time between day and dusk when it was quiet and peaceful. That buzz of adrenaline was fading now that I had crossed everything off my list today. Well, almost everything.

"All that's left is to get the plant and get back before dark."

York nodded. "Just tell me how to help."

I walked a little, searching for the place where Loon and I had almost stepped on the wild parsnip. Then I saw the burst of yellow flowers, but they were smaller than yesterday. I frowned, remembering Nicolas had been holding some. He'd dug up the tallest, most flowered part of the plant. What he left behind didn't look that impressive, but it would have to do.

I pointed it out to York. "It's all that. It's there too. Hand me the burlap. I'll cover it and wrap it up so we don't touch the leaves. Then we'll dig out the roots and wrap them up too."

York followed my lead, helping me dig deeper when I wanted to bring more dirt. It would be heavier to carry, but I couldn't risk killing the plant if I used the wrong soil. I handled the leaves and stem as gently as I could, folding them protectively within the layers of cloth. Then York handed me the twine to wrap it securely. Finally, when the plant was tied up and together, we dropped it into the backpack.

"I can help you carry it," I said, feeling guilty about the weight.

York put the backpack on. "Nah, I got it."

"Ok."

"Ivy?"

"Yeah?"

York smiled softly. "You did good. You're better at this than you think."

Tears sprang to my eyes, surprising me. "Thanks, York. And thanks for coming. I couldn't have done it without you."

"Anytime. You know that."

I nodded. I did know that. I was lucky to have him as a friend.

We made our way back through the forest, toward The Hidden Thorn to drop off the plant. This time, I walked with a weight lifted now that I had something to show for myself. All I had to do was keep this plant alive until Mr. Everett could grade it. At least one part of my test was nearly finished.

Now I just had to study.

And figure out what the owl was a key to.
And read the paper in the cube.
Would it be for me?
I didn't know what I hoped for, I just hoped I wouldn't be disappointed.

NINE

Mr. Taylor was at the kitchen table when I came down for breakfast.

Usually, he was out on the farm by sunrise, or bringing food from the farm to Taylor's Mercantile, but this morning he didn't seem to be in a hurry. His hands were wrapped around a steaming cup of coffee, his body reclined in the chair. His clothes were pressed and his hair combed neatly, as always. He smiled, making the lines around his eyes crinkle, when he saw me.

"Good morning, Ivy. Mrs. Taylor made a delicious breakfast. Will you join us?"

My stomach rumbled. "Of course."

Mrs. Taylor turned away from the stove to nod at me. "Get your coffee. The eggs have but a minute left."

I plucked a blue mug from the shelf and quickly filled it with black coffee, the nutty scent filling the room. I added cream until the color morphed into warm brown sugar. I sipped slowly as I sat down across from Mr. Taylor. His skin was tanned from the sun and I noticed more speckles of grey in his hair. I wondered how long he would continue working his long days.

"Were you successful in finding a plant yesterday?" he asked.

I nodded, relieved. "Yes. I left it outside The Hidden Thorn last night. It's still wrapped, so I need to uncover and pot it this morning."

"It's Saturday. Mr. Everett is opening up today?" Mrs. Taylor asked as she brought us plates piled high with dense pancakes, eggs, and bacon.

"He said he'll be in and out to help," I answered before stuffing my mouth with a syrupy, buttery bite. I would miss Mrs. Taylor's cooking. Thankfully, that wouldn't be for a while.

"Now you can focus on studying for your test." Mr. Taylor cut his pancakes in neat squares. "I know how stressed everyone is over the trade exams. It's good of the Count to host his Wood-working Tournament after, so we can all enjoy ourselves."

I nodded. The Tournament was everyone's favorite time of year. It was the only time the town square was full of new foods, luxurious fabrics, and trinkets from cities across the sea.

This would be the first year York and Percy could enter the Tournament as Carvers, and I was sure one of them would win. Hopefully, this year I would be wearing the new hunter-green vest of an Arborist and have Forest and Fern to myself again. I could hang banners from our front porch, just like my father did when I was younger.

If I passed the test, that is.

Mr. Taylor studied my expression, and whatever he saw must have surprised him. "You're not worried, Ivy? Are you?"

I tried to muster up a smile, but it was hard to lie to him when he gave me his full attention and looked at me like he cared how I felt. So I let myself say something I wouldn't normally admit: "Plants came so easy to my father. The only thing that comes easy to me is horses." I laughed to cover the sting of the truth.

"Your father was a good man and a respected Arborist," Mr. Taylor said slowly as if thinking about how to phrase what he would say next. "But many things that are easy for you were hard for him."

I set down my fork. "Like what?"

"Like understanding people. Your father had difficulty with emotion, but you're the opposite."

I raised a brow. "Are you saying I'm too emotional?"

Mr. Taylor laughed. "Not at all. You've been a ray of sunshine your whole life. Your father may have tended to plants because they were easier than people. But plants aren't the only things that need love and care."

"I'm glad my father can't hear you say that."

His eyes crinkled. "Me too. Even so, you're your father's daughter. You'll be an Arborist too."

I drained the last bit of my coffee and placed my napkin on the table. "I appreciate that. Well, I need to get to The Hidden Thorn. Thanks for the delicious breakfast, Mrs. Taylor."

"Before you go, we wanted to talk to you about something," Mrs. Taylor said, casually.

"Oh?" The realization dawned on me that Mr. Taylor had a purpose for being at the table this morning. A flutter of nervousness filled me. *Did they find out about Nicholas?* "Yes?"

"As we said, you're very close to taking your test. And after, you'll be moving back into your old home, which we know you've been looking forward to."

Oh. Except... I hadn't expected to move out right away. I had planned on working there during the day, but not living alone so soon. I hadn't realized they expected me to. My heart thumped and I wondered if I had done something wrong.

When I didn't speak, Mr. Taylor exchanged a look with Mrs. Taylor. She leaned in.

"We need more help managing the farm. Since it will go to John and Miranda when we can't run it anymore, we all agreed it makes sense for them to move in now and start taking over slowly, with our guidance. Miranda has her hands full with those three little ones and their house in town is too small for them now."

Suddenly, I felt very much in the way. And very aware that this was not my home. I forced myself to smile and nod. "Of course. I understand."

"We don't want you to feel pushed out, but they need the entire upstairs for their family. Especially now that there's another baby on the way."

They beamed at me, clearly elated about having another grandchild to dote on.

My smile stretched thinner. "Congratulations! How exciting for everyone."

"Yes. And timing-wise, it works out," Mr. Taylor said, relieved. "Our support won't stop just because you don't live here anymore. We insist you come back for dinner and stop in to say hello."

All I could do was make myself nod again. I don't know why I felt like I was on a boat whose rope had been cut and now I was drifting out to sea.

Alone.

Again, I had no one.

I understood it wasn't personal. I did. Their real family needed their home back. And everyone assumed Forest and Fern would be mine. But they didn't know how worried I truly was. And I couldn't help but feel hurt and rejected.

I stood before I made a fool of myself. "Just let me know when," I said, carrying my plate to the sink.

"Miranda was hoping it could be as soon as you pass the test. She doesn't want to move when she's any bigger. Oh, what an exciting time it will be for us all!" Mrs. Taylor looked and sounded so happy that I had to look away.

I was the only thing in the way of her perfect family vision. And I hated how upset I felt about it.

"Fine with me. I really need to go. See you later." I quickly stepped outside with a lump in my throat and a pit in my stomach.

I leaned against the door and breathed in several times deeply.

As far as I could see, farmland was broken up into neat patches of yellow and green fields. And in a week, it wouldn't be my morning view anymore.

I'd known it was coming, but I hadn't seen it happening like this. It stung to imagine them discussing how they needed me to leave. It felt horribly awkward to sit there and be asked politely to move out. I didn't want to be hurt over it. I didn't want them to pity me.

I wanted to be happy for them and hopeful for me.

I didn't want to feel any of this.

I waded through the purple fields, trying to breathe in the calming scent of lavender, but it didn't work like it usually did. There was a buzzing under my skin, running through my veins. I wouldn't feel calm again until I got it out.

I shaded my eyes and squinted out into the pasture to find Loon. She ran toward me, her caramel coat shining in the sunlight against her brilliant white mane. I realized that they hadn't said anything about if she could stay here or if I'd have to find another stable. My eyes welled up. I didn't want to move her. Loon loved it here. This was the most beautiful stretch of land outside Windermere, nestled between the sea and the foothills of the mountain.

She reached the fence, pushing her head against me. Tears threatened to spill as I stroked her soft coat and kissed her velvety nose. She was the last piece of family I had left, a gift from my father. He'd said that every child should have a pet, especially when their parents weren't very good company. He'd smiled, but I always thought there was more truth in that statement than he realized.

Sometimes, she was the *only* company I had.

I wanted to ride right now and leave everything behind. Loon could sense it. Her hoofs began to dance on the ground and she dipped her head against me, nudging me to go get a saddle. But I couldn't. Not until I had taken care of the wild parsnip.

My future depended on it now.

"An hour and I'll be back," I promised. Loon lifted her head and looked at me like she understood. Then she pranced beside me as I made my way down the path into town.

———

Outside The Hidden Thorn, the wild parsnip was still wrapped where York and I left it. Except now there was something tucked inside.

I reached down and plucked the note from the folds of burlap. York's handwriting scrawled across the page: *When you're ready*. He'd left his knife with it.

I bit my lip as I tucked the note and knife into my bag with the owl and cube. York was probably already in class with Percy. I doubted I would see him today as I planned to use it to figure out the meaning of the cube and owl. But now I was thinking that some space between us might be a good thing. I could never hide how I felt from York and I didn't want to talk about anything right now.

Before I could unwrap my plant and see how it had fared overnight, Mr. Everett stepped out the door. "Ah. Ivy. Glad I caught you."

I straightened. "Good morning."

"I need to speak with you. It seems some of the students told their parents about your plant and its potential dangers. I'm afraid I've gotten quite an earful already this morning. I understand their concern, and I also know that I didn't put any restrictions on what type of plant students could submit. I hadn't expected anyone to bring in something so harmful... So this is a situation."

Worry clenched in my stomach like a fist. "Are you saying I can't use this?"

Mr. Everett frowned. "No, I'm not saying that, but we do need to take precautions. You can bring it up to the loft and no one will be allowed upstairs. That should ease any fears, and you won't have to continue searching for a specimen. I wouldn't want you to fall behind when this week you need to focus on getting it potted and flourishing."

I nodded. "I'll bring it up now. Where do you want me to

put it?"

A look I couldn't decipher crossed his face. I wondered if I had made a mistake in asking.

"I'll leave that up to your expertise," he said.

I nodded, flushing. Then I remembered something Adeline said once in class. It was hotter up in the loft and certain plants didn't do well with that. I'd better look up wild parsnip to see where it thrived best. I could always request to move it later. Right now I needed to get it in a pot and give it water. I knew that much.

"Ok." I picked up the backpack with my plant and stepped through the door.

But when I walked inside, I noticed that all the empty pots had been filled. They were also hidden behind wood screens. Now I couldn't tell whose plant was whose, or what type of plant others had found. I looked at Mr. Everett, confused.

"When you presented your plant as a mystery yesterday, it captured my imagination," he said, beaming. "It got me thinking. I wondered how I could enhance our test this year. Then it came to me. Instead of students presenting their specimens, the plants will remain a mystery. Now, in addition to the final test, each student will also need to identify each specimen and know an important fact about it. I must say, it's my favorite idea yet. I may continue it every year."

I tried to keep my face neutral as I looked around the room, panicking. Even on my best day, I could only confidently identify half the things Mr. Everett grew in here. How would I ever know what the others had found?

"Well, I'll let you get to work. Please pull a screen around your plant so no one sees it." Mr. Everett said, weaving back through the aisle toward his desk in the front of the room. "And do be careful, Ivy."

I stood there for a moment, wondering how this test could get any worse. Then I picked up my plant and headed to the curving stairs that led up to the loft.

Ten

I had never been up in the loft before, but I liked how narrow and cozy it was.

Floor to ceiling shelves lined the back wall, filled with Botanist's and Arborist's books, and the other side was open. Just an iron railing with more hanging plants that overlooked the bottom level with desks. It was like being up in a tree, tucked away from the world below.

I lugged my plant to an open space and got right to work. The bottom of the bookshelves were filled with the materials I needed to repot the wild parsnip. I was glad I didn't have to drag them each up separately. The plant was heavy enough.

I kept the wild parsnip covered as I put on gloves and rolled over an empty black pot. I filled the bottom with dirt and lifted the wild parsnip into the pot. Careful not to touch the stem or any bottom leaves, I packed more dirt around the roots until the pot was full. Then I emptied the water from a silver can into the dirt, and unwrapped the burlap.

Its jagged leaves were still full, and to my relief, there was no wilting or tears. I noticed some slight drooping in the flower stems, but that should be fixed in a few days. I quickly unfolded the wood screen and set it around the plant so I wouldn't accidentally touch it. Then I searched the shelf for a book on poisonous plants.

I settled down next to the bookshelf, enjoying the peaceful loft and the space around me. For the first time in weeks, I felt a sense of relief I'd found my plant and others were impressed by it. After this, I could focus solely on studying. I just might pull this off after all.

After flipping through all the books and reading everything I could find about wild parsnip, I was even less worried. Wild parsnip liked living in open, warm areas without shade. The loft turned out to be the perfect spot for it. Another stroke of good luck.

I yawned as I reshelved the books. The warm air was dragging me into a nap. Instead, I stretched out my legs and looked over the railing. Mr. Everett was still at his desk. Adeline had come in to check on her plant; a few other people had brought theirs in and were working behind wooden screens. Everyone seemed unaware that I was up here and Mr. Everett looked like he'd forgotten entirely.

I opened my bag and pulled out the cube. This time I noticed that the sanded wood felt like velvet beneath my fingertips. Again, I wondered who'd carved this ... and why did my father have it?

Carving never interested him. As Arborists, we planted and selected the hard and softwood trees for the Carvers to use. Students were in charge of planting new trees for every tree that had to be cut down. Overseeing that grove of trees was the extent of my father's involvement in the Carving trade. Our house had been full of books, empty journals, and plants. I never saw my father pick out anything made by a Carver and bring it home.

But he had this cube. Which meant nothing ... or it meant everything.

But was it the cube he meant to keep safe, or the paper inside?

I wouldn't know until I opened it and read the note.

I pulled out York's knife and unsheathed it from the leather. After a deep breath, I pushed the knife into the same slot York had. It took a bit longer and some extra wiggling before the box clicked open. The top slid back.

I set the knife down and picked up the folded paper. My father had touched this last. What if it changed everything I thought about him and his last days? What if it changed my idea of him: quiet, studious, and dedicated to his work to a fault? Heartbroken over my mother, and unable to entertain anything that reminded him of her?

Part of me was scared to open it. Nicholas had told me my father had been paranoid.

Slowly, I opened the note.

The paper seemed to unfold on its own as if it was glad to be released from its confined space and wanted to be read. I pressed the paper even flatter, reading the words scrawled across the top.

Secrets run through the family tree, but they did not start with me.

Goosebumps prickled along my entire body. I glanced around, making sure no one was eyeing me from below. My heart beat double time as I read those words again.

Secrets run through the family tree, but they did not start with me.

Beneath that were three sketched images. Waves on a beach. A ring of trees. A Carving tool. Each image was enclosed in a circle as if they were meant to be seen as separate.

I frowned. Something was familiar about the images, but I couldn't place it. I knew I'd seen them before.

Beneath the images, ever so small, were the final words: *Open owl.*

My breath caught in surprise. Then every nerve in my body tingled as I pulled my mother's owl out of the bag. Next to the polished cube, this felt raw, untouched by a Carving tool.

No one would know it was an owl, except *me.*

No one would understand this part, except *me.*

I studied the owl. Then I scraped the knife gently over the wood, going as slowly as York did, noting every small change of the surface that could hide a small compartment. But when I had been over the owl twice, I began to worry there was nothing there. Until the knife caught on a slight ridge by the bark. I angled the knife toward the sharp side of the blade and pressed down firmer. My breath caught as I watched a crack spread along the back. I pressed the knife a little deeper and the wood split open.

I dropped the knife and pulled another folded paper out. Again, it was my father's writing. Same hurried scrawl, the same ink color. Almost as if they'd been written with the same pen, on the same day.

*Some things **must** be recorded, even if it is strongly advised against.*

Then there was a string of words: *Forest & Fern. Forest path. Forked tulip tree. Evergreen. Opening in path. Tree Garden. Inside stump. Feed the trees. Don't look, and don't touch with bare skin.* ***Ever.***

I reread it over and over, guessing what it could mean. Finally, I thought it might be steps to a location. And if so, then I guessed I was meant to start at Forest and Fern and use the path there to enter the forest. But why hadn't he made it clearer?

"Ivy? Are you still up there?"

I jumped at Mr. Everett's voice and shoved the paper out of sight. "Yes?"

"I'm closing up for lunch. Since the nature of the test has changed, no student can remain in the building without me present. You'll need to leave as well."

"Oh, OK. I'll be right down." I hurried to gather all my things, feeling disoriented. For a moment, I'd forgotten where I was. All that mattered was what my father had written. And where he wanted me to go.

Mr. Everett was waiting at the bottom of the stairs for me, presumably to escort me out.

"Are you feeling alright?" he asked, concern spreading over his face. "Did you touch your plant by accident?"

"No, no. I'm fine. Just hungry." I smiled, weakly.

"Go get some food in you. Now that your plant is here, you may use the rest of the week to study. Let me know if you have any questions I can answer before the test."

I nodded and left The Hidden Thorn. I cut through town, making my way over to Forest and Fern. I had the entire day left.

I was going to follow the clues my father had left.

Eleven

I made my way to Forest and Fern, passing the shops that sold books, hardware, fabrics, and flowers.

Taylor's Mercantile was also on the way. As I passed by, I spotted Mr. Taylor at the counter talking to John. He was probably telling him he could move in now. I put my head down and walked by quickly. I didn't want to have another conversation about how John's wife wanted my room.

In a week.

I sighed and turned the corner. Forest and Fern was suddenly in front of me. I had been in through the back yesterday but it had been a long time since I'd looked at the front of the building.

My childhood memories were vastly different from how it looked today. Now it was the quietest shop on the street. The black paint, along with our family crest, was fading. The front porch was dusty, the hanging pots that were usually filled with green ferns were empty, and the lights weren't on. I remembered how the inside was covered in a layer of dust. I wondered if I should have asked if I could maintain it. A better daughter certainly would have.

The dust on the porch had also been disturbed by someone yesterday. But why hadn't they waited until after my test to ask me for whatever they needed? Maybe they didn't think I was important. Or that Arborists were important. Maybe they didn't want anyone to know they had taken something. York hadn't seemed concerned that someone had been in there, but I felt uneasy about it still.

Could it have anything to do with my father's clues? Were they looking for the paper he'd left with Nicholas?

Why?

The longer I stared at the front of the building, the more another crest above the door caught my attention. Usually, my eye slid right over this symbol without a thought. Probably because it was everywhere around town. I'd seen it since I was born. But now, all I could do was stare.

My father had drawn those same images on the paper. A wave and a carving tool.

The Count's crest was also made of waves, a carving tool, and a ship.

My father had drawn two of the three shapes in the Count's crest.

Was it a coincidence?

I sank onto the bench outside the flower shop and thought about everything I remembered from before he died. He had been absent a lot, focused on his research in a way he had never been before.

Nicholas also said that he was paranoid. Worried. But there was nothing to be worried about inside the Arborist trade.

Something else, then.

My father hid a piece of paper in a carved box to keep it safe. Was that another clue?

I pulled out the paper again and studied it. The images were the same, drawn identically to the ones in the Count's crest. If I put them together, they were even in the same place as they were on the crest. I sat back, confused. Had my father been researching the Count?

Surely not. I was becoming paranoid too.

I chewed my lip and looked around the street. It was empty, except for a few people milling around. Calmly. Windermere was not a place of intrigue. Everything was what it seemed. Then why would my father feel a need to hide anything, or write so vaguely that his own daughter couldn't understand what he meant?

But maybe that was my fault. I'd never really understood my father or the Arborist trade. There was a good chance I was completely misreading his intention. Maybe Adeline would understand his clues better. There was another image with a ring of trees—I suspected it was an Arborist emblem. I could ask Adeline in a way that wasn't suspicious.

I looked at the other paper with the instructions. If I was right, they indicated that I should start here and take the road out into the woods. It was the same path I'd walked with my father as he went about his work.

The road led past the Carver's Wood Grove and continued deeper into the forest, but I had never been that far out. Especially not alone.

I could ask York to come along. I could ask Adeline what she knew about a ring of trees, but I wanted to prove to myself that I could figure this out. I was strong enough and smart enough to handle this. This had been left to me, after all. Maybe I just needed to believe I could understand it.

I gritted my teeth and stood. Then I walked into the forest.

I passed the grove of trees and followed the path as it wound further into the forest. The quiet and slow pace was exactly what I needed.

I breathed in deeply, letting the scent of moss, pine, and fresh air fill me. I knew the path was leading me away from town, so I did a quick calculation of where the road to the Count's property was. I figured I was walking parallel to it, but was still a safe distance away.

So, then, maybe the similarity of my father's drawings to the Count's crest was just a coincidence and his waves meant something else.

The directions on the paper said to follow this path until I came to a tulip tree that forked. That was strange. Even with the little I knew about tulip trees, I knew they didn't naturally fork. They grew fast, and straight like a pole. I couldn't imagine what it would look like with a fork in it—one that my father might have made. But that was unlike him to change nature. I pondered that as I searched for the wide, blunt-ended leaves that were so different from any other tree. As I walked, I tried not to think about my father on this path and the strange things Nicholas claimed about his state of mind. It was painful to imagine him like that.

Just as I began worrying I'd walked too far from town, or that I had somehow missed it, I spotted a tall tulip tree up ahead with a split in the trunk that forked up into two tall halves. Relief flooded me. I was figuring this out.

I stopped and examined the strange tree. The bark pattern looked like it had been sliced long ago on the inside. Someone had made it like this. I shivered and read the next line of my father's note.

Evergreen.

At first, I thought he'd meant an evergreen tree. But I looked around and saw only oak, hickory, maple, and beech. No evergreens. So, then ... the song, maybe?

Evergreen was also a slow tune about white orchids blooming in late summer. My father would hum it softly as we made his rounds around town, tending to plants and trees. I hadn't heard the song in years, even though it was common enough that anyone in Windermere would know it. But then I realized they wouldn't know how slowly my father had hummed it. He always changed the tune to something slow, melancholy, and haunting.

The hair on my neck tingled. He *had* meant this for me.

I began to hum as slowly as my father used to as I left the split tulip tree behind. As the sad song filled the air, I felt the essence of my father walking on the path beside me. I blinked away the tears as I hummed, thinking how silly it was that a simple song could overwhelm me. Maybe that was why I hadn't been back to Forest and Fern ... Why I hadn't thought of this song in years. It caused all these feelings to surge within me again when I'd worked so hard to pretend I was fine.

But now, I was walking toward a destination my father had planned for me years ago. In a way, he was still here with me, guiding me. I gripped his paper tighter as I finished humming the last few notes.

There.

A glimmer of light shone through a narrow break in the trees. I sidestepped into a small opening that I would have never normally seen. I didn't think anyone would have noticed this; it was invisible from the path. I squeezed beneath a hollow tunnel of branches and bushes, a solemnness stealing over me.

I walked softly until the branches lifted and the tunnel ended abruptly. I blinked, trying to understand where I was. There was no more path. The forest had changed from the predictable spaces of trunks and green underbrush.

Before me was a wall made of trees. Wild and ancient. Thick branches and leaves had grown and woven together tightly to form a living wall. There was no way through, above, or under the elegant tangles they had grown into, except through an archway made from the columns of two entwined trunks. The higher branches joined together in curving points at the highest part, almost like a living gate.

I set my bag down in awe. Then I looked back at the paper, excitement stealing over me. The next line was: *Tree Garden.* I walked forward and examined the archway. Everything here looked older than anything I had ever seen before. I felt like I wasn't in the same forest at all, but one that had been here since the dawn of time.

I took a deep breath, and stepped inside—or, I tried to.

It was like I ran into a solid door, even though there was nothing before me but air. I couldn't get under the arch. I leaned my shoulder in and pushed harder against the invisible barrier, but there was no give. The air was solid, but I could look through the space and see inside. Confused, I stepped back and pressed my palm out again only to feel the same resistance. How was I to get inside?

I must have stood there for a while, my head trying to wrap around the reality that I couldn't physically get through the arch.

Things like this didn't happen in Windermere. Maybe they happened in stories, or maybe they'd happened long ago, but in Windermere, things went as expected. Impossible things were for legends and myths. Not real life.

Then why was this air behaving like a solid?

I tried to walk into the arch again. No luck.

I turned around and picked up my bag. I didn't want to give up, but what could I do? I read the paper again. It said nothing about a patch of air that felt like stone. After the *Tree Garden*, it said *Inside the stump. Feed the trees.*

Feed the trees? I didn't bring any supplies for that. But I couldn't follow the paper any further if I couldn't get inside. I slung my bag on my shoulder and leaned against the strange air. To my surprise, this time I passed through the air easily, as if the invisible barrier had dissolved, and I tumbled to the ground on the other side.

Shocked, I pushed up to my knees. How had I made it? I stood quickly and stuck my hand back under the arch. The air was just a normal breath of wind against my hand, not solid. How had it changed? What was different about this time?

I glanced down and after a moment, I realized I was holding my bag. I stepped back through the arch and the air let me through. Then I set down my bag and tried to walk back inside the Tree Garden. The solid barrier of air was back. Part of me began to panic that I had walked out of the garden before I'd looked around, but something in my bag had gotten me in once. I just needed to figure out what.

There were two things it could be. I pulled out the carved cube and tried to cross through the arch again. The air stopped me.

I returned to my bag and traded the cube for my mother's owl. Nicholas had called it a key. Shaking, I tried again.

The air parted for me and I walked inside.

Relief filled me that the owl worked. But did it work the other way too? I set down the owl on the grass beside me and stuck my hand through the archway. The air wasn't solid, it let me through ... but a pulling sensation crept up my arm. It was sucking me out, without the owl. Before the Tree Garden could spit me back out, I jerked my arm back inside.

Wonder spread across my face in a wide smile. This was incredible. Nothing in my life was extraordinary, so I had no words to describe the feeling of how unbelievable this was. I must have stepped through the opening five times before I dissolved into laughter, unable to help it. What a secret this was! If I tried to tell anyone, who would believe me?

Secrets run in the family tree, but they did not start with me.

I sobered instantly. My mother's owl had gotten me inside the Tree Garden. Then, the secrets started with her? My father had always called it her owl. It had been the key to this place.

I went out one last time, owl in hand, to retrieve my things. Then I walked beneath the arch again, really seeing the Tree Garden this time. I stepped into a circular clearing covered with long, lush grass. Sunlight filtered down through the trees, covering everything in a warm green haze. A gentle breeze fluttered over the blades of grass, making them ripple like ocean waves. Birds chattered softly, high in the trees. Something was different here. It was not natural, but I immediately loved it.

Then, I sank to the ground, speechless.

I was inside a ring of trees.

Just like the image my father had drawn.

TWELVE

It was like I had stepped into another world. A time before people existed.

Ancient trees formed a circle, taller than any trees in Windermere. Wide branches spread outward, weighed down with heavy, oversized leaves. Each tree in the circle had a large hollowed-out hole in its middle.

A peculiar sensation hung in the air. It prickled the back of my neck and made me shiver. As if this place was waiting for something.

I shivered again, staring at the holes, burrowed deeply through the rough bark. They called to me. I stood and walked toward the trees. I wanted to see what was inside. But as soon as I looked inside them, I shrieked and jumped backward.

My heart slammed against my ribs. It was a minute before I calmed down and worked up the nerve to look again.

I hadn't imagined it. Inside the hole, someone had carved a face.

At first, it looked so lifelike that I was sure it was a person. But as I looked closer, it was clear it was formed from the wood of the tree. A face as big as mine, maybe longer. Goosebumps raised on my arms as wooden eyes stared back at me. They were serious and wise as if they had seen all that had happened in this circle. I stared at the man's face, at his elegantly straight nose and a deep, hollow opening for a mouth. His hair and long beard flowed like the wind was blowing through it. It was an excellent carving, with some of the best detail I'd ever seen.

Trembling, I pulled myself away and walked to the next tree. This face was different; it had round glasses and a hat. I moved to the next and the next. Each hole had a face, but the faces were as different and unique as people. Their expressions conveyed different personalities; some were serious, some happy, some curious. I couldn't shake the feeling that they had once been real, or could be real again.

Each had an open mouth. And each had the rings of the tree as strips across their face. There were too many rings to count. The trees must have been thousands of years old.

But the last face was truly unique. This one was the only female. She had owls carved into her hair like bows. Her brows were lifted, as if she had a secret. Her mouth was also an open hole, but the edges lifted in a smile. Instead of a beard, a big knot was hollow at the base of her throat, like a necklace had been lost. I frowned as I studied the shape of the hole—something about it was familiar, but I couldn't grasp what.

Intrigued, I walked to the center of the circle and sat, pulling my knees up to my chest. I felt a strange connection to my mother here, like part of her essence matched the essence of this place. I hadn't felt her inside Forest and Fern; I had felt my father so clearly there. But here—*here* I felt my mother, which was unsettling because I didn't have any concrete memories of her. I couldn't picture her face anymore, or the way she walked. I didn't remember her covered in flour, cooking; or trimming flowers at the kitchen table like Mrs. Taylor. I didn't remember anything about her. Why could I *feel* her so clearly here?

And it wasn't the trees that gave me that feeling, it was the feeling in the air. Of otherness. Of another world.

Another question I needed an answer to, but now the enormity of it all was overwhelming. It was like I'd pulled a thread and the whole shirt unraveled in my hands.

Why did my father know of this place?

Why was it hidden ... and sealed from people entering?

How did *I* possess something that would grant access? *Me?* The orphaned daughter of a respected Arborist without a green thumb to save her life?

I didn't feel equipped to handle any of this. I didn't even understand what *this* was.

But I could try.

I examined the trees again, this time looking past the holes. Large sections of the trunks had strips of bark peeling away, and some leaves on the lower branches were yellowing, even though it wasn't yet fall. Were they healthy? Had my father cared for them?

Then I realized that the trees' mouths were empty. *Feed the trees.*

Oh! But feed them what?

I read the paper again: *Inside the stump.*

I stood, halfway pleased with myself, and walked around the circle. I looked around the trees, wove in and out, but found no stump.

I picked up my bag, making sure the owl was firmly inside, and walked out of the archway. Then I saw it. Near the edge of the wall of trees was a taller-than-normal tree stump. I walked over and brushed the dirt and leaves away, and saw a handle and rusted-through hinges. I took a deep breath and pulled the lid open. Dirt fell into the deep, hollowed-out hole, but it was empty inside.

I shut the lid, disappointed, and walked back through the arch. I sank down in the middle of the circle of trees again, wondering what I should do now that the hole was empty. Maybe something had been inside for my father, but it had been ten years. What if I never made it past this clue?

My stomach rumbled. I ate an apple and some nuts in my bag, thinking that I liked being here. It was peaceful—dreamy, even. I didn't feel alone, even though I was. I felt content. The air here suited me more than the sea air of Windermere. I laid down on the grass and stared above. I traced the web of green leaves against the cloudless, blue sky. Nothing had changed in my life, but everything had shifted since I'd met Nicholas . . .

The next thing I knew, a prickly sensation stole over me and I jolted awake.

A snap of a branch sounded from somewhere in the woods.

My heart jumped wildly, my breathing stilled as I stayed where I was, hidden in the sea of long grass.

Something was moving through the forest. But it was not in the clearing with me—it was outside of it. Then I heard a neigh. A horse. That meant a rider was here too.

The hooves continued, slowly, unhurriedly around the Tree Garden. I pressed myself deeper into the ground, trying to gauge how far away they were. At one point, I thought maybe they'd stopped at the archway. But then the walking continued and eventually faded away. I waited until I was sure the sound of the forest was all I heard. Then I sat up.

I had fallen asleep, and from the look of the sun, it had been a few hours. I needed to get back and study for my test. I had done enough today with the clues and I couldn't do more until I figured out what to feed these trees. Something told me it was not normal tree pellets.

I also needed to figure out how carving fit into this. As I left the Tree Garden, I had the strangest thought. That I belonged here and I shouldn't go. I felt like I was leaving part of my parents behind. A part of them I didn't even know. I promised myself I would come back tomorrow.

I needed to learn what trees like these ate.

———

ADELINE WAS IN THE GROVE OF TREES WHEN I WALKED out of the forest.

Seeing her twisted my stomach as if I was truly in the real

world now and the Tree Garden had only been a dream. An urge to turn around and make sure it was still there filled me, but she saw me before I could react.

"Hey." Adeline tossed a log onto one of the piles she was making. "Where'd you come from?"

This grove was tended to by Arborists for the Carvers. When a tree was felled, the logs and branches were sorted into piles according to the density of the wood. Even though she didn't need the extra credit, Adeline was always the first to volunteer for Mr. Everett. She must really enjoy this. She was a natural, like my father.

Again, I wondered why I wasn't obsessed with the trade like they were. Then I remembered how I had just felt in the Tree Garden. I was captivated by those trees—more than anything.

Was that because they were trees, or because the place they grew was special?

Adeline stopped to look at me when I didn't answer.

"Just a walk," I said, quickly.

"Were you studying?"

"Um, no. But that's a great idea. Especially since part of our test is now identifying everyone else's plants." It sounded like a complaint, even to me.

But Adeline overlooked it and simply nodded. "Practicing in the woods would be more helpful than looking through pages of a book. I would say we could walk together, but I need to finish here first."

I shifted around a pile of logs. "Do you want help? We could quiz each other while we work."

She brightened. "Yes. Especially since we can't use The Hidden Thorn anymore."

"What do you mean?" I asked, confused.

"Didn't you hear?" She handed me a branch, already stripped of leaves, and pointed to the pile. "Mr. Everett won't let anyone in until the test, not unless they still have a plant to bring in. He doesn't want us to share notes about what's inside. He's moving all the books into the town library. He said they should be there tomorrow."

"What about watering our plants?" I asked, thinking about the wild parsnip.

"He said he would tend to them for us. So, at least that part is done, right?"

I nodded, slightly relieved. "Then, we just have to study the rest of the week in the library? There's no schedule for us?"

Adeline nodded. "He suggested making study groups, but our time is to spend as we wish. He said if we can't manage our time wisely by now, then he failed."

I could hear him saying that, and I knew he probably meant it to be funny, but it hit me hard. First the Taylors, now Mr. Everett. Another adult in my life was letting go. I had already been pushed from the nest before my wings had grown, but this felt like I was about to free-fall again. An ache filled the part of my heart that held my parents' absence.

I sighed. "What should I do?"

"Start quizzing. When I need a break, we'll trade." Adeline handed me her book and went back to sorting piles. I sat on a stump and opened it. I searched for a topic we both needed refreshing on but stopped when I saw a page about tree rings.

The Tree Ring Legends. Ten or more specific trees planted in a perfect circle, and through ceremony, transformed into a link to other worlds. The trees must be great oak trees or slender birch trees. But the picture looked nothing like the Tree Garden. And none of the trees had faces in them or holes in the trunks. There was nothing about feeding them anything specific either.

I flipped further, hoping to find something about carving faces into trees.

I wondered if there was something in the Carving trade about that, or its significance. But I couldn't go around asking. I didn't want to draw any attention to the Tree Garden's existence. My father must have had good reasons for hiding it.

"Ready whenever you are," Adeline said, reminding me she

was waiting.

"Sorry! Um … what is the most important food you can feed a tree?" I asked, looking up.

"If it was diseased, or if it needed help growing?"

"Let's say the leaves are turning brown in the summer. And the bark is peeling in large sections. Could that count as being sick?" I clarified.

Adeline's entire attention was fixed on the question now, her piles forgotten. Her brow wrinkled, then cleared. "Sugar and oxygen. A healthy plant will make those from its chlorophyll cells that mix with water brought in through the roots and sunlight. But if it needs more help, you can add a mixture of nitrogen, phosphorus, and potassium to the soil. Among other things, of course, but those three are the most important." She used her fingers to tick off a list. "You can get nitrogen from rabbit manure. Phosphorus from rock or compost, and potassium from rock powders or wood ash. Create a mixture and roll it into pellets, then add it to the soil as needed. You also need to be watering as much as it needs."

I caught my mouth from dropping open. "You know a lot, Adeline."

"I know what we all do." She flipped her shiny hair over her shoulder, casually, but her eyes were bright. "What else?"

I looked back at the book for my next question. I needed to get home and take care of Loon, but studying with Adeline was invaluable. And I wanted help.

"Do you want Botany or Arborist questions?" I asked.

Adeline didn't hesitate. "Both. Your father was brilliant in both too, you know. He was one of the only people in the trade who could effortlessly go between caring for plants and trees. He knew everything."

I nodded, noticing how much Adeline talked about my father. I wondered if that was because she didn't come from a family of Arborists. She would have thrived if she had been my father's daughter.

"I've been meaning to ask …" Adeline said, picking at a leaf nearby. "What do you plan to do with Forest and Fern?"

"Um. I'm not sure. I haven't talked to Mr. Everett about it yet."

Her eyes lifted to mine. "It's the only other Arborist shop in town."

I nodded, knowing that. I waited for her to finish her thought.

"I guess, I'm wondering. Well, would you want help? I could come work with you? Help you?"

"Oh," I said, surprised. She said *help me*. Had she known all along that I was struggling?

"I thought you'd want to stay with Mr. Everett," I said, carefully. "I always thought you'd eventually teach like him or take over for him. You know so much already."

She nodded. "I did too, but he hasn't said anything to me. I know I'd learn a lot from him, but Forest and Fern has all your father's research. You don't have to say yes now, think about it. Maybe I could start with you for a year or so?"

I pictured Adeline at my father's desk, poring over his notebooks while I had to keep pretending to know as much. But maybe that was just my fear. Maybe it wouldn't be like that at all. It would be nice to not have all the pressure of Forest and Fern on me. And maybe after we left our training roles, we could become real friends.

"Of course you can come, Adeline," I said, realizing that I liked the idea the more I thought about it.

"Yeah? Great." She smiled brightly. "Then, which do you think you'll lean towards? Botany or Arborist?"

"Arborist," I answered immediately, even though up till this point, I had only thought about passing the test to get Forest and Fern back. But now, the carved faces in the Tree Garden were calling me.

And I wanted to know everything about them.

Thirteen

I woke the next morning to the same uneasy feeling that I had imagined the Tree Garden.

Maybe it was the mundaneness of everything that came after discovering it; studying with Adeline, taking care of Loon, then studying late into the night. Somehow those normal moments had chased away the surprise and feeling of wonder I experienced there. Even Nicholas seemed like a distant memory.

I had to go back.

I threw off the covers and dressed as fast as my fingers would work. Mrs. Taylor wasn't in the kitchen, so I grabbed an apple and headed out the door. I hadn't seen either of the Taylors since our talk about me moving out. I was avoiding them because I felt awkward. I wished I didn't. I didn't want to leave this house feeling anything but gratitude that they took me in. I needed to focus more on that feeling than the feeling of being rejected.

I shut the door softly behind me. The sun had begun to paint the horizon with golden light, while the air still had a bite to it. I shivered and walked faster to get my blood pumping. I was anxious to be in the Tree Garden again. I needed to feel it.

It seemed I was the only one awake in Windermere, because I made my way into town, past Forest and Fern, and down the path into the forest without seeing a soul. Soon I was humming Evergreen and stepping into the opening of trees. My skin tingled with excitement as I walked through the tunnel. Then I was in front of the archway, sighing in relief.

It was here. It was real. It was just as wonderful as before.

Now I just needed to figure out the part about feeding the trees. I really didn't think the mixtures Adeline suggested yesterday were what *these* trees wanted. That food was practical, meant for normal trees. These were special trees, unlike anything in any book I'd ever read. Besides, just the thought of mixing rabbit poop in anything made my stomach turn.

Before I went under the arch, I decided to check the stump again. Maybe there was a clue somewhere inside that I'd missed. I hoped so. I walked over to the stump and opened the lid again. Delight flooded me.

This time, it wasn't empty.

There was a basket inside.

I lifted the basket from the stump and shut the lid. A stiff piece of paper, covered in interesting handwriting, was laid on top. The writing was not slanted nicely like my father's; it was quick and impatient like a failing grade slashed across a paper. I frowned just seeing it.

Each mouth gets one of both. Put the basket back here and leave when done.

Beneath the paper was a pile of small brown packages, wrapped neatly. Next to them were a dozen acorns.

I sat back, confused but curious. Were these packages the tree food? Or was it the acorns? And why did the person who wrote the letter assume I would obey them without any more explanation?

Because the writing felt like a command, not an invitation or a request.

My brow furrowed as I read the note again. *Leave when done.* Did that mean they knew I'd lingered yesterday?

Someone must have known because the stump had been

empty yesterday and today this basket was inside. I remembered the horse walking by as I lay inside on the grass. Someone knew I had come. But did they know I was following clues from my father?

Trembling, I dropped the note back into the basket and picked up my father's paper. I needed his reassurance.

Feed the trees. Don't look, and don't touch with bare skin. **Ever.**

The stiff new note hadn't warned me not to touch the packages. It also didn't say I couldn't look.

But my father had.

Nicholas had said my father was fearful and paranoid. He hadn't been full of the same wonder that I felt now. It was a reminder that I needed to be cautious and not so easily impressed by things I didn't fully know or understand. I frowned back at the other handwriting. For some reason, I felt like it didn't belong in this place, but why I didn't know.

Still, I couldn't help but be intrigued. I wanted to know what would happen when I followed these instructions. And I wanted to solve this clue.

So I grabbed the basket and walked beneath the arch. As I crossed under it, the same shiver of excitement spread through me and I caught myself smiling. Whatever *this* was ... I was drawn to it.

I marched up to the first tree and that was when my nerves turned into a swarm of bees. *Feed the trees.* I had to reach inside the hole and place the package and acorn into their mouths. My stomach flipped. What if something was hiding in there, ready to bite or jump out at me?

I picked up a package. It was solid but at the same time, it squished slightly under my fingers. I took an acorn in the same hand so I only had to reach inside once. I took a deep breath, and shot my hand into the hole, further inside the mouth, dropped the package and acorn in, and yanked my hand out.

I let out a gust of breath. Nothing happened.

I couldn't help but laugh, and be glad that no one was watching.

I made my way around the circle, repeating the steps over and over. There was one of each for each tree. Twelve total.

It was going well until I surprised a squirrel in one of the holes and it jumped out at me. I screamed and pelted the acorn at it. To my surprise, it grabbed it mid-air, stuffed it in its mouth, and ran up the tree.

I stepped back, surprised. I'd never seen a squirrel do that. It was like it had expected an acorn from me. Was that why I had them? So the animals would take an acorn instead of a package?

Then I realized the squirrel had taken my last acorn and this tree would only get a package. I hoped I hadn't already messed this up. There was nothing I could do but put the package in, alone, and hope it wouldn't matter.

I finished the task, uneasy.

It was only when I returned the basket to the stump that I realized that maybe whoever left the basket couldn't get into the Tree Garden and needed me. And if that was true, they would never know I lost one acorn. Maybe I hadn't made a mistake after all.

They also said I shouldn't linger, but how would they know? I casually flipped my hair over my shoulder and scanned the trees. But I didn't see anything or get the feeling I was being watched. I felt truly alone.

I wasn't sure how I felt about that.

———

I used the rest of the day and evening to study for my test. But the following morning, I rode Loon back to the Tree Garden. I couldn't stay away or think about anything else.

I had to know if the stump had another basket inside. Then I would go to the library and study. The days between me and my test were ticking away. Every moment counted now.

I let Loon graze while I eagerly checked the stump. But it was empty and the basket was gone.

I stared down into the hole, desperation filling me. What if no other baskets came? What if this was the end?

I pulled out my father's note and read it again. But feeding the trees had been his last clue. There wasn't anything else to follow or figure out.

It couldn't end like this.

I hurried into the Tree Garden and stopped, stunned. It was so much greener than it had been yesterday.

Today, thick green moss crept up the trunks like furry caterpillars and the tips of the trees were no longer yellow, but a vibrant green. Even the grass seemed longer as the wind blew through it. And was I imagining it, or were the trees taller too? Whatever was in those brown packages had been special food. Mr. Everett would kill to have his plants thrive like this.

The sight of it almost erased my anxiety. I soaked it in, imagining the trees growing up around me, digging their roots deep underground as they lifted themselves higher into the sky.

It took me a moment to realize I envied them. They were grounded in a way I would never be. If I was a tree, my roots would be shallow and thin, desperately clinging to anything to stabilize me. Nothing grounded me but loss. My parents were missing pieces, forever holes in my life. I would always feel their loss, even if I somehow managed to solve these clues.

I couldn't shake my fear that this was the end as I passed back under the arch and rode Loon back to the farm. I turned her out into the pasture and walked into town. I chewed my lip, worrying the whole way that I had come to the end of my father's instructions and I didn't have any answers to why he'd left me the cube. Or the owl.

I wished I only had my test to worry about, but since meeting Nicholas, my mind was now filled with so many questions about my parents. I had to uncover the answers.

Why had Nicholas found me? Why had my father told me

about the Tree Garden? There was some purpose to the packages in the trees, some reason only *I* could get inside. I was a part of this, somehow. I needed something else to happen that would cast all this into the light.

My feet trudged on to the library. I had been in my own world since meeting with Nicholas and maybe that's why I was stuck. I needed to think about something else and interact with others. Maybe that would help me see whatever I was missing.

Plus, the library also had books on Carving.

The library sat right next to the courthouse, the grandest building in town. Four large pillars held up the second-story balcony, and the Count's crest was carved into each one. It was the only building made from stone like the Count's castle, or so it was said. No one knew what the Count's castle looked like up close except Mr. Mallon.

I stared up at the crests, thinking again how much they looked like the images my father had drawn. Maybe I should turn my focus to them. If I could figure out what those images meant, maybe it would lead me back to the Tree Garden. I had figured out what the ring of trees was, but there were still waves on a beach and a carving tool—

Someone in the window caught my eye, and I realized I was just standing in the street staring into the building. I quickly turned and walked into the library, hoping I didn't look insane.

I stepped into the smell of faded ink, old pages, and the glue of bound books. Large iron lamps were lit all over the room. Every inch of wall space was covered in bookshelves and tables were pressed into nooks. Upstairs there was even more, but I went through two rooms to reach the back, where I found a room filled with tweed vests like mine. My entire class was here, but no one was speaking, and no one looked up at me. It was hard to not feel like I was behind and distracted.

I put my bag on an open seat and walked to the shelves, looking for a book I hadn't tried to memorize yet. I sat and read, trying to absorb all the text until my eyes began to cross. An hour or two must have passed.

I stood up and stretched, thinking I had earned a small break. So, I walked up the stairs to the Carving section.

There were so many more books up here. There were books on Carving tools, Carving techniques, Carving sculptures from Windermere's history, Carving families, and so many more. I scanned the shelves, looking for something about carving faces. As I turned the corner, I found Percy, Bryn, and York sitting at a table. York looked up, and a smile of surprise filled his face.

"Hey," he said, standing.

I smiled back. "Hey."

Percy and Bryn both looked up. Percy nodded and looked back down into his book.

"You must be Windermere's biggest carving fan, Ivy." Bryn sniffed and turned a page in her book as if she couldn't be bothered to say something more insulting.

York moved around the table and stopped in front of me so Bryn was blocked. "Are you studying here too?"

"Yes, downstairs, though," I said pointedly, for Bryn's benefit.

"Then someone should explain to you how the stairs work," Bryn mumbled.

I rolled my eyes and looked at York. "I came up here for a book about carvings in trees. Do you know where that would be?"

"Maybe over here. Come on." York walked with me over to a section of books. He pulled one out and handed it to me as he continued to search through the shelf. "I haven't seen you in a few days," he said, quietly.

"I know. I've been studying."

He looked like he didn't believe that. "Then, everything's OK?"

"Of course." I didn't want to get into it now, especially when I could literally feel Bryn straining to hear us all the way from her table.

"Do these books have to do with the Arborist test?" York asked, handing me another one.

"Sort of. No one is sure what Mr. Everett is adding to the test this year so we are trying to study everything. It's exhausting. Have you ever read anything about faces carved into trees?" I asked, my voice so low I wasn't sure he heard it.

His fingers trailed over the lettering on the books. "Why?"

"Just curious."

His eyes met mine briefly before he looked back to the book spines in front of him. "Do you still have my knife?"

I frowned, feeling like something was off between us, but not sure what. Then it hit me. The note he'd left with the knife. That had only been two days ago, but it felt like months. I'd forgotten to thank him or tell him I got it.

"Yes," I answered, relieved to figure that out. "Thanks for leaving it for me, by the way." I smiled at him to show I was grateful he thought of me.

But York didn't smile back. He focused back on the shelf. "I thought you would have returned it sooner."

I looked at him, surprised, and once again wondered what he meant. Had he needed his knife or was he annoyed that I hadn't asked him to open the cube with me?

Or was he simply pointing out that we hadn't talked since he'd come with me to meet Nicholas? We'd gone a few days without speaking before and it hadn't bothered him then.

Was he actually bothered? I couldn't tell if I was reading too much into this. York was usually easygoing.

"Are you mad at me?" I asked, genuinely curious.

His brown eyes flashed to mine. He studied me for a second before saying: "No."

"OK," I said, still confused. "Well, I'm sorry I didn't return your knife. It's downstairs. I can give it back to you now if you want it."

His lips pressed together in a thin white line.

What had I done now?

Maybe he wanted me to tell him if I had used his knife to open the cube. I glanced behind us. Bryn looked quickly down at her book.

I sighed. I did want to tell York about everything I had discovered, but I didn't feel like answering all the questions right now. I really had to study. I shouldn't even be up here.

And part of me was frustrated that I couldn't tell him I had figured out the clues all on my own.

But this was not the place to talk about it, or about this tension between us. And selfishly, I didn't want to deal with anything more right now.

"I need to get back downstairs. Come get your knife before you leave, OK?"

"OK," York said, sliding a book back on the shelf and walking around me to go back to Percy and Bryn.

I stared after him for a second before I walked away.

I walked down the stairs, not seeing anything but the steps under my feet. When I reached the landing, I didn't notice someone waiting below, blocking the hallway.

When I finally looked up, I found Mr. Mallon, the Count's Regent, towering over me.

FOURTEEN

Even though I'd seen him around town my entire life, I'd never been so close to the Count's Regent before.

Mr. Mallon wore the same black suit and matching hat as always but up close, I saw the vest under his suit jacket was embroidered with a thick silver thread and had a row of matching silver buttons.

I quickly slid to the side so he could pass, but he held up a hand to stop me. I hesitated, surprised, as he studied me a moment longer, pinning me to the ground with his stare.

"Ivy Rune?" he finally asked.

His voice reminded me of a tree shattering as it smashed into the ground. I wanted to flinch away, but I nodded, startled he knew my name. He only associated with the important families in Windermere, mainly the Carvers. I was beneath his notice.

His body sharpened with a new interest as he inspected me. There was a shrewd look in his eyes as they moved over my face and hands as if looking for something. I shifted back on my heel and tried to create space between us. I wished York had followed me.

Finally, he lifted a leather book. "This was found in my collection. Misplaced, I assume."

At first, I was confused, thinking it was a library book and wondering why he was giving it to me. Did he think I worked here? But then my lungs stalled. I would know a book like that anywhere.

My father's office was filled with books identical to this one, each bought from the same merchant during the Count's Woodworking Tournament. I thought of the diagrams and notes scribbled on every page of the leather bound books that lined his shelves.

But why would Mr. Mallon have one of my father's journals?

I realized he was still holding it out to me, so I took it, my hands trembling. The leather surprised me. I'd expected it to feel like butter, soft and pliable like all my father's journals had been from use. But this one was firm and stiff. Which meant, if it was my father's, he hadn't had a chance to use it much. Maybe it was his last one—

"Well, open it. Confirm it's his."

I blinked up at Mr. Mallon, surprised by his impatient tone. I didn't want to open it with him watching me, in case there was another clue inside. But he cleared his throat, pointedly waiting. So I opened the first page and found the neat, slanted handwriting I knew I would.

Suddenly Mr. Mallon and the library faded.

All that existed was my father's writing. I stared at it, hearing his low, calming voice reading me his words . . .

Hedera is an undervalued, overlooked species. It hardly needs any attention and will wreak havoc wherever it chooses to thrive . . .

This time, instead of curiosity and wonder, I felt a lump rising in my throat. This sounded more like him than the secret note I carried in my bag did. Memories flooded me as I flipped through the pages, past sketches of tangled vines, observations, and my father's tips on how to care for hedera.

Tears pricked the corners of my eyes as I leaned in to smell the old pages, partly to hide my emotion, and partly because I hoped to catch a whiff of his cologne. I breathed in the faded ink, just barely catching the woodsy scent of his office . . . and something else. Something sharp like metal.

I pulled back slowly and saw a trail of yellow flecks hiding in the crease between the pages. Was it pollen? But it looked different. Pollen didn't catch the light like that—

"Well, is it his? Do you speak?"

My head snapped up. "I can speak." But my voice trembled. "It's his."

"Good."

I wasn't sure if he was referring to the book or if I could use my voice after all. At that moment, my lungs had begun to tingle. Not painfully, but enough that I noticed and felt uneasy. I patted my chest as if that would stop the strange sensation from blooming out of my heart. When I sneezed, specks glistened in my palm.

"Mr. Mallon!" Mr. Everett was hurrying over. He hastily brushed off his white sleeves and fastened the buttons on his dark green vest. I'd never seen him so flustered before.

"I'm surprised to see you here, with the Count's Woodworking Tournament just days away. Does this mean you've changed your mind? Will I have the honor of supplying the wood for the Carvers this year?"

"No, I have not." Mr. Mallon pulled a heavy silver pocket watch from his vest and flipped it open. The Count's swirling crest was etched on the outside and the watch ticked loudly in the quiet room. "As I tell you every year, the Count does not need help sourcing the wood. I came for one of your students."

Mr. Everett frowned at me, no doubt also confused as to why the Count's Regent would come looking for me. "Perhaps I can help with whatever it is you need?"

"I do not need anything further. I simply returned a book that belonged to her father."

My lungs burned as I sneezed again.

"Ah, the pollen." Mr. Everett glanced down at the open journal in my hands. "I remember how Mr. Rune liked to sprinkle it on the pages. He claimed he needed to be near the essence of the plant at all times."

Mr. Mallon watched me; his expression reminded me of a sly fox.

"But shouldn't this go back in Forest and Fern?" Mr. Everett asked. "As it is an Arborist's item."

I tried to breathe normally through the buzzing in my chest. My eyes felt like they were growing too, widening.

"If it was meant for Forest and Fern, I would have taken it there." Mr. Mallon's voice was sharp as a knife.

Mr. Everett tensed, but I wasn't paying attention to them anymore. For each time I blinked, the lamps along walls flickered brighter . . . The light looked different. Instead of a translucent yellow glow casting about the room, the light felt solid, like I could reach out and grab it. It had changed form and now it seeped into every molecule in the air like golden honey oozing from a hive—

"Now I must go," Mr. Mallon said, abruptly.

I jumped at his voice. When I looked back at them, the light in the room returned to normal. Somehow I had just seen something no one would understand. Something that I couldn't properly explain.

Then I noticed the pinched look on Mr. Everett's face. He was hiding it, but I'd never seen him so upset before.

"There are still a lot of preparations to be made. Farewell." Mr. Mallon turned on his heel and swiftly left the library.

Mr. Everett stared after him. Then he straightened his green vest and looked down at me. "What a find this book is," he said, edging closer to me to peer over my shoulder. "As our most gifted Arborist, your father's notes are most valuable to our trade. And not one has been read since he passed. "

A *find*.

I remembered the journals sitting on his desk in Forest and Fern. I thought about the person who'd come in and searched the room while I had been inside. Had this journal been in the room too? Or had it really been misplaced? Why would the Count's Regent—someone who had the keys to all the shops in town—give it to me now?

Had Mr. Mallon been the one inside Forest and Fern with me?

I shivered at that thought. I didn't want to imagine what would have happened if he had turned the corner and caught me on the stairs.

"Ivy, would you like me to keep this book for you until after the test?"

His tone told me what he wanted me to do: Hand it over. If I didn't, he would think I was getting unfair help on my test. But something had changed in me because of this book. I had to know why. What if there was another clue inside? I couldn't give it up.

"No thank you. Goodbye, Mr. Everett." I snapped the book shut and hurried out of the library without looking at him. I didn't want to see the disappointment on his face.

I hurried past people on the street and the shops without seeing them. I stuffed the book in my leather bag, still feeling the strange sensation around my lungs. I couldn't make any sense of how Mr. Mallon fit into this.

I stopped at the large stone fountain in the middle of the square, unsure of where I was heading. The water spilled out beneath the stone ship, just like the vast blue sea at the edge of town. I thought about the wave in the image my father had drawn. I was jittery and anxious. One thing after another had happened in the last week, and I was spiraling without direction.

I set my bag on the lip of the fountain and plunged my hands into the water, savoring the shock of cold in my fingers. My head cleared slightly and I breathed a little deeper.

Except my lungs were still tingling, expanding at the end of each breath, like if I breathed in any deeper, they might burst. I winced and let out a few buttons of my vest. I should have asked Mr. Everett what kind of pollen he thought the yellow dust was before I ran out, but I didn't want to look foolish if I should already know.

I wiped my hands on my brown skirt. Sunlight flickered in my eyes, and a dull ache began to creep up my neck and make my head pound. Usually, pollen didn't bother me, but perhaps this pollen was from a plant I hadn't encountered before. Maybe it was rare. Maybe that was why Mr. Everett was so interested in the journal.

The glare of light dancing on the water made my head ache. I closed my eyes, but I couldn't escape the hum of energy bouncing between people in the street. From the bits of conversations around me, I gathered that the entire town square was swept up in anticipation of the quickly approaching Woodworking Tournament. I'd been too wrapped up lately to notice it.

My father's journal beckoned me. I turned away from the drops of water and leaned against the lip of the fountain as I pulled the journal back out. The pages crinkled open, but I didn't see any more yellow dust. The pages seemed straightforward, no vague clues for me here. Just one word written over and over.

Hedera.

It must be a tree or plant he was researching. Again, I wondered if it was something I should know.

A prickling awareness pulled me out of the journal. My eyes swept around the town square, and I saw Mr. Mallon standing directly on the other side of the fountain, staring right at me through the droplets of water.

I stood quickly, startled by his frown.

"Did you need something else, Ms. Rune?" he asked.

"No." My face burned from surprise and embarrassment. Did he think I followed him out here?

His eyes narrowed as he shifted impatiently as if *I* was keeping *him* at the fountain. "Then what is it?"

Words stuck in my throat. I didn't know what to say. Why did he think I was following him?

"Thank you for the journal," I managed, holding it to my

chest. That was not what I intended to say, but his sharp expression softened slightly.

"You may keep it and study it thoroughly. We haven't had someone with blood so green since your father, no matter how Mr. Everett tries. It would benefit Windermere to have another gifted Arborist."

I managed a nod as my stomach knotted. I didn't know Mr. Mallon noticed Arborists. And I wasn't gifted. Now I was even more anxious about passing the test.

His eyes darted to my hands ... or maybe to the journal. Then, without another word, he turned on his heel and left. The crowd parted as he passed through and disappeared.

I stood watching him, utterly confused. Nothing about the encounter made any sense.

Then a merchant passed by the fountain; the shine from the large golden pendant on his neck flashed in the sun. A searing pain bloomed behind my eyes and exploded into light.

I gasped and fell forward, gripping the edge of the fountain. The pain stole my breath. I fell to my knees, covering my face.

Then, I saw nothing.

FIFTEEN

It was quiet and something was covering my eyes and forehead.

I shifted, realizing I was lying down. Then I remembered the street, the fountain, and that last moment when I felt the pain burst in my head. Instinctively, I squeezed my eyes shut even harder.

But thankfully, that searing pain was now gone. The relief almost brought tears to my eyes. Even with my lids closed, that light had been unbearable. I pulled in a shaky breath, remembering the strange sensation in my chest just before the pain. That feeling was gone too.

There was a lot to think about.

I reached up and took the cloth off of my eyes.

I was in my bed. In my room.

And I was wearing a nightgown, my hair tumbled around my shoulders in dark amber waves. Someone had changed me and brushed my hair. I shot up, immediately uncomfortable. How had I gotten here? And how long had I been asleep?

The window was open; a light breeze blew against the linen curtain. The sun was high in the sky, but I couldn't tell what time it was. I swallowed and winced as my throat scratched painfully. I needed water.

"Thank goodness, you're finally awake." Mrs. Taylor walked into the room. She put a hand on my forehead and studied me. "How are your eyes?"

"Fine, I think. Why? What happened?" My voice came out scratchy and weak.

I looked around and saw a glass of water on my bedside table. Before I could reach for it, Mrs. Taylor picked it up and handed it to me. I gulped the water down quickly, then winced as my throat tightened painfully. I forced myself to sip slower.

"We don't know. Heatstroke maybe, but more likely, exhaustion. Except you kept complaining about your eyes and the brightness during the night. We were so worried."

"When did I pass out?" I asked, uneasily.

"Yesterday afternoon. Scared everyone half to death. Especially York. He was the one who found you and both he and Mr. Mallon carried you to the Mercantile. We brought you home and Dr. Ray met us here."

My eyes widened. A whole day had passed. That yellow dust ... then the pain. I remembered the pain more than anything. I touched my eyes carefully, but they didn't hurt anymore. Hopefully, they were fine and that would never happen again.

"Wait, did you say Mr. *Mallon* helped carry me?" I asked, disbelief filling my voice.

"Yes. He was in the town square and saw you collapse. He was very helpful. Not that we expected him to be anything less, but he isn't usually what anyone would call warm. He'd order someone else to help, of course, but he did this all on his own."

Mr. Mallon saw me collapse. I thought he'd walked away. Had he been watching me read the journal? Was he also looking for the clues my father had left? Was that why my father hadn't hidden them in Forest and Fern?

The bed shifted as Mrs. Taylor sat beside me. "What happened?"

I hesitated. What could I say? That I'd inhaled something in my father's journal? One that the Count's Regent had given me and Mr. Everett was unhappy about me having? I bit back a groan. Mr. Everett. I should have handled him better, but I hadn't been in my right mind. Hopefully, he wouldn't think I had an unfair advantage with the test now. I'd need to smooth things over with him.

"Ivy?" Mrs. Taylor prompted, waiting for my answer.

"Um, it must have been heatstroke. I've been really tired lately."

What if the journal had really been in Forest and Fern and Mr. Mallon was the one who'd broken in to get it for me?

No, that was crazy. I was becoming paranoid. All the clues had led me to was the Tree Garden. So far.

But there had to be something more I was missing.

I threw my covers back. "Can I get up? I'm fine now and I've just lost a day of studying!"

Mrs. Taylor nodded and stood. "It's alright with me. I'll let the doctor know you're up. He may come check in on you again. Strange. You didn't have a fever or chills. We couldn't figure out what caused it."

I swung my feet off the bed. "I'm sorry for making you worry."

"It's alright now. Oh, and York's here. He's out taking care of Loon for you."

York was here. Good. I wanted to talk to him and fix how our last conversation ended. I stood. "Could you ask him to wait? I'll be down in a second."

"Of course. I'll let you get dressed." When she reached the door, she turned and added, "What a nice friend York is to you."

I nodded. "I know he is."

Thankfully, she didn't say more as she shut the door.

As quick as I could, I threw my clothes on and checked my bag. Everything was there; the journal, the cube, the owl, and

York's knife. The papers were still folded inside their compartments. I grabbed the bag and rushed from the room.

But as I walked down the hall, I slowed, noticing the upstairs rooms were no longer empty.

Trunks of clothes and children's toys filled the first two rooms. Four nicer trunks sat in the biggest room. Miranda and John had moved in while I was out cold.

How worried had anyone really been if they were busy unpacking as I lay unconscious? A flush of guilt crept up my cheeks for even thinking that. This wasn't my home; I was the one imposing on them. Still, I couldn't help but feel crowded in a space that had once been all mine. I flew down the stairs, two at a time so I wouldn't run into anyone.

I bit my lip, worrying now about living alone, cooking for myself, and making money. But that was *if* I passed my test. The best outcome.

Because if I didn't pass, my worries would be even more dire. Where would I go if I lost Forest and Fern? I couldn't stay here. The overflowing rooms made that crystal clear.

I stepped out of the house. The buttery light of the sun didn't bother me and I breathed in deeply, grateful for at least that. I hoped I'd never feel pain like that again. Or fear. Because deep down, when everything had gone white, there was a moment when I thought I wouldn't ever see again.

I made my way through the lavender fields, casting my anxious thoughts behind me like stones. A stone for Nicholas. A stone for my father's secrets. A stone for my mother. For my test. For moving out. For feeling like this was all too much ... I imagined myself feeling lighter as each worry dropped away.

At the end of the field, York stood at the fence petting Loon. When Loon saw me, she left York and pranced over to me.

"Hey, girl." I stroked her soft neck. She nudged my shoulder, pushing her face into my body. "Thanks for helping me yesterday," I said, louder to York. "And for helping with Loon today."

He pushed off the fence and walked toward me. "You're OK now?" He looked relieved to see me up.

I smiled, glad things between us felt normal now. "I think so. Sorry if I scared you."

The tension feathering his jaw disappeared when he saw I was fine. "You did. That was so unlike you."

Then Mr. Taylor walked out of the stable, wearing his work clothes and brown vest. "I thought I heard you, Ivy! Glad to see you're up. Gave us all a fright when you were carried into the Mercantile yesterday."

My stomach dipped. "Was it a huge scene?"

York noticed my embarrassment. "No. I saw you collapse first, but then Mr. Mallon was there. He helped so fast that no one really noticed. Mr. Mallon said you must have been overtired from studying for the test."

I could tell that York didn't believe that at all. I rubbed Loon's velvety nose, unsure what to say.

"Everyone understands. You've been pushing yourself studying so much," Mr. Taylor added. "Probably even strained your eyes from all that reading. At least the tests will be over next week; then we all can enjoy the Count's Woodworking Tournament. Well, I'm glad you're better, but please take it easy."

I promised I would. And when he left, I turned to York. "What's left to do with Loon?"

"Nothing."

"Take a walk with me, then?"

"Sure."

Loon trotted alongside us for as long as she could. We crossed over the bridge and the fields began to morph into shops. As we passed Wilder's, the smell of baking and chocolate wafted out into the street. York stopped and asked if I wanted something. I nodded, grateful when he handed me a cup of a thick, chocolaty concoction. It was warm, spiced with cinnamon, and delicious. I sipped it slowly as we sat on a bench, and felt the tension slowly melt from my body.

"Are you going to tell me what really happened?" York asked.

I breathed out, deeply, glad I could finally spill my secrets to someone I trusted. I didn't have to be alone in this.

"Something did happen to my eyes," I answered. "Suddenly, everything was unbearably bright."

York's brown eyes narrowed. "You screamed. I was terrified for you."

I nodded. The white light had faded, but the memory of pain lingered like a ghost. I'd never forget what it felt like. "I thought I was going blind."

"But why?" York leaned closer to me. "What happened?"

I blew a breath out, wondering where I should start. Everything I was about to say sounded like I was reading too much into things. The sunlight didn't bother me now. The glare on the sparkling water, on the windowpanes we passed, on the jewelry people wore. Whatever happened to me yesterday was gone. My lungs felt fine too. Still, something *had* happened.

I frowned. "I don't know. And I'm not sure why I'm fine now."

"You don't sound happy about it," York said. "Why not?"

I opened my bag and took out the journal. "In the library yesterday, when I left you and went downstairs, Mr. Mallon was there. He brought me this. It was my father's."

York looked surprised. "Why would Mr. Mallon have it?"

I shook my head. "He said it was 'misplaced' in his office."

"It sounds like you don't believe him?" York said, noting my expression.

"Remember when we broke into Forest and Fern? I told you someone was inside."

"Someone with a key." York nodded, connecting the dots. "Have you looked in the journal yet? And what happened with that cube Nicholas gave you?"

I was about to tell him when I saw Mr. Mallon walk out of a shop a few doors down. I shoved the book back into my bag and leaned back so that York blocked me from his view.

"York," I whispered. "Mr. Mallon is right over there."

"Where?"

"Don't look!"

"Why not?" York looked at me, confused.

"He's everywhere now! I've never seen him so much. It's like he's following me or something."

"Following you? He's just getting ready for the Tournament. Of course he is everywhere. This is what he does every year."

"No, it's more than that. I can't explain it. He was so strange in the library. And then I saw him at the fountain after…"

"That's just his personality. We should go thank him for his help yesterday." York began to stand.

"No!" I said, pulling him down. "I don't want to be near him!" I remembered those beady eyes, studying me as if he could tell I knew things I shouldn't.

But what did *he* know?

York frowned. "Ivy, he helped you when you fell. And he gave you the journal. Why in the world would you think he meant you harm?"

I ignored York's perplexed expression and leaned forward to see Mr. Mallon moving down the street, away from us.

"Let's get out of here. I can't stomach another day of studying. Unless you have to?" I asked, realizing I was taking him away from his responsibilities again.

York looked toward The Whittling Wood. Then back at me. "I have some time. Where do you want to go?"

"Somewhere to take my mind off things. Somewhere we never go."

"Then follow me."

When I realized the direction he was heading, I hesitated. I almost said no, because I knew we were heading to another place that brought me no peace, just more questions.

But I followed him, because it was better to go with a friend.

Sixteen

The wide dirt path led us straight down to the harbor.

The sound of rattling carts and busy streets faded into the endless crashing of waves and cries of seagulls. A mist hung above the sea, seeping into the shore and hiding parts of wooden ships as they bobbed gently in the water. Sailors shouted at one another as they crawled over decks like ants. During the winter, this harbor was nothing but dark waves stretching out into the horizon. But in the summer, new energy drifted through the air, the song of faraway lands and untold stories.

And today, I viewed all of it differently. Instead of a pit growing in my stomach as I imagined my mother slipping onto a ship and sailing away from Windermere—away from me—I examined the people curiously.

I now knew there were secrets in the world, like the Tree Garden. That place was special, maybe even magical.

The Count did not want a town rooted in superstition, so our stories and legends centered around Carvers and doing the right thing, or cautionary tales about what happened if we didn't. Magic wasn't a part of them. But sometimes stories with magic would slip in from the merchant children, whispered to us in secret. Once parents heard them, they put an end to it being repeated.

And up till now, I would have said my father hadn't believed in such things either. But he had hidden the Tree Garden from the town, yet he led me straight to it. Why?

I looked around. These ships came from lands where people believed in magic. Could that be why my father had drawn the image of waves—to bring me to the harbor? As I drank in the sight of new people, the scents of exotic food, and studied the rich fabrics worn by merchants, I thought maybe that was true.

I spotted two of Windermere's Dock Masters inspecting the boxes going onto each ship. They wore the Count's colors on their vests: Black fabric with swirling silver thread. They stood with paper and pens, checking off goods on their lists as the sailors carried large boxes aboard. A few merchants stood a respectable distance away, waiting to answer questions if needed.

I was in awe of the sheer amount of boxes being carried onto ships. I knew merchants bought a lot from us, but seeing it in piles like this was staggering. I couldn't even imagine the amount of money merchants brought with them. Windermere's goods could only be acquired here, but once these boxes left our harbor, merchants raised the price exorbitantly. It didn't matter what price we set; the merchants gladly paid.

I realized then that the harbor was not a place where anything secretive could happen. The harbor was held tightly in the Count's fist. He selected and approved each ship that visited, and merchants followed his rules carefully so they wouldn't be banned from coming the following year. Even if I did figure out what to ask, no one was going to tell me anything. Who would risk their favor with the Count for me?

"See that?" A sailor on a boat near us pointed further down the beach to the thicker swirls of fog.

The man next to him frowned. "Glad we're not fighting against that today. I don't like the look of it." He wiped his brow before adding, "There's nothing natural about it."

I glanced at York, but he kept walking toward the fog, unconcerned. I followed, knowing we couldn't go that far. As we cleared the ships and left the crowds behind, York blurted out, "I don't understand why you acted like that with Mallon. There must be things you haven't told me, but I'm not sure why. We've never hidden things from each other before." He looked at me. "Talk to me, Ivy."

"I'm not keeping anything from you," I said, surprised. "I mean, not really. I'm just trying to understand what I'm dealing with first."

"But you don't?"

I sighed. "Not really. I did figure out some things, though." I explained how the paper in the cube led to the paper in the owl, and how the clues led me to the Tree Garden. "I won't describe it, not because I'm hiding it, but because I want you to experience it for yourself," I said, wondering if it was even OK that I took someone there. Then I explained how creepy Mr. Mallon had been when he'd given me the journal, and again at the fountain, ending on the yellow dust changing my eyes and lungs. "Mr. Everett said it was pollen," I finished, feeling like I had been talking forever. But York hadn't interrupted me once.

"And you don't think so?" he asked.

As an Arborist in training, I probably should recognize what it was, but I shrugged, unable to feel self-conscious with York. "I don't know much about pollen and what it does, but it's hard to believe the reaction I had could be caused by a plant."

York nodded. "OK. Then let's get into it." He rubbed his hands together. "Mr. Mallon works for the Count and the Carvers. So why would he bother bringing the journal to you?"

"He said he hoped there was another Arborist as talented as my father in town again."

"Your father was talented," York said, carefully. "But what did he do that Mr. Everett or the other Arborists can't?"

I shook my head. "I don't know. Adeline said he could cure or grow anything: Both plants and trees."

"Maybe Mr. Mallon would care about that in regards to the wood for the Carvers. But the Wood Grove has been fine since your father passed. Not a problem or a shortage. And we know that the Count only cares about the Carvers and the money they bring him. Other than that, he's a recluse who never leaves his castle or lets anyone but Mallon inside."

"All true," I agreed. "What's your point?"

"That those two don't value Arborists, not really. So why wouldn't Mallon just throw out the journal? What's inside of it?"

"Just one plant. *Hedera*. I don't know what it is."

"Exactly. Why would they hand-deliver it to you, a student who doesn't even practice the trade yet?"

I shrugged. "Maybe the Count likes herbs. Maybe he needs them for his old age."

A smile tugged at York's lips. "And they're hoping *you're* the one who will make the potions to keep him young?"

I laughed, unable to help it. I would probably poison him. York laughed too, and I was struck with the realization that only York could make a joke about my biggest insecurity and not make me feel more insecure.

I felt understood and accepted by him.

York didn't care that I couldn't keep up with my father's trade. He liked me for me.

At that moment, as I studied him, something small shifted between us. Here in the fog, it was just the two of us—and the idea of more. The wind brushed over my skin, prickling my arms. The axis of my world tilted ever so slightly, allowing me to peek into a future that I'd never seriously considered before. A future where maybe York could be a possibility.

York didn't speak, but he glanced at me. When he didn't look away, I wondered if he could tell what I was thinking, what I was weighing. The moment stretched on, suddenly serious, heavy with unspoken thoughts that might turn real if the moment continued any longer. I wasn't sure this was what I wanted. So I looked away, breaking the moment.

Only then did I realize how far we'd walked.

Somewhere in the fog, the beach had slowly changed from wide and flat to coarse sand, littered with dark, jagged boulders. A bundle of knobby green seaweed had washed up on the beach and the waves had splashed it against a large boulder. It looked like a vine growing up the rock. I frowned at it. Something about it bothered me, like its image was attached to a memory I'd long forgotten.

"Do you realize how far out we are?" I asked, turning back to York.

Only then did I notice the disappointment on his face before he hid it. He cleared his throat and said, "Not really, not with all this fog. Oh ... wow."

Then I saw it. Pointed tops of several stone towers rose from behind the line of trees off the beach.

"The Count's castle," I whispered. "We're too close."

"We'd better go. They say he has dogs bigger than wolves patrolling the woods." York's voice had a teasing edge.

"And that he's always watching from the highest tower. Waiting to snatch trespassers," I answered back, but my voice didn't sound as light. I swallowed.

Still, neither of us moved. Instead, we peered into the trees for another glimpse of the castle.

Suddenly, York grabbed my elbow and pulled me behind a boulder, scraping my shoulder.

I yelped, startled. "*Ow!*"

"Get down," he whispered.

"What's wro—"

"*Look!*"

I peered out around the rock into the water where he pointed. My eyes widened at the sight.

The strangest, broken-looking ship was drifting in toward shore.

Seventeen

Fog hid most of the ship, but from what I could see, it looked like it had been at sea far too long.

Torn grey sails snapped in the wind, half the railings on the deck were missing, and white barnacles and salt covered the weathered wood bobbing above the water. This ship should be sinking. Instead, it was steadily moving toward our beach.

I peered around the rock, my shoulder pressing against York's. Mesmerized, we watched as the strange ship swayed and dipped in the water.

"Where is it from?"

"I don't know." York's voice was so low I almost didn't hear him. "I can't see its flag."

I frowned, unable to place this ship with any merchant I'd ever seen in Windermere. In our harbor, the wood of the merchant ships gleamed against crisp white sails, crests emblazoned on flags they waved proudly. I'd never seen a ship like this before.

There was something eerie about the way it moved through the fog ... like the air was ripping itself in half to allow it to pass. Even from here, the ship creaked and groaned as it rolled over the waves.

And still, it moved closer.

"I can't believe it's floating," I said, in disbelief. "It looks wrecked—"

A movement on the side of the ship caught my attention. A small boat was being lowered over the side. It splashed into the water. Then a silhouette dropped down the side of the ship as if sliding down a rope, and landed in the boat.

The dark waves parted in that same strange cutting motion as the smaller boat sliced right through them.

This was the moment I knew we needed to decide whether to stay or leave. We should go, but now I was too curious about this ship and why it was all this way down the beach. Were they lost? Was it an almost shipwreck, and they just barely made it to our shore? Maybe they needed our help.

All those reasons made sense, but deep down I thought it could also be something else. And I wanted to know if it was.

York rocked back on his heels. "We're not allowed to be here. And we can't go back down the beach now. We have to use the Count's woods."

My stomach sank at the thought of leaving without learning anything. "Don't you want to know where it's from?"

York shook his head. "Not really."

"But I do. I just want to see the flag, then we'll go," I promised.

The wind swirled behind us, catching my hair and spiraling it out toward the sea. I grabbed the loose strands and knotted them tightly in my fist so we wouldn't be spotted.

"Please?" I whispered to York.

He groaned but leaned back against the rock again.

My heart skipped as the small boat reached the shallow water, and I wondered if we were making a mistake by staying. The boat came closer than I thought it would. We watched as a short man jumped out, splashing, and pulled his vessel into shore. His skin shone dark from the constant blaze of the sun. His head was covered with grey cloth, and gold glinted from his ears, lip, and nose. Jewelry even shone from his bare arms, where it climbed up his limbs like scales.

He was not dressed like anyone I recognized and that unsettled me the most. Our clothes told who we were and where we fit into the world. Even the brightly dressed merchants were walking symbols of their country. But this man wore the color of dusk from head to toe as if he didn't want to be identified.

But the strangest part yet was when he turned and began pulling the large, broken ship in toward shore. Alone.

We watched, speechless. I was sure York's mouth had dropped open like mine. The man was shorter than York and thinner than me. Chills went down my back as I watched the ship glide in closer, pulled by the man with impossible strength.

York's hands gripped the rock tighter and I inched lower. I was sure there was something unnatural about the man, and that piqued my curiosity. This man was different, just like the Tree Garden. Could he be what my father's waves had been pointing me towards? Had my father wanted me to come to the sea, not to see the merchants, but to see someone like this man? But how would he have known about a ship like this? It was either a coincidence or a ship like this had arrived on our shores before, when my father had been alive to see it.

And if it had happened before, that meant people visited Windermere without the town knowing.

York leaned toward me, but before he could speak, the sound of hooves thundered on the sand. The small man turned—the rope to the ship went slack in his hands. We turned our heads too, looking to the path by the woods where a rider sped out of the trees.

Suddenly, my world tilted again, but this was not the small seismic shift I felt earlier. This was a full earth rotation that thrust me into a new orbit. I felt the waves crash, the sand shift beneath my feet, and all my ideas about life simply imploded.

I would never be satisfied living a sheltered life again. I knew it in my bones.

My heart stalled as I watched the rider pull his enormous black horse to a skidding stop. It reared, its magnificent black mane splaying up against the blue sky, and the rider laughed.

A spark deep inside me burst into flame as if the life and power exuding from the rider and horse ignited something within me. In an instant, I knew life could be so much more than what I'd experienced so far.

And while the horse was stunning, it was the rider who captured my attention. I'd never seen anyone like *him*. Whatever future I had just considered with York paled in comparison to the possibility of someone like this.

He was easily the most handsome person I had ever seen. Dark wavy hair, sharp blue eyes, a knowing smile, and an air of confidence made him seem years older than me. He wore a dark button-down shirt and pants tucked into dark leather boots — not black exactly, more like the color of wet, gritty sand. Like the short man, his clothes were also unidentifiable.

I wondered where he was from. He seemed refined, cut from a different cloth than York and I. But he wasn't a merchant, although I could certainly imagine him commanding his own ship, even though he was young. We were on the Count's land ... But why would someone like him work for the Count?

Instinctively, I leaned forward, but York pulled me further behind the rock and hissed, "Stay *low*."

I shrugged him off, straining to see what was about to happen.

The man from the ship squared his shoulders and faced the rider. Next to the rider and his massive black horse, the short man seemed even smaller. Except he didn't look afraid.

A warning tingled through me. I looked back at the rider to see if he was concerned.

But the rider swung down and flashed his white, even teeth in an easy smile. "It's been days. We worried you were lost. Or reconsidered." His voice was like a river flowing over rocks.

"Even I cannot control the weather," the short man

responded in a stilted voice. "And you should know of anyone in this place: We keep our bargains."

The rider nodded and smiled again. "Of course, I know that. And you're here now." His voice sounded like he was used to using it to disarm people—to show there was nothing threatening about him—but I got the feeling that not many people challenged him.

I also got the feeling that the shorter man was used to being challenged—and striking before anyone realized *he* was a deadly threat. My shoulders tensed, and I wondered if York felt the friction in the air too.

The rider gestured to the rope. "Would you like help?"

The small man looked offended. "I would not."

His tone made the hair on my neck raise. York shifted uneasily next to me, but the rider nodded calmly as if he didn't notice. His blue eyes flashed out to the larger ship still in the water.

I was impressed with how composed the rider remained. My heart was racing in my chest, but I had just seen how strong the small man was. Maybe the rider didn't know, or maybe he had a strength of his own. That would explain his confidence.

"Then I'll let it be known you've arrived and return with wagons," the rider said.

The small man inclined his head.

To my dismay, the rider swung up onto his horse, and with a flick of his dark tail, the horse pivoted and thundered off, taking the rider with him.

The beach seemed duller now as if a cloud had passed over the sun. He disappeared like a dream, thrusting me back into reality. I didn't know anything about him, but I knew the image of him on his black horse would be burned into my mind. Everyone would be compared to him from this point on.

Strange, to feel something so intense. I didn't know anything about him, but maybe it was the *idea* of someone like him. Someone vibrant and new, someone who compelled me to jump on Loon and charge down the beach beside him. Someone who made me want to *live*.

I wondered if I would ever see him again—

York nudged my arm. "Let's go."

His voice sounded off, and I glanced at him, wondering if he was scared. But he avoided my eyes. Maybe he was just keeping an eye on the situation in front of us.

The short man shouted something in an unfamiliar language and I jumped. He was pulling the broken ship in much quicker now. It swayed closer and closer, finally breaking free of the hazy fog.

Then I spotted a grey flag fluttering against the sky. It was threadbare; only bits of black marks remained in a circular image, but I couldn't place it. I nudged York and pointed to it.

"Come on, Ivy."

Disappointed that I hadn't learned more about the ship or the rider, I began to turn to follow York. But then I saw a glint of light surrounding the rope in the man's hands. It traveled out toward the ship as tiny shimmers appeared over the dark water. I sucked in my breath, surprised.

"Wait. What was that?" My voice came out in something like awe.

"What?" York asked. But he had turned toward the woods as if he expected the rider to reappear.

"No, by the ship," I whispered, pointing to another shimmer of light before it melted away.

An unwelcome ache filled my head and my eyes felt strained, like I had spent the entire night reading by the light of a candle. I hoped that the pain would not return.

"I don't see anything except the ship getting closer." York sounded frustrated now. "Come *on*."

Another beam of light burst right in front of the hull where it cut through the air and water. "That! You didn't see it?"

"I didn't see anything." Now he sounded confused.

I frowned. Now the ship's hull looked like it was covered by thin threads of light, like a glowing spider web. Another pop of light illuminated the dark water and my eyes strained in response. Panic flooded me as I feared that awful pain was about to come back. *Maybe I should go.* I didn't want to pass out again.

But as the light faded away, I felt like something had *settled* within me. Goosebumps dotted my skin, but an ache still throbbed in my head.

The rest of the ship slowly emerged from the fog. The deck began to fill with people also dressed in grey. A long plank rose into the air and was about to be let down off the side of the ship.

"I don't care what you're seeing, we're leaving. So stay down and follow me." York's hand clasped mine, and I finally let go of the rock. He pulled me along as if he feared I was going to turn back at any moment.

We crept away from the water and I breathed out in relief as soon as we made it beyond the tree line and the pain in my eyes receded.

Then I remembered whose woods we were in.

Eighteen

s soon as we stepped into the woods, I turned back towards the ship.

The light above the water … That webbing of light over the hull … I was seeing light in a strange new way. The ache in my head told me I wasn't making it up. It was similar to the pain I'd felt yesterday, but thankfully, just a duller echo.

This had to be connected to inhaling the yellow dust from my father's journal. Since then, light had changed, but not all light. The new way I perceived light was only triggered around certain things. Things that, so far, were not common in Windermere. A merchant's pendant, and now a strange ship and man.

My father's drawing had brought me to the beach. Had he known about this ship? Was it connected somehow?

How could I leave without knowing?

York stepped closer to me. "Ivy, what are you doing?"

I glanced back at him. His brown eyes looked confused, but his voice sounded slightly annoyed.

"What if my father was trying to lead me here?" I asked. "If we leave now, I'll never know."

York stared at me in disbelief. "You think that," he gestured back to the beach where the ship was. "*This* has to do with the clues your father left *ten* years ago? Ivy, this has nothing to do with us, or with Arborists! We have to leave before anyone sees us here."

"Why? What are you so scared of?"

York hesitated. He looked like he wanted to say something, but all he said was, "Listen."

We stood in silence. Then the hairs on my neck prickled. The woods were eerily quiet and still. There was no wind, no sounds of nature I was used to. It was as if sounds were muffled, and no one would hear what happened inside these trees. Yet, just a short distance away was the beach and the ship. We should hear the waves, we should hear shouts and sounds of the ship being unloaded.

Intrigued, I walked back to the tree line. Through the trees, the ship was being unloaded. I saw the short man yelling orders to people, but I didn't hear him. I didn't hear anything.

I looked back at York, then around us slowly, wondering how this was possible. A short distance away was the path the rider had taken. We hadn't heard him at all, not until he'd been right on top of us at the beach—*then* we'd heard the thundering of his horse's hooves.

No wonder locals thought nothing ever happened on the Count's land; we never *heard* anything. But things were clearly happening out here.

"There's no sound," I said, mystified. "And the fog—do you think that's a cover, too? So no one sees ships come in?"

"A cover?" York's brows rose. "You think someone made a cover with fog? Or they somehow silenced sound?"

"Then what did you mean?" I asked, feeling silly.

"Just that it's quiet now, but that rider is coming back with wagons. And those people on the ship will be coming up the path soon too. I don't want us near here when they do. Now is our chance to walk toward the castle, then cut over toward Windermere. Come on."

York turned and started walking, his strides determined.

But I wanted to stay and watch the ship and see if there was more light around it. It felt wrong to leave now.

I glanced at York's retreating figure, sensing something off again between us. Was it because I saw the light on the beach and he didn't? Or was it because I thought the Count could somehow manipulate the sound or the fog? Or because of everything we'd just witnessed? York didn't seem interested in the way I was, but how could he not be?

I followed him reluctantly. "Who do you think the people on the ship are?" I asked. "And what language were they speaking?"

"I don't know."

"Well, no ship like that has ever come to Windermere before." I ducked under a branch. "That we know about."

"They weren't coming to Windermere," York pointed out.

The words hung in the air. I knew we were both thinking that the ship was coming to the castle. But I wanted to know why, and York wanted to run away and forget it. This was the first time we truly disagreed on something. The feeling was foreign and strange.

The void of sound in the woods made me uneasy. These trees were too still. Watchful, even. A shiver ran down my back. Now I understood why locals kept out. These woods made me want to run far away, back to the safety of Windermere.

I glanced at the path running parallel to us, hoping the rider would appear again before we left the woods. I wished the short man had used his name. Now I would never know who he was. Because I doubted I'd have the courage to explore these woods again. My entire body itched and crawled to get out. I wondered if York felt it too, and if that was why he wanted to leave so badly. But I didn't want to ask, in case he reacted the same way as he had when I asked if the silence and fog were a cover.

"Do you think the rider will be back soon, then?" I asked instead, keeping my voice low.

"I'm not taking the chance to find out."

I stepped over a fallen branch. "Do you think he's from the castle?"

"Who?"

"The rider."

"Probably."

We fell silent again. I decided to stop asking York anything. Maybe I was reading too much into things. Maybe York just needed time to digest this. I had already discovered the Tree Garden, and I was the one who was seeing light now. It was probably easier for me to accept things around us might not be what they seemed. But I felt alone in knowing this and I wanted to share it with someone.

I glanced over and saw York looking around uneasily.

"Do you hear something?" My eyes darted to the path.

He shook his head. "It's just too quiet. But," he pointed ahead, "I think that's the road into town."

Through the trees, another road cut through the woods. My breath stopped as I saw a pale stone arch with two tall iron gates. The iron bars were elaborately formed with the Count's crest and a swirling letter *L*. On either side of the gate, two sea serpents, made of stone, stood with their mouths open, fangs flashing, and sharp tongues pointed. Their talons gripped the stone beneath them.

The Count's gates.

The gates felt ancient and cold, centuries older than Windermere—and nothing like our small, charming town. They made my heart thud. Somewhere behind these iron bars was the Count and his castle. I could only imagine how intimidating his world would be.

And still, it was deathly quiet.

I searched the grounds beyond the gate, looking for any movement. A smooth dirt path stretched into the Count's property and kept winding in the woods, further than I could see.

"Do you think the rider went inside the gate?" I asked, stretching on my toes for a better look.

It took me a minute to realize York hadn't answered me. I

looked back and saw him staring at the gates with a frown. "Why do you keep asking about the rider?"

I flushed, suddenly self-conscious. "I don't keep asking about *him*. I liked his horse."

York blew out a sigh.

"What?" I snapped, tired of his attitude.

"My father was really angry yesterday."

I looked at him, surprised. That was not what I thought he was going to say. "Why?"

"I don't know why." York studied the gates. "But he was ranting, saying people better stay far away from '*that castle.*' My mother calmed him down, said no one ever comes out here." York turned to me. "But here we are."

I frowned, confused. Was *this* why York was acting strange? I didn't ask if his father had been drinking, although I guessed he had. Because what could his father possibly know about the castle that no one else did?

Suddenly, York sank into the brush and pulled me with him.

"*Don't move,*" he breathed.

I looked at where he was staring and froze. Three figures had suddenly appeared inside the Count's property.

I sank lower into the undergrowth like York until we were lying on our stomachs in the dirt. We were far enough off the road that we were hidden, but we could still see through the break in the trees to the road and the gate.

I held my breath, but a thrill went through me as the figures continued toward us.

A high-pitched sound split the air, shattering my nerves, as the gate slowly swung open. It was the first sound we'd heard since we'd entered the woods. So maybe it was only silent near the beach.

To my surprise, a tall, slender woman glided out onto the road. She was nothing like I expected from someone who lived behind these cold gates with sea serpents guarding them. She was lovely, with scarlet lips against porcelain skin, green eyes between thick lashes, and dark, glossy hair piled on top of her head. She wore a fitted coat and a full ruffled skirt the color of rich chocolate. Her dark leather boots gleamed against the dirt on the road.

Two tall men followed her out; neither was the rider. One didn't look much older than York and I. He had wavy brown hair and a jaw set in a hard line. His clothes were cut from the blackest fabric. A silver thread glinted from every seam. He wore thick black gloves even though it was summer.

Behind him came a person I thought fitted with these gates. He was older, with massive arms and a bald head. His features and dark skin reminded me of the small man on the beach, except this man was built as thick as a tree trunk. He pulled the gate shut behind them smoothly with one hand.

To my surprise, instead of taking the path to go down to the ship, they began walking down the road in the direction of Windermere. We waited until they were far enough away to get up.

York turned to me. "I think I recognized one of them."

"Which one?" I asked, surprised. I looked down the road to where they'd disappeared.

"The one with black gloves. Come on."

"We're following them?" I asked, hopeful.

"Not intentionally. We're going back to town."

I sighed as I followed him again through the trees.

"What was that for?" York asked, looking back.

I glanced up at him. He was looking at me curiously, but his mood was still off, so I shrugged. "Nothing."

He turned back around, not pressing my answer.

I just wanted to talk about everything I was discovering. I wanted to tell my best friend about the light I saw around the ship and speculate what it meant. But there was tension between us, and I could feel it stretching thinner. I wished he hadn't hinted about anything between us or put that thought in my mind.

But maybe he hadn't. Maybe I was reading into things.

Maybe I was reading too much into *everything*.

I slipped my hand into my bag to find my father's book, as if that held the answers I needed. This all meant something. It had to.

I chewed my lip, trying to put it all together. Soon the shapes of buildings began revealing themselves through the branches. A few more turns and we were walking in a narrow alley. Finally, we could hear the humming of the town square.

When we stepped into town, it was like I'd imagined everything that had just happened to us. The fog by the sea had not touched Windermere. Here, the sun shone down in a buttery yellow hue, merchants shopped as they always did, and locals were unconcerned about anything except helping them. Nothing was out of the ordinary.

Why had I let York talk me into leaving? I felt deflated being back here, especially after what I'd seen on the beach.

"Should we keep looking for them?" I asked softly, not wanting this to be the end.

York shook his head. "No."

I couldn't hide my surprise. "Aren't you interested in what all this means?"

"What it means? We saw things we shouldn't have. We don't have to investigate it; we'll never see it again."

I faltered. Would York change his mind if I told him about the light holding the ship together or the light that emanated from the short man? How could I make him understand that I thought my father wanted me to figure this out?

But York's face was set like stone, completely shut off from talking more. Something on the beach had bothered him and he was washing his hands of it.

He looked over my head. Carving students were spilling out of The Whittling Wood. Percy walked out with Bryn and when he saw York, he waved him over. Bryn made a face at me.

York waved to them, then looked back at me. "Go study, Ivy. You need to pass your test. What happened out there is none of our business."

With that, he left, leaving me to stare after him in shock. York never acted like this. But he didn't look back to see how his words affected me. I watched him join Bryn and Percy, and the three of them walked away from me.

All around me, normal life in Windermere continued.

Except for mine. I doubted my life would ever be normal again.

My best friend—the person I trusted the most—was upset about things I was drawn to.

And my dead father had shown me things I shouldn't know about. Things I couldn't just ignore.

But I didn't have to. Because just ahead on the street, the three people from the Count's castle were weaving through the crowd, walking further into the town square.

I took off after them.

Nineteen

I followed the group from the castle down the streets of Windermere in disbelief.

All I could see through the crowd was the bigger man's back. It was so wide, it blocked the woman and young man walking in front of him from view. I searched every face that passed the group, but no one looked twice at them. If they did, it was only a quick, admiring look at the woman's beauty. Not because they stood out from us.

Based on their darker clothing, I might have assumed they were merchants from Aedion, if I had not seen them leave the Count's property. Then I was struck by the idea that people from the castle may have always visited, and we never knew because they blended in during the summer.

When they reached Wilder's Bakery, they stopped. I stopped too, causing a merchant to nearly crash into me. I apologized, then turned quickly back to see the younger man saying something to the woman. She nodded and they stepped into line. The big man stepped right behind them, but he didn't stop scanning the crowd on the street.

As I debated getting in line as well, a group of merchants dressed in colorful silks stepped in behind them. Now I would never be able to watch them as closely as I wanted, so I walked past them and stopped at the Carving shop next store. I leaned against a pillar as if I was waiting for someone inside. This was a better spot. Now I could see all three of them.

I picked my nails, pretending to be preoccupied, as I studied their faces. I wished York hadn't left so soon. Maybe if he saw these people in town he would change his mind about this being none of our business. I still couldn't understand his reaction earlier.

The group moved up in line, next to order. The younger man seemed to be searching the people walking past as if he were looking for someone. The bigger man watched him, with tense, tight eyes. It almost looked as if he had positioned himself between the young man and the crowd like a guard. It also looked like he was trying to block them from view as much as possible. But I doubted anyone would approach them with this man looming over them.

When Mr. Wilder came to the window, his sky-blue vest was covered in sugar dust from the delicate cakes and pastries lining the shelves behind him. He beckoned to the group forward, his eyes widening at the woman's beauty, but he quickly composed himself and smiled as he would to anyone else. When she placed their order, the three of them moved to the side of the building to wait.

Now they were even closer to me.

Then the woman turned to look in my direction and I saw her face fully in the sunlight.

I gasped and my mouth dropped open. Not because of her beauty—but because of the way the light suddenly *bent* around her.

An iridescent glow of copper and silver clung to her entire silhouette. Her green eyes locked with mine and she noticed my shocked expression. Her brow floated up in surprise. Or was it recognition? But that couldn't be—we'd never met before.

I stood, frozen, seeing that faint glimmer surrounding her.

My heart pounded in my ears and a dull ache began to creep up my neck and live behind my eyes. But I pushed the discomfort aside as I stared, unblinking. Who was she? Why was there light around her too?

The bald man muttered something to her and the woman looked back at him, severing our connection. Then the light around her simply vanished, ripping me out of the moment.

I blinked, disoriented and feeling like I was coming up for air. The street was suddenly just a street again. I took a deep breath and rubbed my eyes, hoping to calm the small but growing headache. I'd spent all day in bed yesterday, yet today was draining me again in the same way. It had to do with this new light.

I looked back and saw the bald man scowling at anyone who walked too close to them, gesturing to the woman about the younger man. It seemed like he was complaining, but the young man looked unconcerned. Not just that; he looked pleased to be in town.

York had said he recognized him, and something about the young man seemed familiar to me too. When I realized who he was, my knees nearly buckled out from under me.

It couldn't be. But he was.

He was *Carl*.

The boy who dropped out of the Count's Woodworking Tournament a few years ago. The boy who everyone thought had left on a ship. The boy who carved secret compartments in wood … just like the cube my father had given me.

Shivers ran down my body, bumps rose on my skin.

Was *Carl* the one who'd carved the cube in my bag?

But this Carl was an entirely different person than the boy I'd grown up with. In just three years, he had aged differently than we had. I could see why he wasn't instantly recognizable to me or York. His jaw was sharper, his arms and chest were bigger, and he was taller. He looked much more like a man now—and he stood as if he knew it. His sharp eyes scanned the crowd, then a distressed, almost desperate look crossed his face before his features smoothed back into arrogance.

Quickly, I tried to remember everything I could about him. He had been three years ahead of me in school. He was a Carver. He had kept mostly to himself, but York remembered him because of his talent with Carvings. Carvings unlike anyone else's. Carl had been even better than Percy.

I also remembered how quickly Carl's parents seemed to go on with their lives after he left. They never seemed too concerned either. I remembered because, at the time, I'd wondered if I should have been able to move on as easily from my mother leaving me. For a while, I'd thought there was something wrong with me not being able to do the same.

Did Carl's parents know he was at the castle? Were they who Carl was looking for now?

My eyes flashed back to the woman, who now stood as still as a marble statue. The only movement was her skirt fluttering in the breeze. A faint smile remained on her lips as she waited patiently for their order. I hoped she would look at me again, but she seemed to be monitoring Carl. Or evaluating him.

Finally, Mr. Wilder emerged from his shop with a cloud of flour in his wake. He walked over to the group, smiling, with their order. He began to hand the blue box to Carl, who was closest to him. Carl stared Mr. Wilder down, as if daring Mr. Wilder to recognize him, but Mr. Wilder was smiling at the beautiful woman. A look of frustration crossed Carl's face and he reached for the box in Mr. Wilder's hands, but the bald man instantly pushed Carl backward and grabbed it before he could.

The pretty blue box was crushed in the man's large hands and a sweet roll dropped into the dirt. The bald man bent and picked it up, flattening it in his fist as he glared at Carl.

Mr. Wilder looked confused until the woman stepped forward and thanked him sweetly. With a smile, she extended her hand. Mr. Wilder wiped his hand on his blue vest before he shook it. He turned and went back into the bakery.

The woman gave Carl a sad look of disappointment. I wondered if it was for being aggressive toward Mr. Wilder, or for trying to take the box? Then she placed her hand on the bald man's arm and said in a firm, yet pleasant voice, "Let's go. This outing has stretched on long enough."

The bald man continued to glare at Carl. "Just wait till Dr. Ply hears about this —"

Carl's arrogance melted like frost in the sun. "Alright, alright. We can go. I just needed out for a while, Cora. I feel suffocated." He turned pleading eyes on the beautiful woman.

"It's alright, no harm was done," Cora soothed. "But now we really must leave before we draw more notice than we already have."

To my surprise, Cora glanced back at me. Before I could pretend I wasn't watching them, she gave me a small smile. I was too stunned to smile back. Then she turned and led Carl back down the street. The bald man followed behind, still scowling.

I watched them leave, overwhelmed with the urge to follow them. Why had Cora acknowledged me? Simply because she'd seen me watching her, or because she had recognized me?

Instinctively, I reached into my bag, as a child might reach for a parent's hand when feeling uncertain. As I felt the soft leather of my father's book, I realized that the light around Cora reminded me of the light around the ship. I had never seen light like that before in all my life ... until today, when I'd seen it twice.

It was connected. I knew it.

And then I was moving, maneuvering through the crowd, searching for the brown of Cora's clothes in the sea of color. I would make them stop. I would say hello to Carl and ask why he was in town. I would ask if his parents knew where he was. I would ask if he had carved the cube for my father—

Someone stepped in front of me.

"Excuse me," I snapped, tired of people getting in my way. Just as I was ready to dart around the person, I heard a voice that made my stomach pool with dread.

"Feeling better, Miss Rune?"

I looked up to find Mr. Mallon staring down at me. I nodded, my voice suddenly gone.

"And where are you off to?"

I swallowed, unsure how to answer. I couldn't admit that I was chasing a group from the castle ... that I knew about because I had just trespassed on the Count's property.

"Home to study," I said, quickly. "My test is coming up and I lost all of yesterday being in bed."

Mr. Mallon continued to stare down at me, and I had the strangest feeling he had seen everything.

Had he recognized the group from the castle? He might have, as he was the only one allowed onto the Count's property. Maybe he was making sure they went unnoticed by locals.

"Hurry home, then," he said at last.

I nodded, edging around him. Now I walked in the opposite direction to Cora and Carl. I walked through the sea of merchants with arms full of wooden statues and wrapped packages, frustrated by losing them.

When I reached the end of the street, I looked behind me.

Mr. Mallon was still watching.

I had no choice but to turn around and walk home.

TWENTY

That night, I dreamt of the rider.

We were back at the beach, but this time, I rode Loon and he was riding his black horse. He was further ahead, thundering over the sand, but always glancing back at me. Always laughing. An echo of his smile stretched across my face. My heart felt light as my body flew above Loon's. Her white mane streamed out like wispy clouds behind us as she pushed herself faster across the beach.

The rider looked back again. But this time, his jubilant smile flattened into my father's serious, thin lips. My heart stopped as the rest of the rider's face morphed into my father's. His black clothes turned Arborist green. The smile died on my face, but I didn't slow down. I urged Loon faster. We needed to catch him; I needed to know what he wanted me to do next.

Just as I was closing in on him, he whipped his head around. His face had changed again, from my father's into Mr. Mallon's. His clothes morphed from green to black with silver swirls and buttons. His brown beady eyes were angry as he jerked the black horse back. Foam spit at his horse's mouth. He snorted, then reared to a stop.

I yelled at Loon to stop too. My heart was lodged in my throat as Loon began to stumble backward so we wouldn't get closer. Then Mr. Mallon pointed a long, accusing finger at me. Suddenly, the beach disappeared and Loon, Mr. Mallon, and his horse vanished. There was only dark fog and a storm crashing above me. A cold rain pelted me. I stood alone, shivering and soaked to the bone. I had lost everything— somehow I just knew it. I was all alone on the dark, wet sand—

Something nudged me and I awoke in a panic. It took me a minute to realize it was Loon's warm nose. She pushed against me again. I sat up, pushing hair from my face and wiping the drool around my mouth. I was in the barn. I'd fallen asleep on the cushion I'd dragged into the stall last night to study. My books were half open next to me. One had pages missing.

"Hey!" I grabbed the book and smoothed the pages, wishing I could smooth away my unease too. "We talked about not eating books. I need them."

Loon nudged me again and scraped her hoof on the ground. "OK, OK. Got it. Breakfast time," I said as my own stomach grumbled.

I stood, stretching out the kinks in my back. Then I opened the stall and walked down the stable with Loon following me. I picked straw from my hair as we walked, trying to forget the eerie dream completely, but the images were stuck in my mind. I didn't usually remember my dreams, and now I was glad of it.

I opened the gate and let Loon into the large pasture. She took off, kicking and running, to remind me of how much she didn't like being in the stall overnight.

I yawned and went back into the stable. I used a pitchfork to remove any dirty bits from the stall, refilled Loon's water, and added fresh hay. I didn't need to add fresh sawdust because York had done that for me yesterday. I frowned. That was before we'd seen the ship and people from the castle. Before he'd gotten upset. So much had happened yesterday.

But I remembered that York had acted strange in the library even before I'd gotten the journal from Mr. Mallon. Something was off with him. Maybe it was just his father or the upcoming Woodworking Tournament. I knew how stressed I was about my test. Maybe York was feeling the pressure too. I hoped that was all it was. I wished we could talk about it normally.

I sighed, grabbed my bag, and made my way to the house.

But I soon wished I hadn't. John and Miranda's children had left blankets, bottles, and toys strewn all down the upstairs hallway. Inside the rooms, it looked like the trunks had exploded. Behind a closed door, I could hear the children shouting and laughing over Miranda's shouts to get dressed.

I quickly ducked into my room. I brushed all the hay from my hair and watched it float in broken pieces to the floor. Then I swapped my clothes for identical clean ones and checked myself in the mirror. My green eyes stared back at me. They had a frazzled, half-crazed look to them, but my caramel hair glowed from brushing. My white shirt and skirt were pressed, and my boots were shiny. My fingers flew over the gold buttons on my tweed vest, remembering my dream and Mr. Mallon's dark vest. I shook off the lingering unease as I opened the door. The hallway was empty and I flew through it and down the stairs, faster than ever.

Once outside, I sighed in relief. The house was not big enough for all of us. I needed to move into Forest and Fern now as much as I wanted it. I was allowing myself to become too distracted, but now I had to focus on passing my Arborist test. Everything else had to wait until I earned a place to live and had an income to take care of myself and Loon. I flipped my bag over my shoulder and headed into town.

But as I walked, I felt the urge to go to the Tree Garden and check the stump to see if the basket was back. I forced myself to keep walking to the library. Maybe, *maybe*, if I studied and was doing exceptionally well, I could take a little break to check and see if the packages were there again.

But that was dangerous thinking and I put the thought from my mind.

Test. Plants. Study.

That was all that mattered right now.

———

Settling into a classroom setting again felt like walking through thick mud. My brain felt foggy.

There was an empty chair next to Adeline, and I sank into it gratefully. I needed all the help I could in the next week. I cracked my book open and listened to the questions and answers that flew around the table. Slowly, it began to sink in how far I had slipped behind in just a week, while my classmates seemed to have launched ahead. I soon realized our entire class had come to the library every day to study, while I had been out in the forest chasing clues. I gritted my teeth. I was here now and I was determined to focus.

I put my head down, reading intently. But now and then, I glanced up and saw people from other trades walking past. After an hour passed, I glanced up to see Percy and Bryn go up the stairs. But York wasn't with them. I watched the door closer after that, but York never came. I wondered if he was already upstairs, but if he wasn't, where was he?

For the first time in our friendship, I wondered what kind of greeting I'd get once we did see each other. Would he be distant like yesterday? Or could we put that behind us?

I sighed into my book. I didn't want this tension with York. I wanted him to be curious like me. I'd hoped he'd want to help me figure out the Tree Garden, my parents, and the people from the castle. And the light I saw everywhere now. Well, not everywhere. I only saw it around the things I shouldn't know about. I hadn't seen it around Windermere or the merchants in town. I chewed my lip, wondering why.

"Ivy, did you hear me?" Adeline shifted, turning toward me in her chair.

I looked up and realized that everyone at the table was looking at me. Heat rose in my cheeks. "I'm sorry. What?"

"It's your turn."

"For what?"

"The round. We're each sharing a plant and having everyone guess what it is."

"Oh. Hold on." I searched down the page for something to share. But I'd just spent the last hour rereading the same paragraph over and over again. My mind kept wandering back to my father's clues. That gave me an idea.

"OK," I said, slowly, gathering my thoughts to form a question.

"Give us at least three clues," Adeline instructed, leaning forward on her book.

I nodded. "This is planted in a group of ten or more. They're tall with a complicated root system. It can have significance or meaning. Can also be tied to another trade, like say, Carving."

I looked around, only to see blank faces or confusion staring back. A few people looked impressed.

Adeline frowned and repeated what I said quietly as the table listened. Pages rustled. I hadn't wanted to draw attention to the Tree Garden, but I was getting nowhere on my own. Maybe someone at the table knew what I was missing.

"Will this be on the test?" Someone down the table muttered. I wasn't sure who it was, but they sounded frustrated.

I shrugged. "It's in our books."

"What is it, then?" Adeline asked, closing her book.

I looked around, but no one had the answer. Once again, they all thought I knew more than I did. "A tree ring."

"Oh, that's part of the ancient legends," Adeline said, relieved. "We're not covering that. Mr. Everett said it has no significance to our trade. Actually, your father was the first one to say that, did you know? I read his paper about it. Said there was no point wasting research on it or replicating anything to study."

"I didn't know that," I said, surprised.

Then it was Adeline's turn to ask the question. Only when she gave her clues did I realize what everyone at the table was really doing. They were giving hints about their plants, without saying what they were.

They were helping each other. And I was the only one who hadn't said anything about my plant. Or paid attention to clues that might have helped me pass later.

Now it looked like I didn't want to help them, or that I didn't approve. I shifted uncomfortably. I hadn't meant to do that. I would've gladly told them about the wild parsnip I found if I'd known that's what we were doing. Another mistake. I needed to pay attention.

Yet, I found myself thinking about what Adeline said about my father telling the Arborists not to look into tree rings.

He'd *known* about one.

He'd known it was more than a legend, and yet he'd claimed it was nonsense. At the same time, he'd revealed it to me and led me right to it. Why? Had he intended it to be my way to make a name as an Arborist? Did he mean to clear the path for me?

The more I thought about it, the more unsure I was. If I did reveal the existence of the Tree Garden and the very real tree ring within it, I would be saying my father was wrong in some part of his research. That would throw into question all his other research and his reputation. Surely he didn't want that. There must have been some other reason I was meant to know about it.

Maybe I needed to start thinking about why my mother's owl was the key to getting into the Garden.

And how did the Count fit into all this? And the image of the carving tool?

Mr. Everett swept into the room. He smoothed his hunter-green vest as he looked around. I hadn't seen him since I'd abruptly left the library with my father's journal the day before, ignoring his offer to keep it for me. When his eyes rested on me, a frown creased his lips, just for a moment. It was enough for me to know he still was unhappy about my decision to keep the journal.

Then he clapped his hands together.

"Class, it seems we are all here today. Finally. I have an

announcement. As you know, trade tests traditionally take place just before the Count's Woodworking Tournament. I know that meant it would be at the end of this week, but I think you are all ready. So our test is now set for tomorrow morning. I know it's sudden, but I believe you are all up to the task."

Whispers spread like wildfire through the room. Most people sounded relieved to get the test over with and have the rest of the week to enjoy the festivities. But I was stunned.

I had just lost a week of studying for the biggest test of my life.

And now I had only half a day left to prepare.

TWENTY-ONE

I spent the rest of the day in the library, pushing myself through any book I could get my hands on and joining every group discussion.

Part of me wondered if Mr. Everett had done this so I wouldn't have a chance to read the whole journal. But he didn't need to. The only information in the journal was about one plant that my father seemed fixated on: *Hedera*. I doubted knowing about one plant would give me any sort of edge over anyone. But from the way Mr. Everett avoided me as he made his rounds, I was more and more sure this was why he'd moved the test up.

At the end of the day, Mr. Everett stood.

"Alright, class. Time to let the library close. Make sure to rest tonight. I hope to see the highest marks ever this year. We all know that the Carvers consider themselves the most important trade in Windermere, but our work is important too. For without us, Carvers would have nothing to whittle and sell, nature would overtake our town, and half of us would be poisoned by mushrooms found in the forest." He smiled at his joke and a few students laughed. "So come in tomorrow prepared to earn your green vest. You are dismissed."

I swallowed and slowly closed my book.

My head was throbbing and I was starving, but instead of heading straight home, my feet carried me over to Forest and Fern. Something inside me needed to see it one last time before my test. I leaned against the flower shop across the street, inhaling the sweet scents of jasmine and rose as I stared at my childhood home.

Although now the building's black paint was fading, I imagined it ten years ago when it was my home.

Lamps glowed in the windows and green ferns hung in a neat line down the porch. My father, bent over his desk, visible from the window. And somewhere upstairs, I played, unaware that my life would never be so simple again.

I'd spent the last ten years pursuing a position within the Arborist trade so I could make this house my home again. I'd never given up, even when it was so much harder than I thought it would be. Even when it felt like I was a square peg trying to fit into a round hole.

Everything was riding on tomorrow. If I passed, this place would be mine after the Count's Woodworking Tournament.

But what would my life look like then?

I would have the responsibility of an adult, of making an income, cooking alone, and contributing to the Arborist trade. Becoming an Arborist might erase my fear of losing my home and continuing my father's legacy, but it would also erase my dreams.

Dreams I didn't even have yet, but ones I knew were bigger than this town.

Was I willing to give up my future to put the ghosts of my past to rest?

As if summoned, the rider charged into my mind like he had that day on the beach. The same flush of excitement and nerves filled me. I'd never felt my world focus down to one singular moment like that before. As if it was just the two of us, and all I felt was alive and curious.

He was a question I wanted to answer. Not because he might be part of my father's clues, but because of the feeling that overwhelmed me. It was a feeling I couldn't forget.

I wanted to feel it again, even if it was impossible.

I sighed and kicked off the wall to head home, leaving that daydream behind.

No one risked a life beyond Windermere. Everything we needed was here. The merchants told us every summer how lucky we were to be born here.

I needed to be content with earning my Arborist vest and make the most of this opportunity. I knew I was lucky to be eligible for a trade that took talent. Some people were not as lucky. I needed to focus on that, not imagine things beyond my reach.

I walked down the next street and then heard my name. I looked up. York was heading toward me. For a moment, I felt nervous, until I saw his father behind him. Then I knew we would not be able to talk about anything.

Mr. Pembroke looked nothing like York. His wiry black hair stuck out from his head and his deep-set eyes cut sharply to everyone in their way. He worked at the harbor on ships, so the lines on his face, hands, and under his fingernails were always filled with dirt and salt, giving him a harsh, wild appearance.

I swallowed the other nervous feeling that always came when I was too close to him. Mr. Pembroke was never unkind to me, but he wasn't warm either. He was deeply suspicious of people and he had a way of making me feel like I was thinking something I shouldn't, or was about to do something wrong.

"Hello." Part of me was surprised that York had called after me, especially after leaving so abruptly yesterday. But I was glad; maybe he had changed his mind.

Mr. Pembroke nodded toward me, the best greeting I would get. Then he gestured to Taylor's Mercantile behind us. "I need to pick up some things." His voice was rough and low.

York nodded. "I'll wait here."

Mr. Pembroke grunted and went inside. York turned to me. I wondered where he'd been all day, given that I hadn't seen him at the library. He had on his tweed trade vest, but his hair was tousled and he looked unkept enough to make me think he had been working with his father today at the harbor, not Carving. When I found no trace of sawdust on his pants or shoes, I knew he hadn't. I frowned. York should be practicing as much as he could.

He gestured to the steps. "Do you have a minute?"

I nodded, thrown off by his formal tone. "Sure."

We sat on the steps. An unusual silence descended on us. York shifted, uneasily, as we watched the street together.

"Where are you heading?" he asked, after a minute.

"Home to study. Mr. Everett just announced the Arborist test is tomorrow."

York's brown eyes widened. "Wow. That's soon."

I nodded, and my stomach dipped. "I know. I thought I had till the end of the week. I've been way too distracted lately to study as much as I should have been," I admitted. I wondered how to bring up yesterday. York was the only one who knew what I knew, and I was dying to talk about it.

York picked something out of my hair. "With Loon?" He asked, letting a piece of hay drift to our feet.

"No, with the Count," I answered, sharper than I intended.

York stiffened and looked around us. "Ivy, be quieter."

I tried to lower my voice, but I was frustrated. "How can you not want to know what yesterday meant? I do."

York looked back into the street, his jaw clenched. "I want everything we saw on the beach to stay there."

I frowned. What did he mean by that? Did he mean he didn't want me to talk about the light I'd seen? Because he hadn't seen it too? Maybe he didn't believe me.

That made me so angry that I blurted out, "Well, too late. Because after you left, that group came into town, and guess what? That boy you recognized? It was *Carl*. Remember him? He was supposed to be on a ship, except he's really down the road at the Count's castle."

York looked at me, surprised. "They came here? And you're sure it's him?"

I nodded. "I'm sure. He was looking for someone and he said he felt suffocated. Then they took him back to the castle. And remember when you said Carl was the only one who made secret compartments like the one in my cube? What are the odds of Carl showing up in Windermere right after Nicholas gave me a cube that Carl himself could've Carved? My father's clues are leading to the Count. And I'm going to figure out why."

York opened his mouth to speak, but then he closed it. It was like he didn't know how to respond. Then he stared back out into the street, his face unreadable.

"Say something." I nudged his shoulder. "Why are you acting like this?"

When he finally spoke, his voice was hard. "Why does it matter?"

I leaned back, surprised. "It matters because you're my best friend. And you're the only one I want to help me figure this out."

He looked back at me, his eyes conflicted. "*Why?*"

I angled my body so I faced him rather than the street. Our knees touched. "Because you're about to become a Carver. And if something is happening with the Count, with the Carvers, don't you want to know what it is? Even Mr. Mallon might be in on it."

Before York could say anything, a door behind us slammed.

We both jumped and saw Mr. Pembroke standing there, wide-eyed. I didn't understand his expression, but York leaped up, away from me. Our conversation was clearly over.

Mr. Pembroke stomped past us and down the stairs without looking back. But I thought I heard him growl "Home" to York.

York went down the steps quickly too. But then he turned. "All you should be focusing on is your test. Good luck, Ivy."

Then he disappeared into the crowd after his father.

I stared at them, confused. Then I let out the breath I was holding. The door opened again and Mr. Taylor walked out of his store. "Hello, Ivy. Are you heading home now? I can give you a ride."

"I am, but I think I could use the walk. Thanks, though." I smiled at him and picked my bag off the bench.

"Will you be at dinner, then? We haven't seen much of you lately. Are you feeling better?" He looked concerned, and I wondered if he was trying to make sure I didn't feel hurt that he'd asked me to move out. Or that his family had already moved in.

I nodded. "My test is tomorrow. I've been trying to study as much as I can."

His face cleared with understanding, "Of course you are. Well, come home and get a good dinner. I'll make you an entire pot of coffee and you can have the big table all to yourself tonight."

I smiled. "I will. Thanks."

After he left, I stared again in the direction York and his father had disappeared. York was acting as strange as his father was.

But for the life of me, I couldn't figure out why.

THE NIGHT BEFORE MY TEST FELT SURREAL.

Throughout dinner, one thought kept running in the back of my mind. If my parents were still alive, I'd be having dinner at Forest and Fern with them. After, my father would sit in the office with me and work late into the night as I studied. Maybe he would even pause his work and quiz me himself. I'd like to think he would have. And my mother... Maybe she would be making me corn muffins with butter and honey like Mrs. Taylor was now, and putting them on the counter in case I was hungry later.

Eventually, I pushed those thoughts from my mind, because I had to admit, it was a perfect night. John, Miranda, and their children were at John's parents' house tonight, so it was quiet and peaceful—just like the past ten years of my life had been. I wondered if the Taylors had done that on purpose, to give me one last night with them. I was touched and grateful. I would miss living here.

There were moments when I almost asked about Loon staying, but I didn't want to spoil the mood. I would ask tomorrow if I could keep her at the farm. The way they seemed sad for me to leave made me hopeful they wouldn't mind. Then I would have a reason to visit more often without feeling like I was imposing.

Just like he promised, Mr. Taylor brewed a fresh pot of coffee for me, and then they wished me luck, leaving me with the big kitchen table. I laid out all my books and set weights on the pages to keep them open as I drank coffee and focused on identifying plants. Adeline said Mr. Everett planned on focusing on fungi too, so I studied pictures of mushrooms and noted all the differences.

The night crept on until the pot of coffee was nearly empty and my yawns were much more frequent.

My eyes started to droop. It was too late to think clearly anymore, but a new hope filled me. Somehow I felt ready for the test and I was sure I could pass it.

I cradled my head in my elbow and fell asleep at the table. As I slept, I dreamt about identifying every plant right tomorrow and becoming an Arborist, just like my father had wanted.

I was ready for the next part of my life to start.

Twenty-Two

Green flags rippled above The Hidden Thorn, signaling the Arborist test was today.

Down the street, the deep purple flags of the fabric shop, Threads, were also displayed. All week, flags would be added to each shop, showing which trade had its test and by the end of the week, the town would be full of color.

The Count's black flags would fly last, above the courthouse, where the Woodworking Tournament would be held. After the Carving winner was announced, all other trade results would be posted on the courthouse pillars. Then, the celebration would take place. Lights were already being strung above the streets and soon vendors would set up booths. Trade vests would be handed out during the night, and the next day, new careers would begin.

After a deep breath, I walked into The Hidden Thorn. Somehow, I didn't feel as nervous as I thought I would be today. I was ready.

The shop was crammed with my classmates and all the plants we'd brought in from the forest. Mr. Everett wasn't joking about us needing to prove we were ready to be Arborists, because any plant that was possibly poisonous had not been labeled or moved out of the way. It was on us to know which not to touch. But it was so crowded, it was going to be hard not to bump into leaves. That made me jittery.

Everyone had gathered in front of Mr. Everett's desk. I saw Adeline, and she waved me over.

"How do you feel?" Her eyes were bright, but she was bouncing on her feet.

"Ready," I said, honestly. A calm had settled over me. I brushed a strand of hair away from my face, knowing there was nothing more I could do now.

She nodded. "I am too. But I don't like not knowing exactly what he's going to ask."

Mr. Everett stood. Suddenly, The Hidden Thorn was so quiet we could hear the plants growing.

"Good morning, class. How do you feel this morning?"

There were nervous mumbles around the room. Mr. Everett listened for a moment before holding up his hand for silence again.

"Good. Then we will begin. You have two hours for the test. As you can see, I've moved your plants to different locations around the room, and I have repotted them so they are not in the same pots you originally used. You also have to identify your own plant. In the week that they have been here, some have grown a foot, or bloomed, and they will look different. I have already graded you on your plant and it will be added to your score. I have made sheets with numbers that coordinate to the numbers on the pots. You do not need to go in order, just start where you are and mark down every plant with a fact. Take a pencil and paper and get started. And remember, no talking. If I hear anything, it is an immediate disqualification. No questions asked. Do you understand?"

We each nodded.

"Also, please take care to not bump classmates into plants. I don't want any emergencies. Go slow and be respectful. Best of luck to each of you."

I took a paper and pencil from Adeline and we all fanned out into the room. My first plant was number forty-three. I smiled. It was a tulip tree. I tried to conjure up a good fact about it, then I remembered they could grow forked if manipulated. I wrote that down, silently thanking my father for his clues as I made my way to the next pot.

I paused at the next nearest plant and waited for John, a classmate I didn't know very well, to finish. He looked up, then he gave me a strange look as he passed me. I frowned, wondering why. Then I thought I knew when I got closer to the plant.

I was sure this one was my wild parsnip. But the yellow flowers had already fallen off. It looked different, much taller and fuller than it was before. But the leaves had roughly the same shape I remembered. I was careful to stand a good distance away as I wrote down its name, along with a fact I had learned from Nicholas.

It felt like I was starting on the right foot as I made my way to the next pot.

An hour later, I was stuck behind a wall of leaves, frowning at the two identical pots in front of me. A cluster of white mushrooms had pushed up through the black dirt in both of the pots and I had to work to see the differences between them. Even though I had identified most of the plants, there were still some I didn't know.

I pressed my lips together, smothering a frustrated sigh. I still wasn't sure which one to choose and I had spent too long here already.

"Hello, Ivy."

I jumped as Mr. Everett pushed around the plants to peer at me through his thick glasses. It was the first time we'd talked since the library. I smiled nervously. I hadn't noticed him stopping to talk to anyone else, but then again, I had been intently focused on the test.

He adjusted his deep green vest and I instantly smoothed my tweed vest and the collar of my shirt beneath it.

"You seem confident today," he observed.

He sounded like it was a bad thing. Was he insinuating I had help from the journal? "I studied a lot," I clarified politely.

"Is that so?" He gestured to the pots in front of me. "Then you've identified which is the death cap?"

Uh oh. "This one." I pointed to the larger mushrooms.

Mr. Everett edged around the plants to stand next to me. "Class," he said in a louder voice. "Who else has marked this pot as death cap?"

Everyone looked up from their papers in our direction. I reddened, glad I was mostly hidden behind leaves. Slowly, a few hands rose around the room. I felt better when I saw others had answered as I did.

Mr. Everett frowned. "Then according to almost half of you, I can safely eat this mushroom right now and live. Shall I try it now? Or should I pick one of you to?"

He glanced at me, his fingers hovering just over the top of the mushrooms as if he were going to pluck them from the dirt. My heart raced, wondering if he was going to ask me to try it. The room turned quiet and tense. From his tone, I knew we'd picked wrong and that the death cap should have been easily identified.

"No, I don't think I'm prepared to die today. Those who raised their hands should be grateful for the opportunity to change their answer. And even more grateful that someone's life wasn't lost from your lack of knowledge. Continue, please."

I shifted uneasily as Mr. Everett looked back down at me. There was a look on his face like he was dumbfounded I hadn't known that. I flushed and looked down at my paper.

"If you cannot spot the subtle difference in yellow color, then use your nose. Death cap will have a faint, sweet smell, almost like honey."

I looked up, surprised by his gentler tone. "Thank you."

"Well. We may have had a disagreement, but that doesn't mean I want to lose you to another trade. I'm sure your blood runs green just as your father's did. It may simply take some time to develop. Perhaps his notes would be helpful to you."

I swallowed the dread that was slowly rising. If my green thumb hadn't developed yet, I wasn't sure it was going to. But he was right. When I became an Arborist, I could access all my father's research. That would help me be successful too.

"Five minutes left," he said loudly to the room. Then he disappeared around a pair of stone pots growing a colorful plant I couldn't remember the name of, but I was sure was poisonous.

Maybe.

I marked the correct mushroom on my paper, relieved to know another answer was right. Then I made my way down the next aisle and froze. My wild parsnip was sitting in a big pot by the window. My stomach dropped. The plant I'd seen earlier *hadn't* been my wild parsnip, then. I waited anxiously for my turn as a few students inspected it from a safe distance. When they were finished looking, they passed me with the same odd look that John had given me earlier. I touched my face, wondering if something was on it. Then I decided it wasn't important. I had only a little bit of time to finish.

I walked forward, staring at the yellow flowers opened like sparks of light, remembering meeting Nicholas in the woods that day.

I thought of York next to me. He had been so ready to help me then, when it had just been about my father. But when we got to the beach, he didn't want anything more to do with it. Was that because the Count might be involved? I remembered how he said what happened on the beach needed to stay there. That was such an odd way to put it—

The clock chimed again.

I jumped, startled out of the thoughts that had nothing to do with my test. I cursed under my breath as I quickly scribbled the wild parsnip down on my paper and a fact about it. Then I quickly erased my other answer as I ran back to the earlier plant and studied it again. Once I wrote down a new answer, I scanned the rest of my answers to make sure I hadn't made another mistake.

Then Mr. Everett's voice boomed through the room.

"Time's up everyone. You should all be proud of your hard work, and those who earn their green Arborist vest should be proud of their achievement. I will start grading tonight, but the scores will not be posted until after the Count's Woodworking Tournament at the end of the week. Best of luck to each of you. Place your tests on my desk as you leave. I can't believe this is my last time saying this, but you are all dismissed."

The sounds of relieved voices filled the room. My legs felt like jelly. I couldn't believe it. My Arborist training was officially over.

I slid off my stool and followed the line weaving past ferns and mounds of green moss for the last time. Adeline stood in the line in front of me, and when she turned and saw me, her smile was less bright than it had been earlier.

"How did you do?" I asked, instantly concerned by her expression.

"Fine," she said, eying me. "Some plants weren't what I expected, though."

"They weren't?" I thought back over everything, thinking I was only really stumped by my own plant. "Well, I'm sure you did great. If you want, we can meet by the results after the Count's Tournament?"

"Sure."

That was odd, but then the line moved forward. I placed my test on top of the others and made my way back down the aisle to the door.

There was nothing to do now but pray one last time that I passed.

Twenty-Three

I stood on the street, feeling strangely empty.

Now that I didn't have to worry about finding a plant or studying, what would I do with my time?

I could ride Loon to the Tree Garden, but I didn't feel like being alone. I was still on a high from completing my test, and for the first time in a long time, I *wanted* to be in Windermere. This was the one time of year that everyone in town shared the same experience.

Around me, anticipation for the Count's Woodworking Tournament filled the air and the excitement would only grow as trade tests were finished. At the end of the street, flags the color of sawdust flew over a temporary shop that was cleared for Carving contestants. Only the best Carving students were invited to participate in the Count's Woodworking Tournament. They could also set up a booth to showcase their skills and sell their carvings. Merchants swarmed the place, placing bets on the winner by buying up all their carvings, in hopes they would be worth even more after the Tournament.

I wondered what York had carved; it was strange I didn't know. Either I really had been in my own world lately, or things were more off between us than I realized.

I started walking in that direction, planning to visit his booth, until I saw Percy's father's shop at the end of the street. I hadn't visited him in a while either, and I missed talking with Mr. Gable. He always made time for me, and I was also curious about what he had carved this year.

I headed toward Mr. Gable's shop, planning to visit York's booth after.

I reached the glossy black door, admiring the jaguar knocker. Its emerald eyes glittered in the sunlight, the head carved from the finest cream marble, streaked with ribbons of grey. Below it, gold cursive swirled: *Gable's Emporium.*

A low growl snarled overhead as the heavy door opened to the finest Carving shop in Windermere.

The busy street vanished into quiet as I stepped inside the room. My mood turned almost reverent as I walked beneath dimly lit chandeliers through rows of white, polished statues displayed on matte black shelves. Velvet drapes gathered in elegant tassels draped beautifully to the floor beneath the windows.

I pulled my hands in close. Each figure I passed looked more fragile than the last. No one knew exactly what material they were carved from, but some merchants swore they were bone bleached a brilliant white. And they were the most unusual figures in Windermere. Mr. Gable carved his statues with oversized ears; elongated noses; or large, sullen eyes; making them seem like they had emerged from another world.

I leaned down to look closer at a deer so small it could fit into the palm of my hand. The white ears were larger than its body and the nose ended in a point so sharp I was sure it would pierce my skin.

A *tink-tink-tink* echoed from the back of the shop. I set off towards it, to the real masterpieces—the life-sized statues.

I passed a white lion, a bear up on two legs, a zebra with black and white stripes, and a baby elephant. Gold chains hung around each statue with a sold tag. As always, the merchants were snapping up statues as soon as Mr. Gable finished. Most of those large boxes being hauled onto the ships were from this shop.

"Morning, Mr. Gable," I called, turning the corner. Then I stopped in surprise.

Percy and York were sitting by his workbench. York looked up, then smiled at me. Except his smile didn't feel as genuine as it usually did. I suddenly felt like I was imposing.

"Oh, hey." I twisted my hands, feeling the awkwardness from yesterday resurface between us.

"Hello, Ivy! This is a treat." Mr. Gable beamed at me, his blue eyes twinkling. They matched his deep navy vest of crushed velvet. A row of matte black buttons ran down his black collared shirt. I always thought Mr. Gable was the best dressed man in Windermere.

I smiled, bigger this time. "Hello, Mr. Gable. Percy."

"Hey." Percy barely looked up from his carving. I noticed that York was making something too, but he cupped his hand around it protectively.

Mr. Gable blew some fine white powder off the statue he was working on. I bent closer to look so I could ignore that York was hiding something from me.

I stared at a tiny hummingbird, caught mid-flight. Its body and head were regular-sized, but the wings were enormous and arched gracefully up into the air.

"It's beautiful." My whisper came out in awe.

"Thank you, Ivy." Mr. Gable straightened his arm and inspected the leather cuff that stretched from his wrist to elbow. Only Master Carvers wore these. The tools they carried were custom-made for each Carver who wore them, and priceless. His fingers ran over the row of tools until he pulled out a chisel and began to wipe it with a soft cloth.

"What are you up to today?" he asked, returning the chisel to his cuff and pulling out another tool I didn't recognize.

"I just completed my Arborist test."

York's head snapped up.

"Excellent!" Mr. Gable put down his tools, giving me his full attention. "And how did you do?"

"I hope I did well." I shrugged. "But I can't lie, I'm relieved it's finally over."

"Of course you are. Trade tests are designed to be almost impossible, so don't fear. There is no reason the daughter of our most knowledgeable Arborist would be anything else."

I smiled, hoping he was right. As Mr. Gable began cleaning his tools, he asked me more questions about my day. York lowered his head and continued carving, but I could tell he was listening too.

As Mr. Gable and I talked, I couldn't help but wonder how different my relationship with my father would have been if he had listened to me this well. He had been a man of few words, preferring reading to conversation, so I never remembered him talking very much. Would I understand his clues better if we had spoken this easily to each other?

"These two are working on their carvings for the Carver shop," Mr. Gable said, gesturing to Percy and York. "Tomorrow the merchants will be able to purchase them."

"What are you carving?" I asked them both, but I looked at York.

He hesitated, his palm curling around his carving again. Then Percy answered for him. "He's carving horses."

"Really?" I said, surprised. I recalled the small statue of Loon York carved for me years ago, and I'd bet the one in his hand now was so much better. I was dying to see it.

"It's just one of them," York muttered. "There are other animals."

It was clear he didn't want to show me, and I tried not to feel hurt by it. "What about you, Percy?" I asked, looking away from York.

"It's a surprise, but the merchants will love it." Percy's chin jutted out as he studied his carving. "There's not much I haven't mastered. I'm sure to win this year." After a pause, he added, "No offense, York."

York shrugged. "I hope you do."

An awkward silence descended. I wanted to say that York had just as good of a chance of winning as he did, but I knew York didn't want me to. Instead, I glared at Percy, wishing he had half of his father's graciousness. Mr. Gable was the most sought-after Carver in Windermere, but he never acted superior. As if sensing my disapproval, Percy glanced at me. Then he looked away.

"Percy, where are your manners?" Mr. Gable asked.

"Sorry." Percy dropped his tools with a clatter. "I'm starving. Can we eat lunch now?"

Mr. Gable frowned. "Have you invited Ivy and York to join us?"

"I assumed they were coming!" Percy huffed.

"Assuming doesn't equal an invitation," Mr. Gable said, sliding his tool back into his leather cuff.

"Would you two like to join us for lunch?" Percy said through gritted teeth.

"How nice of you to ask, Percy. Ivy, I didn't want to assume, but should we?" York grinned at me—but this time, it was genuine.

I smiled back, amused by the shade of red Percy had turned and relieved something had thawed between York and me. "Sure."

Percy took off up the stairs, not waiting for any of us. His shoulders were stiff from being corrected.

Mr. Gable sighed as he signaled to the store manager that we were heading upstairs. Then he unbuckled his leather cuffs and placed them in their case on the wall. He closed the glass doors and locked them with a silver key. The leather cuffs and the silver tools gleamed in their case like their own works of art. Mr. Gable turned and smiled, gesturing for us to follow him up the stairs.

Above the store was a spacious apartment where Percy's family lived, very different from my old home. These rooms were filled with lavish furniture, thick carpets, and mirrors. Every fabric was either dark silk or velvet. Percy's mother had exquisite taste and owned Threads around the corner.

"Excuse me for a moment," Mr. Gable said, leaving us by the bathroom as he walked further into their private rooms. I wondered if he was going to check on Percy.

After York and I washed our hands, we waited in the dining room. Silence stretched between us. We were still unsure what to say to each other.

I scanned his face, looking for clues about how he was feeling. He looked tired. His hair had a slept-in look and the skin under his eyes was blueish-purple. Maybe he was more nervous about the Woodworking Tournament than I thought. Maybe I should have been paying more attention. I shifted in my chair, feeling guilty.

"Are you going to show me what you're carving?" I asked, breaking the silence.

"Eventually." York grinned at my glare. "What? It's not finished."

"Are you still upset about everything?"

"No, I'm not upset," he finally said. "My father is, though."

"What?" I asked, startled. "Why?"

"He heard everything you said outside Taylor's Mercantile." His voice lowered. "About the Count."

"But why would that matter?" I asked, genuinely confused.

York shrugged and looked down at the table, tapping his thumb against it absently. "All I know is that my house isn't the most pleasant place to be right now. I cleared out early today and plan on getting home late tonight."

His words hung in the air. It was the most he'd ever admitted about his father's temper. York was careful with what he said. In Windermere, we were taught never to mention unpleasantness. It would threaten the perfect image and quaint atmosphere the town created for the merchants.

I swallowed. "I'm really sorry, York. I didn't know he would hear."

Before he could respond, Percy and Mr. Gable walked in. Behind them was their house manager, Reya. She smiled at us as she filled the table with an assortment of cheeses, fruits, cured meats, and a large roasted pheasant. A slab of honeycomb was placed next to a loaf of warm bread. Mr. Gable even opened a bottle of sparkling durian, an expensive rarity purchased from a merchant ship, and poured it into four glasses.

"I thought we should celebrate Ivy's test, and the upcoming Tournament, for good luck." Mr. Gable raised his glass. "May Ivy earn her Arborist vest and may the best Carver win!"

I smiled and lifted my glass, tipping it toward Percy.

Percy looked surprised, but pleased at my gesture.

York shook his head, fighting a smile, which had been my real goal. But I wished I could do more than make him smile—I wished I could take all his worry away.

I took a sip from my glass. It tasted like creamy vanilla custard and sparkles. I knew I wasn't the only one who made themselves sip slowly.

As platters of food were passed around the table, I was suddenly struck with how much things would change by the end of the week. York and Percy would finish the Count's Tournament and earn a navy vest like Mr. Gable, while I would wear a hunter-green vest. In a week, we would all start new trades, and our lives as students would be over. I wanted to savor the time left before everything changed.

Percy began to speculate about the rules and requirements for this year's Tournament. York ate quietly, hardly adding anything to the conversation and again, I wondered why his father would be upset about what I said. I remembered that York had said in the woods that his father had been upset about people going near the Count. So I guess it made sense he didn't like hearing that York or I had an interest in the Count.

"Speaking of the Tournament," I said, seizing an opportunity to talk about the Count without suspicion, "does anyone remember Carl—he dropped out of it a few years ago? What happened to him again?"

York shot me a look of warning. Percy stopped eating and looked up.

Mr. Gable thought for a moment. "He went to work with a merchant from Langview, if I'm not mistaken."

I nodded, knowing he was wrong. The whole town was wrong. Carl was just a short distance away in the Count's castle. "But why did he leave the Tournament early?"

"That was just a rumor." Percy scoffed. "Why would anyone who qualified to compete leave before the Tournament was over?"

I shrugged. "I don't know. And if he was so talented, why would he leave a job as a Carver to work somewhere else? Even if he didn't win, he would never have worn a white vest."

"Who cares?" Percy said, clearly frustrated with the way the conversation had turned.

Before he could steer it back to himself again, I angled myself toward Mr. Gable. "You must know something about the Count, since you saw him when you entered the Tournament, right?"

Mr. Gable looked amused. "I've never said he was there, Ivy. No Carver would ever confirm if he was at the Tournament or not."

"Then you never saw him?" I pressed.

York frowned and pushed his food around his plate.

Mr. Gable toyed with his glass as he answered. "I don't think anyone in Windermere has actually seen him — besides Mr. Mallon. He's the only one who goes to the castle anymore."

"Hey! You just gave away that he never comes to the Tournament!" Percy complained.

I ignored Percy and leaned in. "I thought you would know more about him than anyone since he orders from your shop and no one else's."

Now Mr. Gable laughed. "That's just a rumor. I'm afraid no one knows much about the Count beyond our trade association." He rubbed his chin. "Everything is speculation or inflated stories now. The only truthful part I know is that his ancestors came from a faraway island. They built Windermere and established our main trade of carving, trading to ships that stopped for supplies. Eventually, they made Windermere famous for its carvings. They say the Count visited the wood shops when he was young, but then he never came again. There are also rumors that the people who work for him come from a particular land, and its ship comes here every summer. However, it's never stopped in our harbor."

York met my eyes. The ship covered in barnacles and the short, strong man flashed across my mind. The strange light and the rider. A cloud passed over York's face and he looked away.

Mr. Gable lifted his glass and took a sip. "Of course, if that's true, they must be very discreet because in all those years, no one has ever spotted a ship destined for the castle. And the rumored people who work in the castle never come to town."

"Who cares about all that!" Percy interjected. "The only thing worth talking about is the Count's Tournament, which I intend to win!"

I glanced at York. He looked weary. Even though Percy was his friend, I couldn't imagine putting up with his arrogance and competitive nature daily. I was beginning to tire of him too. How much worse would he be if he won?

"I'm sure you'll do very well, Percy," Mr. Gable commented, drily. "As will all the other contestants who have worked hard all these years alongside you."

Percy flushed, but then the sweet rolls from Wilder's Bakery were brought out, toasted and warm. The conversation turned away from the Count and I relaxed in my chair, knowing I would not learn anything more.

I bit into the sweet icing and flaky bread, wondering if Cora and Carl had eaten theirs on the walk back to the castle, or if they had waited and toasted them too. I'd never eat another sweet roll again without thinking of them.

York ate his in silence. I wondered what he was thinking.

I knew the next few days would be busy for him, but maybe after the competition, York and I could get back to a normal place in our friendship. Somehow everything had gotten off track. Now I wanted more than ever to start my trade and settle into my new life. Then I would use my free time to figure out if my father's clues really led to the Count, and why Carl was at the castle.

Eventually, I'd convince York to help me. I knew he would.

TWENTY-FOUR

Loon and I thundered down the field, past the land used for growing crops and apple groves.

Today, we were the only ones enjoying the morning beyond the endless green grass for the chickens and cattle. Loon was as happy to be out as I was; this was one of the rare times I felt she had wings.

As the wind whipped my hair behind my head, I felt happy and free. A whole week ahead of me and nothing to fill it with but things I enjoyed. First on my list was Loon. Then I would rest, maybe in the Tree Garden with a book that had nothing to do with plants. Something with adventure. It had been a long week and only now I realized how much I needed the break.

But still, my thoughts kept wandering back to my father's journal. I had looked over it again last night, flipping through the pages, looking closely for the pollen, or whatever that dust was that had made my body react. But I saw nothing until a scrawled sentence on the bottom of the page caught my eye.

Hedera is a plant that has lots of tricks up its sleeve.

I read it over and over, frowning at how my father described this plant. He acted like it was something more. Why was the whole book about *hedera*? Were all his journals like this, focused solely on one plant? I made a note to compare this journal to the others when I inherited Forest and Fern at the end of the week. But *hedera* had fascinated my father enough that he'd spent the last part of his life studying it.

I knew it was silly to be jealous of a plant, but the feeling of never measuring up still festered inside of me. Nothing about me had ever fascinated my father. And now, when I was about to accomplish what he'd always wanted, he wouldn't see it. He would never see the progress I made or how hard I'd studied to be an Arborist. I would never be able to change the way he viewed me.

And when I passed my test, I wouldn't watch his face light up with pride. There would be no celebration between us like Mr. Gable would celebrate with Percy. That hurt to think about.

But perhaps becoming an Arborist would heal something inside me, so I could move on and let go of all the hurt I carried.

I certainly hoped so. And maybe if I figured out what my mother had to do with the clues my father had left behind, I could find more closure with her too.

My thoughts turned to the broken ship, the short man and rider on the beach, Cora and Carl, the Count's castle . . . and most of all, the light I had seen. Questions erupted within me. I had a whole week to think of nothing else. I toyed with the idea of going back to the beach, or maybe even back to the Count's woods. I wanted to see the gates again.

And the rider.

As I rode, I thought back to the rider's fearlessness on his horse and couldn't help but feel impressed. His horse was much bigger than Loon, and Loon had never reared on me. She was swift, but I always felt safe riding her. I wondered if I would ever be able to ride the way he had.

In the distance, I saw a figure waving at me. I gently nudged Loon, and we took off in that direction. As we got closer, I saw it was Mr. Taylor. We stopped by the fence and I leaned down to pat Loon's neck.

"Morning, Ivy." Mr. Taylor smiled up at us. "It's been a while since I've seen you two out here."

I nodded, catching my breath, although Loon had done all the running. "Good morning. Before I forget, I wanted to ask if you would mind if I kept Loon here when I move to Forest and Fern. I'd pay, of course," I added quickly. "If not, I'll use my time this week to make other arrangements. I'll ask some of the other stables."

"No need for that, Ivy." Mr. Taylor took Loon's reins as I slid down. "We love having Loon here, and it will keep you coming by to see us too."

I breathed out a huge sigh of relief. "Thank you. She loves it here so much and I'd hate to move her. Whatever you think is fair for her board, just let me know."

"That won't be necessary," Mr. Taylor said. Seeing I was about to protest, he added, "No, I insist. You'll have enough to figure out with your income, your new trade, and taking care of Forest and Fern. As long as you take care of Loon as always, we'll keep a stall in the stable for her."

"Are you sure? I can at least provide the hay and pay the friar."

"All in good time, Ivy. We don't have to rush this. By the way, Mr. Everett asked for you to drop by The Hidden Thorn this morning. He wants to talk with you."

"Really?" I asked, surprised. "Why?"

"He didn't say. He just said to please come before lunch."

"Oh. Ok, I'll head there now, then. Thanks for letting me know."

He nodded and gave me the reins.

I wondered what Mr. Everett could want as I led Loon into the stable and tackled my daily list of chores. I was grateful I didn't have to worry about moving her. This farm was as close to my home as Forest and Fern was. It was perfect, and now I wouldn't lose either of them. With Loon here, I could visit anytime even though I'd be living in town again.

Loon crunched the carrot I gave her. As I headed inside to

clean up, it hit me that Mr. Everett probably wanted us to relocate our plants now that the test was over. I frowned, wondering how I would do that now that the wild parsnip had grown so tall and the pot was so heavy. I didn't feel comfortable asking York to help this time. Hopefully, Mr. Everett wouldn't mind if I just disposed of it now that there wasn't any need for it.

Then I realized that probably wasn't what a real Arborist would do.

I sighed and headed into town.

———

I pushed open the door to The Hidden Thorn and walked inside.

It was empty of people, but still overflowing with all the extra plants. Walking through the aisles felt familiar but also different. I was now on the other side, no longer a student walking into a classroom. I was something bigger now, although I had not grown at all.

Mr. Everett was at his desk. He stood when he saw me. "Good morning, Ivy. Thanks for coming." He gestured for me to sit in the chair across from his desk.

"Morning," I said, realizing I'd never sat at his desk before. In class, we usually stood all around the room. This felt very formal, like a meeting, but from his serious expression, I realized we *were* in a meeting. Because why would he have me sit just to ask me to get rid of my plant? He wouldn't.

Maybe this was about the journal. He still wanted it.

My blood pressure spiked as I twisted my hands in my lap. I took a deep breath and told myself to stop thinking the worst.

Mr. Everett folded his hands on the table. He sighed, making my heart race faster. "Normally, I don't do this, but you are a very unique case. I decided to grade your test first because of the situation with Forest and Fern and all your father's research. I needed the time to make preparations for the building to be transferred to you."

I nodded, now relaxing. He just wanted to discuss my taking over Forest and Fern. Well, he would be happy to hear I was fine giving most of the research to the Arborist trade because I knew that he wanted it. After Adeline read it, of course. Mr. Everett would do more with it than I could. I just wanted the sentimental things.

"However—well. There is no easy way to say this, so I'll just tell you. You did not pass the test, Ivy."

My smile stayed plastered on my face. I was sure I heard him wrong. "What?"

He frowned and shifted uncomfortably. "I'm very sorry."

The chair I was sitting on suddenly felt like it had been pulled out beneath me. I gripped the handles. This wasn't happening.

Mr. Everett looked at me sympathetically. Then he took off his glasses and cleaned them on his shirt, sighing again. "I was just as surprised as you were. As you know, half your grade was the plant you brought in. However, it was not wild parsnip, as you labeled it. It was Golden Alexander. There are only two months in the plants' lifecycles when the two are nearly indistinguishable from each other, and I might have been able to overlook this, however, many of your classmates identified the plant correctly. So I was left with no choice but to give you no marks."

Suddenly, it dawned on me; why everyone was giving me strange looks during the test. Why Adeline had acted less friendly to me. They had known my plant was Golden Alexander, and not poisonous like I said. They thought I was trying to confuse them.

How could they think that? I filled with indignation that quickly dissipated. Deep down, I knew how. I'd kept a careful distance my whole life because I feared if they really knew me, they would discover I was an imposter. That no matter who my father was, I didn't belong with them in this trade.

"And when I graded your test, I even checked to make sure it was yours. Several specimens were misidentified, and most facts were slightly incorrect. I tried to grade in your favor, I did. And I tried to understand how you came to your conclusions, but eventually, I had to face the realization that you do not truly understand our trade. Particularly the poisonous plants that grow around our town—I can't take a chance with that. I wish it was a different outcome, Ivy, I do. You're a nice girl and a hard worker. I do believe you gave this trade your best. Unfortunately, it just isn't a fit."

His words doused me like cold rain. He had voiced every fear I had ever felt and laid them out bare. Everything I had tried to overcome. Everything I tried to hide. Even after my hard work, I still wasn't good enough. I sat in the chair, stunned, feeling every part of me shut down. I had nothing left to say, no fight left to give.

"I'm letting you know before everyone else because I want you to have time to prepare what you will do next. I will keep these results to myself until after the Count's Tournament when I will have to post them. But for now, you have this week to decide what you will do next. What trade or what work you may want to pursue."

It was hard to breathe. So many people just assumed I would pass my test.

Even *I* had assumed I passed my test.

I told Mr. Gable, Percy, and York yesterday that I did well. But I *failed*. A knot twisted in my stomach. No matter who my father was, now I would be given a white vest . . . I winced, unable to believe this was happening to me.

"It's alright," Mr. Everett said nervously, as if he thought I was about to cry. "I've thought of a few options for you. The Taylors could offer you work in their Mercantile. Mr. Gable might need someone to help manage his shop. I know he is fond of you, and he may create a position for you. Otherwise, I have a list prepared of other work needed around town. If something catches your attention, I can talk with them on your behalf, discreetly. This way you'll be ahead of everyone else who will be needing work. It's the least I can do for you."

He quickly slid the paper to me, along with a box of tissues. I took the paper and ignored the tissues, and scanned the list. They were all menial jobs. Nothing that required talent. I didn't see anything that caught my eye. But if I picked one, I wouldn't have to wear a white vest. Now I swallowed back the tears threatening to form.

I made myself take a breath and steady my voice before I asked, "Forest and Fern is going to another Arborist?"

Mr. Everett shifted, clearly uncomfortable. "It must. The Count held it for you, but the time has come to let it be used by another Arborist. I'm very sorry, Ivy. "

"Who?" I managed to get out.

He frowned. "It has yet to be determined. When it is, I will let you know, before it is posted as well."

"I want to go there. Now." I stood. "I want to claim my family's things before you let someone else inside. I deserve that much." My voice cracked, and I clamped my lips shut, glaring at Mr. Everett. If he said no, I'd go anyway. I stared at him through watery eyes, willing my tears not to fall.

To my surprise, Mr. Everett stood too. "Of course. I can't imagine how difficult this is for you." He took a key from inside his desk. "I'll take you now."

"Really?"

"Yes. Mr. Mallon dropped off the key this morning. I asked him if you could gather some things, and he agreed. I'll accompany you just to ensure nothing you take is valuable to the Arborist trade, and then the shop will be cleaned and passed on."

"Mr. Mallon already knows?" I didn't know why that made my stomach sink.

"He is the only other person who knows, besides me. Let's hurry. It's nearly time for lunch and everyone is preoccupied with the preparations in the town square. No one should notice if we slip in the back."

MR. EVERETT UNLOCKED THE BACK DOOR AND LET ME inside first.

"I'll stay here to give you space, Ivy. Just bring back what you want and I'll try my best to approve it."

I nodded and turned away, unable to endure his pity one more second. I went into the hall and upstairs first, feeling like a shell. Numb. But when the stairs creaked beneath me, a sob almost escaped. I covered my mouth to stifle the sound and hurried the rest of the way into my father's room. This would be the last time I was here.

He had left a long time ago, but now I had nothing to tie me to him anymore.

His bedside table was nearly empty. The drawers held a few pencils and a gold watch. I picked it up and turned it over in my hands. It was a dull gold, with no inscription. I slipped it into my bag. A few shirts hung in the closet, but I left them. There was one brown blazer he always wore when he was at home. I took it.

I knew my room was already empty of everything from the last time I was here, but I checked it quickly as well before heading back downstairs and into the office.

The street outside was quiet. For now, I was safe from curious or pitying eyes.

I heard Mr. Everett clear his throat behind me.

I turned, trying not to glare. "Yes?"

"I'm afraid the books must stay. As must his journals. But if there is something else you'd like from his office, just ask."

I waited until Mr. Everett went back into the kitchen before I turned around and faced the office again.

I went to the desk, running my fingers over the glass jars lining the back and the three journals stacked on top of each other. I opened the drawers, remembering how I'd heard them open when I'd snuck in. I wasn't able to touch anything then, but now I touched everything. I was remembering this place, committing it to memory. Because I knew when I left this time, I'd never set foot here again. It was too painful to think about anyone else using these things and making this house theirs. I didn't want to see the changes they'd make.

I could still envision my father here, bent over his books late into the night, recording things I never understood—and still didn't. I could still feel what I'd felt ten years ago like time hadn't passed.

But time had passed and everything had changed.

I moved to the shelves with the books and trailed my fingers over the spines that I would never open. Heartache and guilt threatened to overwhelm me and spill out of my eyes. There was also fear so thick it could choke me. Who would I be now?

I didn't know.

I took another moment to look around the entire room. Then somehow I was able to compose myself and swallow down everything I was feeling. I would fall apart later, alone.

I stepped back into the kitchen and announced calmly, "I'm done."

I held out the bag so Mr. Everett could inspect it. I knew he had to make sure I took nothing that had to do with the trade, but it still felt wrong and unfair.

He must have felt the same way because he glanced inside very quickly. "I'm so sorry, Ivy. Please come see me in the next few days to talk about what to do next. You're not alone in this, no matter how you may feel right now."

I didn't respond.

My feet felt heavy; each step landed like lead as I reached the back door and walked out of my family's home for the last time.

Twenty-Five

I remembered nothing about my walk home, but somehow I made it back to the Taylor's farm.

I avoided the house, fearing they would immediately sense something was horribly wrong. Instead, I went to Loon's stall and sank into the corner with my knees pulled up to my chest. But the tears I had been holding back never came. I just rocked myself in silence, my mind stuck in an endless loop.

I failed the Arborist test.

I failed.

This was not a worry anymore: This was my reality.

I would never go back to Forest and Fern.

All I had left of my family was in the bag next to me. Everything else was gone.

I failed.

I'd always worried I might, but deep down, I'd never really thought they would let me. I thought my father's name carried too much weight.

It didn't.

I didn't matter anymore.

I pressed my forehead into my knees and squeezed my eyes shut. *What now?* This wasn't how my life was supposed to go. My future had only been centered around becoming an Arborist. Forest and Fern had always been my future. It had always been waiting for me. Now, at the end of the week, someone else would move in. And I wouldn't.

I would never fulfill my father's wishes. I'd lost every connection to my past and burned the bridge to my future.

I imagined the town gathered around the pillars of the Courthouse after the Count's Woodworking Tournament, straining to read the list. And next to *Forest and Fern*, they would read someone else's name, maybe Adeline's, but my name would be nowhere. My stomach rolled nauseously.

Everyone would know I failed.

This morning I had been so happy riding Loon, and now my world had turned upside down.

Where would I live at the end of this week? John and Miranda had already moved in and were waiting for my room. Where would I *go*?

Sometime after dark, I got up and went into the house. Everyone was asleep. I hid under the covers and pulled my knees up to my chest.

There was something wrong with me. Things that happened to me never happened to anyone else. Maybe it was because I poisoned everything like Bryn said. My mother left because I had been a disappointment, or was too much of a burden. My father died, leaving me nothing but a dream of his to chase and clues I didn't understand.

The tears came. And they didn't stop.

When I woke the next morning, my pillow was still wet.

———

I spent the morning with Loon, avoiding everyone, but I didn't have the energy or heart to ride.

Nothing could lift me from this fog. Despair was my constant friend, its heavy arms around my shoulders like a weight. It stopped me from drawing in full breaths.

Eventually, I decided to reconsider Mr. Everett's list and try to formulate a plan. I walked into town. Every face and building I passed was a blur. I couldn't focus on anything.

I wandered, trying to think of a trade or job I could do that would also provide me with a place to live, but it was miserable trying to change course now. Asking for help felt even more crippling. I couldn't bring myself to tell anyone.

Around me, Windermere was sparkling with life. Colorful banners now waved from almost every building, and crisp white tents had been erected for merchants. Children laughed, playing around the fountain without a care in the world. Everywhere I looked was bright and cheery, but it felt like I was seeing it behind clouded glass. On my side of the glass, I was alone.

Even the scent of sugar coming from Wilder's Bakery had no effect on me. In the space of a day, Windermere had turned into a place I was no longer part of.

I was adrift again, just like when my father died. A deep sense of loneliness curled around my heart, but I couldn't bring myself to talk to anyone; I couldn't admit this failure. Not even to the one friend who truly understood me.

York.

I missed him so much that my chest ached. But I was also angry at him. Why hadn't he made things right between us yet? Didn't he care? We'd never had a fight last this long. And it wasn't even a fight—it was just a disagreement. Maybe I didn't matter to him. He was going to become a Carver and all his problems would be solved. He wouldn't need a friend like me anymore.

By the end of the day, I'd accomplished nothing except somehow avoiding everyone.

I went back to Loon's stall and took her for a ride before darkness fell. I steered us away from the forest and the Tree Garden. I didn't want to be near anything of my father's. I was angry at him too.

I'd worked *so* hard to be like him, but following in his footsteps had only grown seeds of self-doubt and unworthiness in me. I would never prove to him—or myself—that I was enough.

I'd lost myself ... Or maybe I never really *became* myself. I had always been a watered-down, lesser version of *him*.

Maybe I'd never really been anyone. Just a physical body following a ghost.

And now I was nothing more than a shadow.

Without a trade, I wasn't anyone. I was a white vest, a blank space.

I stayed in Loon's stall until everyone was asleep, then crept into the house. I knew I couldn't keep this up much longer, but I didn't see how I was supposed to move forward either.

In bed, I pulled out my father's journal. His methodical and serious writing mocked me. Just reading through his extensive notes and the way he examined this plant, *hedera*, made me realize again that I was never going to succeed. Why had I thought I could be like him? My father was a scholar. His passion was discovering how nature worked and how plants thrived.

But he had fixated on this plant, and whatever he had found out about it, he hadn't finished... Instead, he'd left me clues to finish for him.

As I flipped to the end, I noticed writing that seemed to confirm Nicholas's claims about my father's state of mind. Some of my anger bled out as my heart sank.

A type of obsession had set in. My father had written the plant's name over and over, with darker strokes and underlines. His descriptions became more colorful too. One line in particular stuck out to me:

Hedera is generally considered to be bad luck . . .

I frowned and closed the book. My father almost sounded superstitious, but I'd never known him to be that way. Had this plant been his bad luck?

That night when I slept, those words mixed with Bryn Bryer's nasally voice calling me poison ivy and bad luck.

When I woke, my pillow was soaked with tears again.

The next morning, I walked back into Windermere. I needed to find a job and claim it so when I talked to the Taylors, I had a plan about where I'd live. I still felt utterly defeated, but I couldn't allow myself to be inactive anymore. I didn't have that luxury. So I forced one foot in front of the other, feeling like I would have to do this for quite some time.

Just as I passed Wilder's Bakery, a delicious scent hit my nose. Then my stomach growled. I couldn't remember the last time I ate.

"Ivy! Come over here."

I looked up. Claire Wilder was leaning out the window of the bakery. Behind her, the ovens glowed, and sugar and flour filled the air like snow. Her father, in his light blue trade vest, was just behind her, forming the puffiest balls of dough. That scent—and the feeling of happiness—was what pulled me in.

After two days of living under a dark cloud, I was drawn to the light.

Then I noticed the blue flags waving above the bakery. Their trade test was today. I took a deep breath and prepared myself to wish Claire luck. But as I got closer, I noticed she didn't look nervous; she looked radiant.

"Good morning." I was proud my voice sounded normal after not talking to anyone in days.

"Eat this." Her blue eyes sparkled as she pushed a warm golden croissant into my hand.

My mouth watered instantly. "OK." I bit through the crusty layers into a sweet chocolate middle and tasted something new. A sweet floral burst.

I moaned before I could help it. It was so good, tears sprang to my eyes. I'd had plenty of chocolate croissants, but none like this. I'd overheard merchants claim that food from Wilder's had a way of making fears and worries melt away with just a bite, and for the first time, I felt like I understood that. Just the care it took to make this ... it felt like the gaping hole inside me was slowly stitching up, even if just a little. Enough that the despair had lessened and a bud of hope could grow.

The past few days, I'd felt like my life was ending, but now I was reminded that there were plenty of reasons left to go on. And lots of delicious food left to savor.

"This is incredible. What's different?" I asked through bites.

Claire looked like she couldn't hold it in anymore, pleased by the way I was inhaling her offering. "It's an old family recipe, but my trade test was to improve it. So I infused orange pieces and zest in the dough and chocolate."

"It's incredible. I can't believe you made this." I lowered my voice. "I think it's even better than the original."

"I heard that, Ivy," Mr. Wilder called from inside the room.

"Sorry!" I winced, but Claire laughed. For the first time in days, I smiled.

Mr. Wilder appeared next to her, a smile on his face as he wiped flour from his hands with a white-and-blue striped towel.

"No need to apologize. That's the biggest compliment you could give me. All I want for Claire is to build upon what I taught her and go further. And Claire's creation is better than the original, so I've decided it will be on the menu from now on."

"I passed?" Claire squealed, throwing her arms around her father in a hug.

He laughed and held her close before he released her. "Without a doubt. Think of a name and then go get measured for your new vest." A beep sounded in the room, and with a wave goodbye, Mr. Wilder hurried to save whatever it was from the oven.

I smiled, genuinely happy for Claire. I could see the wheels spinning in her head as to what she should name her first recipe. I was struck: This was what earning your father's respect looked like. Someday, he would trust Claire to take over completely.

I swallowed the lump in my throat.

Even if I had passed my test and continued my family trade, I would never have *improved* my father's work, like Claire effortlessly had.

I'd struggled for years.

I'd been drowning for years; only now did I see that.

Tears filled my eyes. Suddenly, I couldn't stand the thought of being alone in this any longer. I needed to find York. He was the one person who would understand why I felt so misplaced standing outside the bakery. I felt like I was always looking in on someone else's perfect life. York got that.

"Ivy, what's wrong?" Claire said, her voice full of concern.

I'd forgotten I was staring at her. Tears threatened to flow, but I pulled my face into a tight smile. "I need to find York. Has he been by?"

"Oh, no, not in the last few days. He's probably at the harbor."

"The harbor? This week?" I asked.

"Yes. Haven't you heard?"

At first, I thought she was talking about my test. Had the results been posted early? My stomach sank—but then I realized she was talking about York. A new type of dread filled me. "What?"

Claire frowned as if she didn't want to gossip. "It really is unfortunate. York's father said he can't be a Carver. He's not entering the Count's Tournament anymore. I guess he's helping his dad with the Shipping trade now."

I was so surprised, I dropped what was left of my croissant. I picked it up quickly. "*Why?*"

Claire shrugged. "No one understands. No one agrees with him." She looked back into the kitchen and lowered her voice. "My father said some Carving parents even tried to talk to Mr. Pembroke, but he got so angry. He kicked all of them out."

I thought back to the last time I saw Mr. Pembroke. He seemed mad when he came out of Taylor's Mercantile and stomped off. I thought that was strange. York said he was angry after hearing me talk about the Count.

This was all my fault.

"I can't believe it," I whispered.

If I had caused York to feel the way I had the last few days, I would never forgive myself. All this time I was worried about me, and mad that York hadn't found me, but he had been going through the same exact thing.

Except *I* had done this to him.

"Me either," Claire said, "I'm really sad for York. Tell him that when you find him, will you?"

I looked toward the building the Carving contestants were using to sell their carvings before the Woodworking Tournament. "I will. Congratulations again on your test, Claire. You really deserve it."

She smiled and handed me a small cup. "Here, for the road."

I could smell the cinnamon and thick warm chocolate drink inside. "Thanks," I said, gratefully. "You're the best."

"Consider it good luck for this week, even though I know you're probably not nervous at all about your test results. You'll be wearing a new vest soon too!"

The smile dropped from my face as I hurried away. Except I wasn't panicking about everyone finding out I failed anymore.

I was thinking about York, and praying I hadn't lost him his trade too.

Twenty-Six

The chocolate Claire gave me warmed my throat, but unlike her food, it did nothing to ease my fear.

Nothing else mattered except York. Not my failed test, my uncertain future, or my father's clues. All that could wait.

I would never forgive myself for this. I remembered Mr. Pembroke's face when I saw he had been listening. Even in my memory, he'd looked furious.

I tossed the cup into the garbage and looked around. Where should I go? I bit my lip as I debated checking the harbor or going to York's house. I saw the contestant's Carving shop up the street. Merchants congregated outside as if something inside had them excited. Without hesitating, I wove through the street toward the open doors. First I would make sure York wasn't inside.

Maybe Claire had misunderstood. I'd never heard of a parent forbidding a student from becoming a Carver, especially when they were as talented as York. Surely Mr. Mallon would intervene if this was true. He wouldn't want to jeopardize Windermere's most profitable trade.

I stepped into the Carving shop, into the aroma of wood and hints of wood stain lingering in the air. Booths lined the walls and created aisles in the middle of the room. Every booth showcased a contestant chosen for the Count's Woodworking Tournament. Statues, jewelry, vases, and other items filled the tables. Merchants browsed slowly, occasionally plucking things up to inspect them.

One booth had more of a crowd around it than all the rest.

I hoped it was York's. All I could think about was how he'd hidden whatever he was carving from me inside Gable's Emporium. Percy had claimed it was a horse. I wondered if it was a better version of Loon. I had to see it.

I got closer and my heart dropped when I saw it was Percy's booth. Disappointment pulsed through me as I pushed my way over to it. The sign on his table said *P by P* and under that was *Perfection by Percy*.

It took everything in me not to roll my eyes or laugh. I wondered if York had seen this sign yet. I looked around for him, but this row was filled with other students. I spotted Bryn and quickly looked away before she saw me.

York wasn't here. This was serious.

As much as I didn't want to, I stepped up to Percy's booth. I had to ask him about York.

Percy's theme was the sea. He'd carved octopi, ships, coral, fish, and whales. But unlike Mr. Gable, Percy's carvings lacked any whimsy or charm. They were literal and realistic, technically perfect, even, but nothing that inspired wonder as Mr. Gable's creations did. I wondered why he had chosen to carve wood instead of bone, like his father. He could have stood out even more, but maybe Percy didn't want to live in his father's shadow.

He also had the most items to sell of any Carver in the room. There wasn't an empty spot on his table. I watched as merchants purchased statues as quickly as he put them down. He must have been carving this entire year in preparation. Part of me had to admire his determination, although grudgingly.

"Oh. Hey, Ivy," Percy said, noticing me.

I tried to muster up some enthusiasm. "Hey. These look great."

"Thanks."

A new pin stood out on his tan vest: A gold plate stamped with the seal of Carvers; a chisel, ship, and a tree branch wound intricately around each other. It gleamed dully. It must have been this year's pin marking him a contestant in the Woodworking Tournament.

York should have been wearing one.

"So, the sea, huh?" I asked, to fill the awkward silence. I only talked to Percy when York was with me, and now I felt York's absence.

"It was Bryn's idea."

"Oh." I guess I really had been preoccupied lately. I hadn't noticed Percy and Bryn getting so close. "Well, they look good." My praise sounded hollow, even to me.

"Thanks. So, I haven't seen you around lately—"

"Have you seen York?"

Percy's eyes flickered past me into the crowd. "Of course."

I frowned at him. "Where's his booth?"

Percy picked up a narwhal and began to polish it. "He didn't set one up."

"Why not?"

"He's not going to enter the Tournament after all."

I didn't respond, forcing Percy to look at me. There was guilt in his eyes.

He was *glad* York dropped out. It gave him a clear shot at winning. And today, the merchants were all at his booth instead of distracted by anyone else's.

I gritted my teeth and tried to stay calm, but I was too upset. This might have been all my fault, but Percy was a selfish friend and York deserved better.

"Do you know why? Didn't you ask?" I asked, pointedly.

"His father changed his mind and wants York to work in his trade," Percy said, his voice strained. He knew this was wrong.

"That's what Claire said, but I didn't want to believe her," I said, frustrated.

Percy shrugged. "You know how unpredictable his father is."

"York must be upset." I held Percy's gaze. "Have you checked on him?"

"He's fine," Percy responded, defensively.

Before I could respond, another group of merchants crowded the table and began snapping up Percy's carvings. I moved back to give them room, watching Percy's face light up at the attention. Anger flickered inside me as I watched them buy almost everything on his table. I knew if York was here, his table would sell just as well. That made me feel sick too.

This was *wrong*. I could understand why I hadn't become an Arborist, but York was meant to be a Carver. He was talented. He could have won the Tournament. And after, he could have opened a nice shop like Gable's Emporium, instead of becoming a Carving instructor or giving tours to merchants—the destiny of many Carvers without talent like York's or a family like Percy's. After the Tournament, York shouldn't have had to work for anyone ever again, especially not his father, doing hard labor.

It burned me up to see Percy's smug expression as he filled his table back up with more carvings. He was so sure he would win the Tournament. Now, he would have his father's undivided attention. I felt bad about that thought, but it was true. Percy had never shared Mr. Gable's attention well with York.

As if it couldn't get any worse, Bryn was suddenly next to me. "If you're not here to buy something, you should leave. Otherwise, you're just taking up space, and it's very crowded." She narrowed her eyes at me, daring me to argue.

But I didn't care about her anymore. I had bigger problems. Still, I couldn't resist saying, "I can see that. It's very crowded, except at *your* booth, Bryn. Is that why you have time to bother me? No customers?"

Her eyes opened in surprise, but before she could speak, I added, "No customers mean the merchants don't think you'll win. That's too bad."

"Why, you little—"

"Quit it." Percy took my elbow and steered me through the

crowd. I looked back as Bryn stared angrily after us. It took me a minute to realize it was because Percy was with me, not her. I snorted. She could have him.

"Stop, Ivy. You're making a scene."

I snorted again.

Outside, Percy dropped my arm. "Look, I understand how that sounded, and I'm sorry. I do feel bad for York. But he has his family's trade. He still won't get a white vest. So he's *fine*. He's better off than most. Disappointed, but not destitute."

That word hit me hard and made me want to lash out. *I* was the one destitute.

"And now you'll be able to win because you were never sure you could beat him. Everyone knows you're a poor loser."

Percy looked shocked before he shrugged. "Sorry you feel that way." His voice was tight as he moved further away from me. "What's wrong with you, anyway? You're more upset than York was."

I took in a deep breath and let it out slowly. I needed to calm down. "If he was unbothered, it was an *act*. As his friend, you should know that. He doesn't want to upset his father. But it doesn't mean he doesn't care."

Percy mindlessly reached for his pin and began to polish it, as if there were invisible fingerprints on it. "I need to get back. See you at the Count's Tournament."

"Hope not."

"Oh, grow up, Ivy," Percy scoffed. But he didn't turn around as he walked inside.

I stood on the street, fuming and thinking that he and Bryn were perfect for each other. But it hadn't always been like that. Percy had changed too.

We all had, in different ways.

I spun on my heel and took off in the opposite direction. All I cared about now was York.

And I was going to find him.

TWENTY-SEVEN

York's house was four blocks from the town square, at the end of a narrow street.

It was a small, extremely well-kept cottage. It should have been charming; the yard was green and a path of stones led to the front door, but it felt far from inviting. Like whoever lived inside was insisting, *Nothing to see here.*

But Windermere was too small for Mr. Pembroke to hide the truth. He existed in a grey area—not exactly dangerous to others, but not an upstanding citizen either. We avoided him, but went out of our way to show kindness to York and his mother. Most people thought it was just a matter of time before something set Mr. Pembroke off for good.

Yet, here I was, standing outside his door when he was upset with me.

But I had to see York. I had to fix this if I could.

I knocked and stepped back quickly, praying York would answer.

The door swung open, and to my relief, it was not Mr. Pembroke. It was York's mother.

The difference between York's parents was striking. Mrs. Pembroke was round and so short her feet didn't touch the floor when she sat; they just bobbed above the ground. Every time I saw her, she was fidgeting. Perhaps the years of living with Mr. Pembroke had been hard on her nerves—I really couldn't blame her.

"Good morning, Ivy," she said, softly, tugging the collar of her dress straight. Then she tugged it again, crooked. Her eyes looked tired. "I haven't seen you in a while. Come in."

"Thank you. Is York here?" I asked.

She nodded and gestured for me to follow her. We passed through a small sitting room with windows overlooking the street and walked into the kitchen. The homey scent of cooking that filled the Taylor's house was absent. This house was too clean, too sterile, like it was hiding something.

York sat at the round table, finishing lunch. He was wearing a dark blue collared shirt rolled to his elbows, blue pants, and heavy boots. These were the rough spun clothes he wore when he worked down at the harbor.

I missed his tan Carving vest. I wondered how he would feel about my change of vest at the end of the week.

York looked up, surprised. Then guilty. Then curious. "What are you doing here?"

"Hello to you too, " I said, stung. "I came to check on you. I was just at the Carving shop. You didn't have a booth."

York shifted in his chair, his eyes flashing to his mother.

"York's busy with the shipping trade now. How did your test go, dear?" Mrs. Pembroke said, sweetly changing the topic to me.

It worked. I hesitated, immediately reminded that I failed and was hiding it from everyone. I swallowed the lump rising in my throat as I glanced between them. I wanted to say it was fine, but she was looking at me with such kindness, I didn't want to lie to her. I couldn't admit I failed either, though, not yet.

"We'll know when the list is posted," I finally said.

York frowned as if he sensed something off. Then he stood. "I'll walk you out."

"Oh. Are you busy?" I asked, hurt by how fast he was dismissing me.

He hesitated. "I —"

Footsteps filled the hallway. My stomach sank into my boots as I turned around.

Mr. Pembroke towered in the doorway, glaring at me like he never had before. I cringed away, shocked by the intensity of a grown man staring at me like this. Then he looked at York, seeing that he was about to leave.

"And where do you think you're going?" His voice was harsh and severe. "I need your help with that large ship that docked last night."

"I'm just walking Ivy out." York gave me a pointed look. "She's leaving."

I nodded, knowing York wanted me to go quietly, but I couldn't help saying, "I'd like to talk to you first, York. If you have time, that is."

"Not about Carving," Mr. Pembroke growled. "We've talked about it. It's time to give that up."

York sighed. "I know."

"And no more about the Count's castle either!"

I gulped and looked at Mr. Pembroke. "It was an accident. We didn't mean to walk that far. It was all my fault, not York's."

"Oh? Did you force my boy to follow you, then? Pull him along like a puppy?"

"Um..." I glanced at York, unsure what to say. I didn't want him to get in any more trouble. Beside him, Mrs. Pembroke wrung her hands.

"I told you. It was an accident," York said, frustration leaking out of his voice.

It seemed to trigger Mr. Pembroke, whose anger rose up in him like a bear. His voice filled the room. "I forbid you to have anything to do with the Count! Do you hear me?"

York flinched, then caught himself.

I hated how small he looked.

Anger propelled me forward. I stepped in front of York and glared up at Mr. Pembroke. "We're not going by the castle or to a Carving shop!" I said, staring straight up in his face.

Mr. Pembroke looked startled and backed up a step.

"We'll just talk in the yard. We didn't mean to get so near the castle. We're sorry. *I'm* sorry!" I said, firmly.

"Oh. Well, good," he muttered, moving away from the door. Everyone in the room seemed to exhale, until he said, "That Count is dangerous. There are terrible, terrible things going on inside that castle."

Startled, I took another step forward. "What do you mean?"

"Let me fix you something to eat," Mrs. Pembroke said to Mr. Pembroke, gesturing for me to leave.

Mr. Pembroke sank heavily into the chair, muttering about the *terrible, terrible Count*. I didn't move, even though Mrs. Pembroke flashed me another look of warning.

What did he mean? What did he know?

York took my arm and pulled me out of the kitchen. I twisted, wanting to ask again what Mr. Pembroke meant, but York's grip was firm. Just before the front door closed, I heard something about *lightning and unnatural trees*.

I'd never been so relieved or so frustrated to be outside.

York dropped my arm. "Sorry about that."

I nodded. "Is he OK?"

York ran a hand through his hair and sighed. "He's always been difficult, but it's gotten worse the older he gets. Or maybe, the older *I* get."

I frowned, not understanding. "What do you mean?"

"I mean the closer I get to taking my Carving trade test, the worse he's become. Especially about the Count."

"Why does the Count make him so upset?" I asked, genuinely wondering.

York glanced back at the house. "He thinks he knows things no one else does. He's angry that no one pays more attention to the castle."

I wanted to ask what things, but York looked at me. "When my mom asked about your test, you seemed off. What's wrong?"

"Nothing," I said, quickly. "We were talking about you. Tell me you're still going to enter the Tournament."

York shook his head. "I can't."

"Because of how your father feels about the Count?" Disbelief colored my voice.

York shrugged. "You saw him in there. Seems like a pretty good reason."

"But this is your only chance to become a Carver! And you've already qualified! If you win, he won't be able to control you anymore. You can open your own shop."

York rolled his eyes. "That's the best-case scenario, Ivy."

"For other people, maybe, but not you. You're better than everyone. You're so talented, York."

His eyes flashed to mine. "I'd have to beat Percy."

I scoffed. "I hope you do. Look, Carving is your chance to control your future. And I know you don't want to work with your father. What if you can't handle it and you end up in a white vest because you quit?"

A flush crept up York's neck. "You're one to talk. You've lived your whole life doing what your father wanted you to do too."

And look how that turned out, I wanted to shout. But I took a deep breath, willing myself to stay calm. "York, if you enter the Tournament, everyone will support you."

His anger calmed too, but his eyes were still clouded with worry. "But my mother would still be here. Who'd support her?"

"We would," I said, firmly, holding his gaze.

"He'll never let me through the door again," York whispered. "I can't. It's not worth it."

I didn't know what to say to that. But I knew how powerful fear was. It could make you think there was no hope when there was always hope. Even in this situation.

Even for me.

"Didn't you plan on getting away from him eventually?"

"No one gets away from anyone in Windermere." York looked away. "Stop trying to convince me. It doesn't matter anymore. It's already decided."

"It does too. It's not too late. You'll always regret it if you don't enter!"

York avoided my eyes and all I wanted to do was throttle him.

"Fine! We'll both be wearing white vests, emptying moldy sawdust bins from Percy and Bryn's fancy wood shops for the rest of our miserable lives!"

York's gaze snapped to mine. "What do you mean *we*?" He asked, slowly.

As soon as I realized what I'd said, I knew I couldn't take it back. I froze, trying to think of a way to spin it. But York's face fell—he had already guessed the truth.

So I turned and ran.

Twenty-Eight

My eyes were blurry with tears as I tore through the trees down the dirt path.

But it didn't matter that I couldn't see. Somehow, I knew my way through this forest, even blind. I knew every dip in the path, where to jump over every hidden log, and where to avoid slippery moss.

It didn't occur to me to wonder *why* or *how* that was.

Why today, I ran surefooted like an arrow shooting toward a bullseye. I didn't even need my father's clues to direct me. I just *knew*.

I could hear York far behind me, crashing along the path as he struggled to keep my pace.

"Stop, Ivy! Where are you *going*?"

My voice would betray how devastated I was, so I said nothing.

At the familiar glimmer of light shining through the trees, I sidestepped into the opening in one smooth movement, as if I had done it a hundred times. Only I hadn't. I'd visited the clearing just before the Tree Garden only three times before, and each time I had to carefully search for it.

Strange.

York thundered past. I stepped out. "Hey, back here."

He turned, nearly slipping, and walked back to me, breathing hard.

I pulled him inside the opening with me. Wide-eyed, he looked back at the nearly invisible part of the trees and then back at me.

This opening had always been invisible to me too, especially without singing Evergreen. But today, it was clear as day. And I'd seen the light from the opening further back than I ever had before.

I stared at York, knowing I looked disheveled. My hair had come loose and was tumbling around my head. I breathed heavily too, and then my eyes began to burn with tears. I blinked to hold them back.

"*Ivy.*" York sounded heartbroken for me.

His voice made it worse. I covered my face with my hands and tried not to lose it, even though I knew he wouldn't care.

"Are you sure?"

I nodded.

"How do you know before the Tournament?" he asked, quietly. Hopeful it wasn't true.

"Mr. Everett graded my test first. Because of Forest and Fern. He wanted me to be able to prepare. I don't think he thought I would be prepared to lose everything publicly, though." I removed my hands and took a big, shuddering breath. The anger helped me not fall apart.

York looked like he wished he could help me but didn't know how. He reached out and took my bag off my shoulder and put it on his. His eyes were full of concern, not pity. "What if it was a mistake?"

"It's not." A tear escaped and slid down my face. "I failed. I just ... don't know what this means yet—what it means for me."

"It means you'll find something that suits you better," York said, more firmly. "I can't imagine how it feels to lose Forest and

Fern, but Ivy, you didn't like being an Arborist. You don't have to pretend anymore."

"I don't know what else to do!" I said, frustrated. "This is all I ever wanted."

"Is it? Because I remember how you used to want to be a Pryer. Remember when you wanted to open a shop and investigate all the town's problems?"

I shook my head and smiled at the game we played as children. I always had a knack for figuring things out. I loved unraveling the threads of problems to find the knot, but plants had always evaded me. "Yes. But my father said I couldn't make a trade out of being nosy."

"I don't think you were being nosy," York said. "You just wanted to help people."

"I was a kid," I said, wiping my eyes. "At least as an Arborist, I would have fulfilled my father's last wishes for me."

"What about the clues he left? You seemed to enjoy following them?"

I chewed my lip. "Yes, but I've reached the end and haven't gotten any further. Plus, his clues can't give me a place in Windermere. The Taylors expect me to leave at the end of this week. Where am I going to go?" I sniffed.

"The Taylors will let you stay. They'll give you a job at the Mercantile. You could do something with horses. Or help take care of John and Miranda's children. Mr. Gable would probably even hire you." York folded his arms. "You're not alone, Ivy. Maybe you've felt alone because you haven't talked to anyone about it. But no one is going to leave you to figure this out by yourself."

I stared at him. "I wanted to talk to *you*."

He shifted, uncomfortable. "You could have."

"No. It's been so awkward. You've been upset and I'm not sure why."

York sighed. "I know. You're right. I'm sorry."

"What's wrong?" I pressed.

York's hand swept through his hair, and he looked away from me to the trees around us.

"It started when we saw the ship by the Count's woods," I prompted. "Was it because I said I saw something and you didn't?"

York looked surprised. "What? No."

"But you pulled me off the beach so fast. And then you didn't want to talk about it after. Every time I brought up the beach, you acted strange. Then you just started ignoring me!"

A flush spread across York's cheeks. "It wasn't because of that. It was because … well," York huffed out a breath. "You want me to be honest?"

"Please," I said, even though my heart began to pound.

"Fine. It was because I saw how you reacted to someone else."

My mouth dropped open. "What?"

"I saw the way you looked at that rider on the beach," he said in a rush, looking down. "I've never seen you look at anyone like that. I guess I was jealous."

I flushed, embarrassed by his confession, and that he'd noticed. Deep down, I'd known this was the reason.

But I hadn't trusted myself when it came to York's hints about his feelings. Now I didn't know what to say.

"It's fine now, Ivy," York said, quickly. "For a second, I thought maybe we could be more. But then I realized you've never looked at me that way and it was probably because you see me as a brother. It just took me a while to accept you probably wouldn't look at me that way. Ever."

He paused like he was waiting for me to confirm.

I realized that he *needed* me to confirm it. He needed and deserved honesty from me too.

I nodded. "I'm sorry."

"Right." York lifted his chin. "Yeah. So, I just needed some time to get over it. And now it doesn't matter how I felt. You're my best friend and I don't want to lose you. I'm OK with us just being friends. I promise."

I sighed, relieved that we were finally being honest, even if it was a little uncomfortable. "I'm sorry too, York. I did consider it, I did. I should have told you right away that I didn't feel the same way. I just didn't want to ruin anything or disappoint you. I was scared."

"I know. It's OK. I just want our friendship back to how it was."

"Me too."

I threw my arms around him, and he hugged me back, resting his chin on my head. For a moment, everything bad that had happened slipped away. All I felt was my relief and the beating of York's heart along with the sounds of birds in the trees.

Somehow, everything would work out. I still had my father's clues to follow, but for now, I had another purpose. I had to get York back in the Carving trade. No matter what, I couldn't let him lose his chance too.

Finally, York released me. "So, what now?"

I knew he meant about my future, but I didn't want to talk about it right now. There was an itch under my skin to see the Tree Garden and I wanted to spend time with York without worry.

"How about we forget our life-ending problems for a second? Right now, I want to show you something."

York grinned. "Fine."

"Come on, then."

He followed me beneath the tunnel until the branches lifted and ended at the clearing in front of the Tree Garden. The wall of trees rose before us, its branches and leaves wound and tangled tightly together. It was more green than ever.

"Where are we?" York asked, looking up in awe at the thick archway of branches ending in a curling point. "What is this place?"

"This is what I said you had to see to believe. It's where my father's clues led me. This is the Tree Garden."

The awe I felt the first time I stood here spread through me again. But this time, there was a stronger pull from inside. I turned to York.

"Want to see something unbelievable?"

He nodded, his eyes following me as I walked up to the archway. It'd looked intimidating to me at first but now it was lush and inviting. I no longer felt a warning pulse through me. I heard a welcoming song.

I turned back to York. He still had my bag on his shoulder—the owl was inside it.

I grinned mischievously. Then I stepped up to the archway slowly, ready to lean against the barrier and watch York's reaction when he saw me resting against nothing but air.

I folded my arms and let my weight fall backward. It felt like an eternity as I waited for something solid to catch me and keep me out.

But to my surprise, I tumbled backward into the Tree Garden.

Twenty-Nine

I lifted my head out of the grass, shocked. I was inside *without* the owl.

York was laughing. I looked in disbelief at where he stood, just outside the arch, still holding my bag.

I got into the Tree Garden all by myself.

"Are you OK?" York sounded amused. "Why did you do that?"

I sat up. "York, put my bag down, and come in here."

"What?"

"Just do it."

I could tell he thought I was acting strange, but he set my bag on the ground and walked up to the arch. Then he smacked his head against the hard air. This time, I laughed.

York lifted his hand in disbelief, feeling the solid air press back on it. "What? *How?*"

I stopped laughing and got up. I walked to the arch and held my hand up to the air. I waited for the sucking sensation to overcome me and spit me out, but it was gone. The Tree Garden wasn't trying to push me out anymore.

I felt welcomed. It *wanted* me here.

But what changed?

Earlier, I'd found my way here without help. As if I'd been coming here forever.

York held his hand up to mine, but I couldn't feel it. Wherever his hand went, the solid air formed. He couldn't touch me. We stared at our hands in wonder, then I reached through the air and touched his skin.

His eyes widened. "What's happening?"

I shook my head. "I'm not sure. I've never been able to get in here before. Not without ..."

I crossed under the arch, but again, it was as if there had never been any barrier at all. With the owl, I'd always felt the air *split*, as if I was allowed to pass through it. Now, the boundary was gone.

Was *I* a key now, like the owl? The only thing that had changed about me since the last time I was here was seeing that mysterious light.

"Um, Ivy?"

I glanced at York; he looked spooked.

"Hold my bag and it will let you in," I said quietly, still wondering how this was possible.

York picked up my bag and walked to the archway. This time, the air parted. He stepped inside, shivering as if he felt cold.

I stepped inside too. The light in the clearing looked different. It glittered and shimmered, not only the sunlight filtering down through the leaves but something else. It covered everything in a new, green haze. I hadn't noticed it before. I recognized it—the same light I'd seen around Cora and the ship.

Whatever I'd inhaled from my father's journal was in me now. Had it given me the key to this place?

Next to me, York looked wary but intrigued. A breeze fluttered through the long blades of lush grass, birds chattered softly high in the trees, and the smell of earth and nature eased something in me. It was so peaceful here that for a moment, I didn't care how I got inside. I was just glad to be here.

Then I realized that York was just staring at the holes in the trees.

"Wait until you look inside," I said, a teasing dare in my voice.

York rolled his eyes as he made his way over to a tree and looked inside. He jumped backward, just like I had the first time.

I laughed again.

"What are *those*?"

"I don't know. What do you see?" I chuckled, wiping my eyes. It felt so good to laugh after this week.

"Faces. Eyes." York looked again. "They're incredible, but who carved them? What are they?"

"Tree spirits, I think. I can't seem to find anything more than that about them in the library."

York turned to look at me. "How did your father know about this place?"

"I haven't figured that out. He said the owl was a key. It was my mother's."

York stilled. "You never talk about her. Even when you brought the owl to Nicholas, you never told me it was hers."

I shrugged. "That's because I don't know anything about her. Still don't."

"Tell me what happened after we saw Nicholas. You haven't told me anything."

"Well, I read the note my father left in the cube. Those clues led me here. But after I fed the trees, I hit a dead end. After we saw Carl leave the Count's castle, I thought about how the cube had a secret compartment, just like the ones you said Carl carved. There was also a drawing of the Count's crest in my father's clues. I think it's all connected, but I'm not sure how. That's why I was so interested in the Count."

"Wait, back up. *Feed* the trees? Is that an Arborist thing?"

I sank to the ground and opened my bag, pulling out the owl, cube, and journal. "Someone left a basket with packages and a note, telling me to put them inside the trees."

York frowned like he didn't know what to say.

"Don't get weird on me now. There's more."

"I'm not." York sat down next to me. "What else?"

I hesitated, not sure how he would react to this part. "Do you remember how Nicholas acted like my father wasn't dead?"

York nodded.

"When I told him my father was dead, he didn't believe me. He said my father had thought something might happen to him. That he'd been preparing for it."

"OK," York said, neutrally.

"And you and I saw Carl ... and Carl wasn't across the sea like he was supposed to be. He's been at the Count's castle this whole time. I've been wondering if maybe the same thing happened to my father. That he's just somewhere he shouldn't be too." I sighed. "It sounds dumb now that I'm saying it out loud. I don't believe it."

York blew out a breath. "It's not dumb. Maybe ... unbelievable. But all of this," he gestured around us, "is kind of unbelievable too, and we're here."

I nodded. "I know."

York looked around, thinking. "How old is this place?"

"Must be thousands of years. Maybe more."

"How many times have you been here?"

I paused. "This time makes four. I came after we met with Nicholas."

"Why didn't you bring me before now?"

"I wanted to. But at first, I felt like I needed to follow my father's clues on my own. Then, I thought you were upset about me seeing that light on the beach, and I didn't think you'd appreciate the air keeping you out of the Tree Garden."

York looked back at me, confused. "What do you mean about the light?"

"It's why my eyes hurt, that day that you and Mr. Mallon saved me. When I inhaled the dust, or powder, or pollen, or whatever it was in my father's journal, something about the way I see light changed for me. I saw it on the beach around the strong man's hands, then the ship. Then around the woman from the castle who was with Carl—Cora."

"What does it look like?" York asked, intrigued.

"It depends on what it's around. Above the sea, it was shimmers of gold. But around the ship, it was threads like a spider's web. And around Cora, it was a silver and metallic outline."

"Huh."

York didn't sound like he doubted me; he seemed to be thinking about everything in a completely new way. And it felt nice to confide in him like I normally would.

"And you don't know why?"

I chewed my lip. "I think if I can figure out the clues, I'll understand. The light changing, and what it means. The problem is I'm not an Arborist, and these clues were meant for someone who thought like my father. I clearly don't."

"Let's try together, then. Tell me what else was in the clues."

I shrugged. "Things I don't understand. Images. Here—you look." I handed the cube and the owl to York.

He opened them with his knife and read both pieces of paper slowly. Then he looked around, thinking.

"I don't get it either," he finally said. "And why is this place even here? Who made it?"

"I don't know. All I know is that after I fed the trees, the grass and leaves grew, and now it kind of glows."

"Glows?" York peered up into the trees. "Like what you saw around the ship?"

I shook my head. "No. This is like sunlight, but brighter, softer, and *greener*, somehow."

York looked perplexed. "And you'd never seen anything like this before the journal?"

"No, it started after I passed out. The day I woke up, we saw the ship."

"And you don't see it around Windermere," York clarified.

"No."

"It's only around things or people that have something to do with the Count?"

I stared at York, taking in that realization. I hadn't thought about it like that. "What do you think it means?"

"I don't know. My father would say it's not good. What does this part mean," York looked back at the paper, "*Feed the trees*?"

"I may be able to show you."

I jumped up and walked back out of the archway. As I walked toward the stump, I saw the handle was uncovered. Usually, leaves or dirt were hiding it. I glanced around, but I didn't feel or see anyone. When I opened the lid, I found another basket inside.

My heart jumped excitedly. It wasn't the end of the clues after all.

York eyed the basket as I walked back into the clearing. "Where did you get that?"

"In a stump just outside the arch. I think whoever left them can't get inside." I paused. "And now I can get in all on my own."

"Did your father do this too?" York asked.

"He must have. How else would he know about it?"

"Do you think he got in here with the help of the owl, or by himself?"

I froze. "Wow. I never thought about that. Good question. I wish I knew."

York was still reading the clues. "If he insisted on the owl, then he probably needed it too."

"Maybe. Or he just assumed I would." I sighed. I wished things were more clear. "OK, watch."

I walked to the first tree and took a small package wrapped in brown paper and placed it inside the tree's open mouth. Then I added an acorn. I walked to the next tree and repeated the process, not feeling as jumpy as the first time with York here. Around the circle I went, placing a bag and an acorn in each tree's mouth.

Just as I put the final package in the final tree, York asked, "What's in the packages?"

I turned back to look at him. "I don't know."

York was surprised. "You haven't looked?"

"My father warned me not to—"

York shot up from the ground. "Behind you, Ivy! Watch out!"

I shrieked, covering my head with my hands and turning to see whatever had scared York. But all I saw was a black bushy tail disappearing up the tree.

"What was it?" I asked, my heart racing.

York reached me and peered up into the tree. "I'm not sure. Something came down so fast and shot into the hole before I saw it. I only saw something black come out."

My heart dropped. "Oh no! Did it take the package? I think it was supposed to only take the acorn." I looked down. I was still holding the last brown acorn. "That must be what he wants. These are oak trees, but they don't seem to grow acorns."

"I'll get it back!" York jumped up and grabbed a lower branch before I could stop him. He swung himself up, balanced, and grabbed a higher branch. Then he disappeared in the leaves.

It was quiet. I couldn't believe how thick the leaves were or how quickly they'd swallowed up that animal, York, and any sound. I strained to hear.

"See anything?" I called up.

York's voice sounded far away. "Not yet. Wait, what's that?"

"What?"

The leaves swayed above. "Get away!" York called. There was more rustling and shaking of branches above me. Then, "Ivy! There's a nest. It's filled with those packages."

"Don't touch them!" I yelled.

"Don't worry."

"York, I'm serious!" I yelled, louder.

He didn't respond. But a second later, he dropped from the tree and crashed down next to me.

"Hey," he said.

"What do you mean, 'Hey'!" I said, swatting him. "Did you touch them?"

York looked down at his hands as if inspecting them. Then he shook them out as if they were on fire.

"What's wrong?" I said, worry filling me.

"Nothing. Look." He reached into his pocket and held up something for me to see.

It looked like a round stone, but golden. My breath caught. An undeniable, unmistakable light was coming from inside the stone. Maybe I was imagining it, but it seemed to pulse with light.

"What color is this?" I asked, in awe.

"Gold?" York said.

"Shiny or flat gold?"

"Flat."

"Hmm." To me, the stone was shiny. Again, I was seeing something York wasn't.

Something didn't feel right. I looked up. Only then did I notice that York was staring at the stone like he was mesmerized.

"You're touching it," I said, panicking.

Whatever hold he was under broke. York looked at me, surprised. "How else was I supposed to pick it up?"

"But I told you not to. My father said not to touch anything with bare skin."

York shrugged and looked back at the stone. "I'm fine, nothing happened."

I looked at York's hands. They *seemed* normal. "Were there more?"

He nodded. "There was a lot." He reached back into his pockets and pulled out more golden stones.

"Can you put them in the basket now?" I asked, feigning calm when all I felt was dread spreading through me.

I felt York hesitate like he was about to protest. I looked up at him, but to my relief, he slowly dropped them into the basket. It looked difficult for him to let them go.

"I'll hurry up and finish," I said, wanting to get them out of sight as quickly as possible.

I covered the extra stones up in scraps of paper I had in my bag and stuffed them inside the trees, getting them away from us. I didn't think it mattered that I was doubling up; these were supposed to go in the trees anyway, I assumed, but they'd been stolen.

York hovered close—closer than he needed to be. I casually moved the basket to my other hip, away from him, and he tracked the movement. I had a terrible, sudden feeling that he was going to try to take the gold stones before I could finish putting them in the trees. I stepped away from him.

Alarm bells rang through my head, warning me that York had touched the stones with his bare hands. Now he wanted them. What if he tried to steal them from the trees? How would I stop him?

My body wanted to run; we needed to leave. Once I got him out of here, York wouldn't be able to get back in.

That thought startled me.

I saw York shake his head, and his expression cleared. He smiled his normal smile and I smiled uneasily back.

But what had just happened? Was it just paranoia?

"I'm finished. Let's go," I said, walking quickly to the arch. York followed me without complaint.

I breathed a sigh of relief when we walked outside the Tree Garden. I put the empty basket back in the stump and took my bag back from him. We walked down the tunnel and onto the path to Windermere. Now that we were away from the packages, York seemed back to normal. He was even whistling.

But every so often, he shook his hands out.

"What's wrong with your hands?" I asked.

"They're tingling. You know that weird prickling feeling you get when your leg falls asleep? They sort of feel like that. But hot."

An uneasy feeling crept over me. "York, you shouldn't have touched anything."

"I'm fine," York said, dismissing my worry. "Hey, we should see Mr. Everett tomorrow."

I looked at him in surprise. "Why? It won't change anything. He already let me collect my things from Forest and Fern."

"Then we'll go around town and see about a job for you. I'll help you get it figured out before anything is announced."

"We only have tomorrow. The Woodworking Tournament is in two days," I reminded him.

He nodded. "It'll work out. I know it."

"We need to get it worked out for you too," I said, pointedly.

"Maybe I'll become an Arborist. I really liked the Tree Garden."

"It's a secret. Other Arborists don't know about it," I said, frowning.

York laughed. "It's a joke, Ivy. And I won't tell anyone."

When we reached town, York and I split up, making plans to meet tomorrow.

As I walked home, I replayed over and over how strange York had acted. I knew I wasn't being paranoid—something had happened to York in the moments after he'd touched the stones. Or something had happened up in the trees. I hadn't asked him what the nest was like, or if he'd seen whatever had taken the packages.

Even if his hands looked fine, something didn't feel right.

York couldn't get back inside the Tree Garden without the owl. He knew it, too. I didn't like not trusting him, but I had to believe my instincts.

From now on, I would keep the owl close to me at all times.

THIRTY

Merchant tents circled the stone fountain and fanned down the street toward the Courthouse.

Booths were not allowed to sell goods until the Woodworking Tournament, but that didn't stop the townspeople from coming to see what was being offered. Merchants displayed their samples, and locals made plans about what booths they would visit first tomorrow.

York and I decided to walk through the booths before we looked for a position for me. I kept a lookout for the merchant my father had bought his special white orchid seeds from. Maybe I should stop by and ask him how I could plant the bulbs I'd saved without killing them. I also hoped the leather merchant would set up his booth again. Last year, he'd had the most beautiful selection of bridles and saddlebags.

I was grateful for one last day in Windermere when no one knew about my failed test. My stomach twisted every time I thought about tomorrow. I didn't think I had the guts to be in town when the news spread. I thought about spending the day in the Tree Garden, but I didn't want York to ask to come. Not after yesterday.

"What?" York said, startling me.

"Huh?" I asked, wondering what I'd done. We were just walking.

"That's gotta be the fifth time you've stared at me like something's wrong. So, *what*?"

I swallowed. "Sorry. I was just thinking about your hands. How are they?"

"Oh." York clasped his hands together and rubbed his thumb over his palm. He seemed agitated. "They're fine."

"Really? You're about to rub a hole in them."

York dropped his hands and sighed. "They feel itchy, or maybe restless is a better word. Like they have all this energy that needs to be used. I think carving would help; it would settle them. But I'm not supposed to be in the shops anymore."

"Why don't you whittle, then?" I asked.

York looked around us. "Not in front of everyone. Not when they know I won't be in the Tournament tomorrow. I'm not supposed to *want* to carve anymore."

I stopped. "York, you have to enter tomorrow."

"And you need to find a position today," he shot back.

"If I do, will you enter?" I asked, stubbornly.

"Did I miss something? Did you somehow clear up all my family problems so I can?"

I stepped back, stunned. York had never spoken to me like that before.

He saw my widened eyes and immediately said, "I'm sorry, Ivy. I didn't mean to snap at you. I'm just on edge today. I've been looking forward to tomorrow my entire life. I always thought I'd be going inside the Courthouse with everyone. I can't believe I'm not."

I swallowed. "I understand."

York grimaced. "I know you do. You're the only one who can."

"Except I had my chance and *I* messed it up. You're letting someone else mess up your chance for you."

York looked weary. "Can we drop this? I don't want to fight today."

"Fine," I said, suddenly tired too.

We walked together in silence for a while.

We passed Wilder's Bakery; the line was so long that Claire smuggled out some sandwiches for us, and we sat on a bench eating them. It would have been a perfect day if York and I weren't so miserable about what would come tomorrow.

Tomorrow would be hard—unbearable, even. York would watch his classmates enter the Tournament without him, left behind. And everyone would know I'd failed and that Forest and Fern was going to belong to someone else.

As if he could read my mind, York asked quietly, "Do you want to break into your father's shop one last time?"

I shook my head. "I already got what I needed. I have to get used to the fact that it's not mine. It never really was."

"I'm sorry."

I nodded, keeping my eyes on all the color and excitement in the street. "Me too."

York crumpled up his paper and took mine, throwing them both in the trash as we stood. "I guess it's time to talk about things again. Like where we should start looking for a job for you."

I sighed. "Mr. Everett made a list. I guess we should go get it now."

"Lead the way."

I glanced at him. "Do you want to go to a Carving shop? One last time?"

"Maybe." York rubbed his palms together. "Honestly, it's getting hard to think of anything else."

I frowned. "Do your hands still tingle?"

"Yes. And they're hot."

I stopped walking. "Still? From yesterday?"

York nodded, but then Mr. Gable appeared in front of us. In

the sunlight, the deep navy of his vest caught the light and shimmered lightly in its velvet crevices.

"Good morning, you two," he said, his blue eyes twinkling as if he was happy to run into us.

I smiled back. "Hello, Mr. Gable."

"Hello." York looked behind him. "Is Percy with you? I haven't seen him in a while."

"He's still at the Contestant's shop, selling quite a bit and carving even more. Are you ready for the Tournament tomorrow, York?"

"I'm not entering," York said, but he sounded less certain than he had earlier.

"What a pity. I heard that and hoped it wasn't true." Mr. Gable frowned. "Any particular reason?"

"My father." York didn't offer any more of an explanation.

"Ah." Mr. Gable hesitated for a moment as if debating what to say. "You know, I've always thought that a life is built on the actions we take. But it is also built on actions we regret *not* taking. You're reaching the point where your life is starting to build itself . . . What direction it goes now is up to you. For only you will suffer the consequences now—not your parents."

York nodded, clenching and unclenching his hands. I was becoming antsy just watching him.

"You're uniquely talented," Mr. Gable continued. "There is not a single Carving student in town who would qualify for the Count's Tournament only to pass it up. You are one of the fortunate few who were invited to participate, and I'd hate for the opportunity to be lost due to ill guidance or a lack of support. If this is a matter of practicing before the Tournament, you are more than welcome to use my shop. You may also stay the night with us if that makes it easier for you to get to the Tournament."

York looked surprised. Gable's Emporium was right across from the courthouse. Mr. Gable was offering him a way to get to the Tournament without having to sneak away from home.

I looked at York, hopeful.

He just nodded. "Thank you. I promise I'll consider it."

Mr. Gable put his hand on York's arm. "Many people have high hopes for you, York. And you, Ivy, anything you need as well. You know I feel protective over both of you and anything I can do to help, just ask."

"Thank you," I said, touched.

I stared after Mr. Gable as he headed back to his shop. He couldn't know how much his words and support meant to me because he didn't know about my test results yet. *Maybe I should tell him and ask for help.*

I was just about to ask York what he thought when I heard another deep voice.

"Ivy Rune. Here you are."

My stomach sank like a stone. I turned; Mr. Mallon stood behind us. The sight of his black suit with silver threads sent waves of anxiety through me. What could he want now?

I was struck by a worse thought: Was he going to ask for my vest back? Surely it would not happen like this. I searched his hands for a white vest and backed up slightly. My mouth went dry as sawdust.

"You were not at the Taylors and I feared I would spend the whole day trying to locate you out in the forest. Hello again, York Pembroke. I've heard about your unfortunate change in trade."

York shifted, uneasily. "Oh. Um, I'm sorry about that."

I stared at Mr. Mallon. What did he mean about me being out in the forest? How did he know where I'd be ... unless he was watching me? I finally found my voice.

"You were looking for me?"

Mr. Mallon glanced down at my bag before he turned his dark eyes back on me. "Yes. I heard about your Arborist test."

My stomach lurched, but my hand curled around my bag to protect my father's journal. "You can't have the journal back! Even if I'm not becoming an Arborist now, it's still *mine*."

York looked startled at my outburst, but he took a step closer to me.

Mr. Mallon seemed surprised too. Then annoyed. "Keep your voice down. I wouldn't do that. I was simply looking for you to ask if you've told anyone else in town about your test. I assume you've told York."

I nodded and tried to speak more calmly. "Only he and Mr. Everett know. I've told no one else."

"Good. Keep it that way. I am not pleased that Mr. Everett told you early, but I'm glad to hear you can hold your tongue. Now, I want you to meet me before the Tournament on the front steps of the Courthouse tomorrow. Ten minutes before it starts. Do not be late. Do not tell anyone you are meeting me either."

Before I could respond, he looked at York. "I would like you to come as well."

He stared at us, waiting for our answers. We both nodded, shocked. He looked satisfied but gave us a parting look that promised consequences if we did not obey. Then he walked away.

York and I both remained frozen, looking after him. Merchants began to weave around us, their overflowing carts rattling after them.

Then York turned to me. "Ivy, you just yelled at the Count's Regent."

"I didn't mean to. I couldn't help it." I shook my head. "Why do you think he wants to meet with us?"

"*You*, not me, I don't think. He invited me as an afterthought."

"No, he wanted you to come too," I said.

York turned to me, he looked hopeful. "He said he wasn't happy with Mr. Everett. What if he intends to override your grade? Maybe he's going to let you become an Arborist after all."

I blinked. "Why would he do that? Why would he care?"

"He gave you the book. He helped you when you were hurt. Maybe he's not as bad as you think."

"Then why ask me to keep it a secret?"

"Think about it. He made sure you didn't tell anyone you

failed. He probably doesn't want it to look like you're getting special treatment."

A small part of me felt hopeful. "Do you really think so?"

York looked at me, sympathetically. "I don't want to get your hopes up, but I can't see why else he would want to meet with you. Tomorrow, trades are announced at the end of the day. He has to meet with you before the Tournament because he's inside with the contestants all day."

"Maybe he's offering me another trade and he wants my agreement before he announces it?" I said. That seemed more likely.

York nodded. "Maybe. Either option is good though. What a relief."

I knocked him with my shoulder. "Hey. Were you worried after you told me not to be?"

York rubbed his arm and laughed. "Ow, and yes. I'm relieved for you. Plus now you don't have to look for a position anymore. You can't, if he doesn't want anyone to know. We'll have to wait and see what he says tomorrow."

"Yeah, you're right," I said, slowly. "You know, after what Mr. Gable said to us, I was going to ask him what I should do. If he could give me a position."

"Ask him tomorrow if whatever Mr. Mallon says isn't what we think," York said.

Then he looked past me, and I turned to see what caught his attention.

The faded sign of Whittling Wood swung in the breeze. Sunlight flickered against the image carved into the wood. Just like the image my father had drawn in his journal. I still had all that to figure out; it would be nice if Mr. Mallon stepped in and solved at least one of my problems.

York rubbed his hands together and looked back at me. "Hey, I'm going to Mr. Gable's to carve before my father needs me. Do you mind?"

"Not at all. I should go take care of Loon anyway."

"Then, we'll meet on the steps before the Tournament?"

"Yes. See you tomorrow."

As York disappeared down the street, I couldn't help but hope that he was right.

Maybe tomorrow wouldn't be so terrible.

Maybe I would become an Arborist after all and then the last week would be nothing more than a bad dream.

THIRTY-ONE

The morning of the Count's Woodworking Tournament arrived, along with grey clouds that smothered the sky like a heavy blanket.

I walked into town as dark splashes of rain began to hit the ground. All night, I'd wondered what Mr. Mallon wanted to talk about, but now, all I worried about was York. Today was supposed to be the biggest day of his life—and it probably still would be, but not for the right reasons.

If I couldn't convince him to join the Tournament, he would remember this day, every time it came each year, as the day he gave up being a Carver. I chewed my lip, going over arguments in my mind—how could I make him see it would all work out in the end? I knew that York wouldn't enter if he thought he was protecting his mother from his father's wrath. And I couldn't blame him, but I wished things were different. Less complicated.

When I reached the town square, the sky looked like it might open and downpour at any moment. Gusts of wind rippled the tops of tents and rattled the buildings, but that didn't deter the entire town from showing up. Everyone was here. Any open space around me was quickly swallowed by a new body jostling to get by. It seemed everyone was heading where I was—the Courthouse. But while I went to meet York and Mr. Mallon, they gathered to watch the contestants enter the Tournament.

A group of Carving students and their families stood closest to the steps, anxiously waiting to see if they had been awarded the extra ticket. I hadn't given the extra ticket a thought this year; I'd been so consumed by everything else.

On the day of the Tournament, the Count always awarded one extra ticket to a student who hadn't qualified. The students invited to the Tournament today had already earned the Count's seal, which meant they could start selling their carvings after the Tournament. The contestant who won the Tournament earned the title of a Master Carver and were given their own Carving shop. Everyone looked forward to the extra ticket, especially if the person to whom it was awarded won the Tournament—but that had only happened once. I wondered: If the Arborist trade awarded extra tickets, would Mr. Everett have given it to me? My stomach soured. It wasn't fair that only the Carvers had this extra chance.

From what I heard from the conversation around me, everyone thought the extra ticket would go to Mira, a talented Carving student who surprisingly hadn't qualified. She stood by the steps with her father and mother, stamping her feet to keep warm. She looked nervous and my heart went out to her. I really liked Mira. She was not from a Carving family and I remembered York saying how much she always practiced. I hoped she got the extra ticket.

I pushed my way up to the Courthouse. Just up the steps were four large pillars that held up the grand balcony. In a short while, Mr. Mallon would greet the crowd and announce the winner of the extra ticket. Then the Tournament would start. Later this afternoon, he would return to announce the Tournament winner.

But right now, he wanted to meet *me*.

It was the most unlikely thing I ever thought would happen today.

It was almost ten minutes till the start of the Tournament,

but I still hadn't spotted York anywhere. I made my way over to the side of the building, clutching my jacket tightly against the wind. There was York, waiting behind the back pillar. I hurried up to him, relieved.

"Does your father know you're here?" I asked, stepping behind the pillar to hide from the crowd beside him.

York shook his head, his brown hair tumbling across his forehead. He looked like he'd walked here in the rain too. "No, he was still asleep when I left."

"You didn't stay at Mr. Gable's. Does your mother know?"

"She knows I came to town. I'll go back after we talk to Mr. Mallon and make sure my father doesn't suspect I came here."

I nodded, taking a breath, ready to launch into my best argument for why York should still enter the Tournament when the side door swung open and Mr. Mallon walked out. When he spotted us, his pinched expression smoothed, but my stomach dropped as he walked toward us.

I panicked—what if York and I had it all wrong? How could I ever think this man would rescue me from my failure? He looked like he wanted to give me a white vest before the day even started. My cheeks burned.

"Good, you're both here," he said, stopping in front of us. But his expression looked anything but glad; he looked as cold as the air around us. "Have you told anyone about this meeting?"

We shook our heads.

My pulse raced. This was it.

"Good. Ivy, I am here to inform you that you have been awarded this year's extra ticket to the Count's Woodworking Tournament."

My mouth dropped open. I was sure I'd heard him wrong, but York looked just as shocked as I was.

I didn't understand.

Mr. Mallon wasn't letting me back in the Arborist trade; he wasn't even helping me with a new position. He was offering me a place in the Tournament. As a Carver.

Me. I hadn't even touched a chisel since being reassigned to the Arborist trade. My eyes flew down to Mira and the other Carving students waiting for this announcement.

"Why me?" I managed to say. "A Carving student should get it."

Mr. Mallon's eyes narrowed. I could feel his annoyance that I dared to argue with him. "You've had the early training just like everyone else."

I gestured to the crowd. "But there are a dozen Carving families waiting down there, hoping for this chance. No one like *me* should get it! I'm not a Carver."

"Regardless, the spot is yours."

"Please," I said, panicking. "Please give it to Mira."

His lips thinned and pressed together until they turned white. "This is my decision. And I expect to find you inside."

I looked at York, completely at a loss. He stared back, speechless.

An idea struck.

"Then let York come with me," I blurted out.

"Ivy!" York protested, surprised.

Mr. Mallon's eyes narrowed in irritation. "You are not in a position to make demands, Ms. Rune. York's father has made his position quite clear."

York quickly nodded. "Yes, he has."

Mr. Mallon frowned. "Then you agree with his decision?"

"Oh, no. Not really."

"You were *invited*." He studied York intently now, making him shift uncomfortably. "No contestant in the history of Windermere has *ever* declined an invitation to the Count's Tournament."

"He doesn't want to decline," I said in a rush. "He wants to participate, but his father will punish him if he finds out. Can't you protect him somehow? York is the one you want in the Tournament, not me."

Mr. Mallon pinched the bridge of his nose and huffed out a

breath. "Ms. Rune, are you always this difficult? Anyone else would be grateful for this chance, especially when they have *nothing else*." He bit out the last two words cruelly.

I cringed. "I thought you were going to offer me another chance at being an Arborist," I said, quietly.

"No. That is not possible."

I drew in a breath and mustered up every ounce of persuasion I had. "I promise never to argue with you again. I'll go willingly, even though I don't understand why you want me to. I don't care what happens to me. Just let York have his chance too. He could win."

Mr. Mallon looked away from me and out into the crowd. I knew my time was running out. But I stared him down, unwilling to blink, ready to put up a bigger fight if I had to.

York stared at me, eyes wide.

Mr. Mallon said, "Very well. I have every intention of taking care of this situation, York. I planned a demonstration at a later date for the town to witness. However, Ms. Rune's idea might be a more discreet option for all involved. So you will enter the Tournament. Your father will understand this was on my orders and that we do not, under any circumstance, defy the Count's wishes."

He was saying the words I wanted to hear, but a chill ran through me. What kind of public demonstration had he planned for York's father? I glanced at York, wondering if he'd caught that too, but he was just looking at Mr. Mallon in disbelief.

"This conversation is over. Wait here. Someone will be out shortly to collect you." Without another look at us, Mr. Mallon headed out to the steps to greet the crowd.

We only had minutes before the Tournament started.

Blood pounded in my ears as I turned to York. "What just happened?"

York ran his hand through his hair. He seemed as confused by this turn of events as I was. "You just got me into the Tournament."

"Are you OK with that?"

"Yes. My father knows I can't ignore Mr. Mallon's orders," York said, excitement beginning to light in his eyes. "Thank you, Ivy."

My heart lifted as I smiled back. "Well, I *did* create this mess in the first place. I'm glad to fix it, but now I have to go in too. And I can't carve!" I groaned. "What am I going to do?"

"You still know a little bit. And you don't have to carve anything complicated, I don't think."

"But when everyone sees my terrible carving compared to the real contestants, they'll be angry I took this spot from a real Carver. I can't open a Carving shop after this, and that's the only reason to compete. I still need a position, but I'll never be offered a job by anyone after this!"

"No one will talk about what you carve in there. It's a secret."

"Bryn will for sure, and others might. How could they not? This has never happened before."

York frowned. I was right.

Mr. Mallon's voice boomed out over the crowd.

"Greetings! Welcome to the Count's Annual Woodworking Tournament. Our competition is about to begin. I know you are all waiting for the announcement about the extra ticket. However, this year, the Count has decided not to reveal the winner publicly. The person awarded the extra spot has already been informed and will take their place in the competition without any fanfare."

Surprise sounded in the square. My stomach churned as I watched Mira's face fall in disappointment. Her parents hugged her, their upset evident too. The crowd scrutinized the group of contestants standing on the bottom steps in front of Mr. Mallon. Everyone wanted to know who it was . . . but why hadn't he announced it was *me*?

York met my eyes, thinking the same thing. Mr. Mallon had just made everyone's curiosity worse by not revealing who'd received the extra ticket. Now this was all anyone would talk about today: the mystery of who'd gotten the ticket and why.

My blood went cold as the large doors swung open, signaling that it was time for the contestants to enter. The crowd surged forward, everyone straining to watch each person who walked up the stairs.

I twisted my hands. "I'm going to be sick."

"It's OK. I'll be with you." York looked at me, determined. "And I'll make sure Bryn doesn't say a word about you or what you carve."

My knees buckled. "But York..."

He squeezed my arm. "Take a deep breath. It's going to be OK, I can see that now. If I win, I'll give you a position in *my* shop. You won't have to worry about a job or a white vest anymore."

"Why is Mr. Mallon doing this? It doesn't help me at all. He can't expect me to win...so what *does* he expect?"

York frowned. "I don't know."

The rest of the contestants were almost in the door, and Mr. Mallon stared over their heads at us. When the side door opened again, a woman I'd never seen before beckoned for us to follow her inside.

With a bewildered glance at each other, York and I quickly slipped from behind the pillar through the side door. As soon as the door closed behind us, the noise of the crowd disappeared.

I stood in the dark hallway of the Courthouse, thinking that *this* was now the most unlikely thing I ever thought would happen today.

THIRTY-TWO

A light shone from the end of the dim, narrow hallway.
It was the main entry, where the official contestants had just entered. I wondered if the woman would take us that way, or if we would be kept separate. Would Mr. Mallon keep us a secret from the town? I frowned. York didn't need to be kept a secret from anyone but his father. He had earned his place in the Tournament. I worried that if he won, people would wonder why they hadn't seen him walk in with everyone else.

The woman continued walking. She still hadn't turned around to greet us. York and I stared at her back as we followed her toward where the contestants were gathered. I felt a little relieved that we were going toward them after all. York deserved this, even if my stomach sank at the thought of facing everyone.

The woman turned to us as she reached the doorway. I knew I'd never seen her before. She was unremarkable in every way. Her clothes were simple and dark. She wore no vest. Her features were so bland that I wondered if I would even be able to remember her if I had to.

"Wait for me here and don't make a sound." She turned and walked into the entryway, then pulled a tall wooden screen across the doorway so we would not be seen. The screen was carved in an intricate design with holes to look through.

York and I glanced at each other and quickly stepped forward, pressing our faces against the screen to peek out.

The air seemed heavy with nervous expectations. The contestants had formed a line in front of the single table and chatted as they waited. I could only see walls of wood paneling, old paintings in gilded frames, and a tall tree in a corner. It looked grand, though.

York and I jumped away from the screen when we saw the woman return.

She pulled it shut behind her and handed each of us two bags.

"Do not open these. Follow me." She pushed past us and led us to the end of the narrow hall. An old staircase wound up around a large wooden chandelier that needed dusting. We climbed the stairs silently behind her.

Why was a stranger allowed here? I didn't think she was a Carver, or even from Windermere. Who was she that Mr. Mallon trusted her with this?

When we were far enough behind her on the stairs, I pulled York's arm and whispered, "Who is she?"

He shrugged. "I'm not worried about *her* right now, Ivy. And you shouldn't be either."

He was right, so I tried to put her out of my mind and focus on why we were here and what I was about to do. The stairway twisted as it rose to the higher floors. My heart pulsed nervously with each step, but I reminded myself this was not my trade test— it was York's. All I had to do was avoid everyone and carve something simple. If I could manage that, this might turn out alright.

After three flights, my legs burned and my breath came faster. I huffed in relief as we reached the landing and the woman opened a door. She looked inside the room first. Satisfied, she gestured for us to follow her in.

We entered through a side door. There was a large set of double doors across the room. My eyes rose to the impressive high vaulted ceilings and wooden beams that crisscrossed above our heads. One wall was full of large arched windows that faced the street. I could imagine when it was sunny, the room was warm and inviting, but now, the light was weak and grey. Rain pattered against the glass, making the room feel cold.

No one was here besides us, but I could hear footsteps coming from beyond the double doors.

Several large work tables were spaced evenly around the room. Each table had four individual workspaces, separated by large panels of wood so that we could not look over and see what another contestant was doing. The woman gestured to the desk closest to us, at the very back of the room.

York and I sat down next to each other, hidden behind the large panels of wood. Mr. Mallon was trying to keep us undetected. My stomach flipped uneasily.

The woman cleared her throat. "Wait here. Do not change workstations. Do not open this bag until the competition starts," she said, pointing to the smaller bag. "The other one has your tools, so you may open it now and arrange your table however you like. Good luck."

She pivoted and left through the side door. There was nothing to do but open our bags. We found black leather cuffs with four carving tools strapped to it. It was not as elaborate as Mr. Gable's, but still, it was fine leather. There was also a black vest with a pin with the Count's crest. York put on his right away.

"It's nicer than our student vests were," he commented, feeling the fabric. "It feels good to put a Carving vest back on."

I didn't respond. Hesitantly, I slipped off my tweed vest and put on the black vest. It was strange to wear a Carving vest and the Count's crest. I felt like an imposter and I didn't want anyone to see me. I tried to breathe deeply as I laced up the leather cuff on my left arm. The room began to fill with contestants. I peeked up above the wooden panel, unable to resist. A few people looked at York in surprise, but no one noticed me. To my relief, as soon as they sat down, they began strapping on their cuffs and inspecting their tools, and no one looked around at all.

Then Percy and Bryn walked into the room. I ducked my head quickly, my heart thumping. They sat at the empty table across from us but didn't spot us. I tightened my cuff nervously, hoping they wouldn't look our way.

Then I heard Percy's shocked voice. "York! You're here."

York's chair scraped the ground. "Yep," he answered.

I tried to hunch into my workspace, but Percy noticed me. "Ivy? What are *you* doing here?"

I looked back, sheepishly. Before I could answer, Bryn's head whipped around and she stood up to see me better. "Impossible!" she hissed. "Don't tell me *she's* the one who got the extra ticket? Is this a joke? This is so insulting to our trade!"

"Bryn." York's voice was quiet. "Don't say another word to her. It wasn't Ivy's choice."

His tone sent a chill through me, and it must have affected Bryn too, because she sat down in a huff. She grumbled behind her workstation. I noticed York pressing his hands against his thigh like they were bothering him again.

"Relax, York," Percy said, as he noticed York fidgeting too. "You're probably just feeling unprepared because you haven't practiced or sold anything. But I'm sure you'll still do a decent job."

He might have meant to be encouraging, but it sounded condescending. A flare of heat torched my chest over his arrogant assessment of York and the way his shoulders relaxed when he found what he perceived as weakness. Percy looked away to judge the other contestants, sizing up and dismissing the competition. Another swell of anger flooded me. I wanted York to beat them.

I wanted to beat them.

I'd never wanted to win so badly at something in my entire life.

This wasn't my trade, but somehow I had gotten this chance too. Maybe this could be *my* moment. The moment when something unexpected and amazing happened to me. *I'd* win the competition and get the respect I'd always dreamed of. I couldn't help but imagine everyone's surprise and awe. No one would care I'd failed as an Arborist; they would only think about how I had been destined to be a Carver.

A small flame of hope lit in my heart. Maybe I could pull this off.

I used to enjoy Carving. I'd never thought I was that terrible before I was moved to the Arborist trade. Maybe I just needed more time. Now was my chance to prove I could be in the prestigious trade. My heart began to race with new purpose as I tried to remember every Carving technique I'd ever learned.

The room faded as I studied the tools in my cuff and looked at the smaller unopened bag. From its size, I knew the statue would need to be carved very small. That meant every detail mattered.

I glanced at the clock—only a couple of minutes to go. York was wiping his hands on his pants as if they were burning or sweating. I tried to catch his eye, but he was focused on breathing and staying calm. I was overwhelmed with guilt, seeing how his hands were affecting him. His hands wouldn't be bothering him right now, if not for me taking him to the Tree Garden.

Mr. Mallon and another judge stepped inside the room.

The Count's Woodworking Tournament was about to begin.

THIRTY-THREE

Every voice faded into silence as Mr. Mallon walked to the center of the room.

He took off his hat and wiped his forehead with a handkerchief, already looking hot in his suit despite the chilly weather outside.

"Contestants, welcome to the Count's Woodworking Tournament." His deep voice carried across the room. "First, I'd like to congratulate each of you on passing Qualifications. You would not be sitting in this room if you were not extremely talented. But as you know, only the very best will win today, and only a few will be able to fulfill the rigorous requirements of this year's Tournament. The requirements this year are perhaps the most difficult in Windermere history. The item you must carve is a ship, representing Windermere's trade. The ship must not be taller than five inches. The sails must also be in perfect proportion to the body. The ship cannot be any wider than 3 inches—"

A few huffs of disbelief filled the room. Mr. Mallon paused, waiting until the room was silent again.

"Yes." His eyes glittered, his voice quiet. "As I said, only the best of you will win."

The room had become so silent we could hear the rain hitting the windows. A chill went through me as I looked at York. He was focused only on Mr. Mallon. But he didn't look discouraged; he looked ready to grab his bag and start carving. I was glad.

"These challenging measurements are to ensure the winner has utterly perfected this trade and can uphold the title of Master Carver. We will judge you on the originality of design, execution, and finish. The ship should also demonstrate a certain difficulty in skill set. Be sure to remove all blemishes and sawdust from your work. It could mean the difference between first and second place. I will be walking among you, observing. Cheating will be dealt with most severely. This includes copying another's work, watching another for inspiration, or using tools that were not included in your cuff. If anyone is caught breaking these rules, they will clear their table immediately and leave the Tournament. Their career as a Carver will also be over. Does everyone understand?"

His eyes scanned the room as we each nodded. Satisfied, he continued.

"You each have the same wooden block and limited tools. Your skill alone will make your ship stand out above the rest. The ship with the most detail and most accurate measurements at the end of this Tournament wins."

The other judge behind Mr. Mallon rang the bell to start the Tournament.

I nervously tore my bag open along with everyone else. A small piece of white wood thudded onto the table. Surprised, I picked it up, marveling at its unique color and softness. Where had this come from? I'd never come across or heard of a tree that produced wood like this in all my Arborist training. It was so soft, almost velvety. I wondered if this wood was used in every Tournament.

My newfound hope of winning plummeted. This was the smallest piece of wood I had ever worked with. It meant that every cut would have to be chosen carefully.

I slipped a protective glove over my hand and pulled out the tools in my cuff. There were only four variations of a knife and chisel, the same we all started training with. Thankfully I had used them all before.

I felt a little bit better when I heard sighs of frustration around the room. They were probably disappointed to be using beginner tools when they were so much more advanced. However, York was already bent into his workstation, undeterred.

I took out a pencil and began to lightly trace the outline of a ship. The wood was so white, that the charcoal lines showed up easily. I frowned as even the lightest touch of the pencil made an impression on the wood. I would have to be very careful when I carved. I could see that the tools would push further into the wood than I wanted them to.

It was another hour before I slipped the first chisel from my leather cuff and began carving.

The room was filled with the sounds of Mr. Mallon's footsteps, the clinking of tools, the scraping of wood, and the steady pounding of rain on the roof. I wondered if the crowd had been washed away, or if they were still huddled around the merchant tents, buying their yearly goods.

My neck was sore and tense. I rolled my shoulders and wiped my forehead with my arm. I wasn't hot, but my forehead was damp from stress as I concentrated on making the finest cut in the wood. I'd forgotten the strain I felt from Carving, how my shoulders reflexively pressed up to my ears, how my hand clenched the tools as I tried to catch any mistake before it happened. I was not a natural at this; it was even worse than being an Arborist. I liked watching others because they made it look so easy, and I loved the smell of wood. But being the one holding the knife and concentrating on the work was hard.

I held my breath and scooped out the tiniest piece of wood with my knife, trying very hard not to dig too deep. I sighed. I was never going to finish if I was too scared to make a proper cut. Then I remembered Mr. Gable once saying, *Try to imagine the shape inside the material. It's easier to carve if you imagine what the figure will look like.*

I closed my eyes and imagined the ship I had designed. It was the broken ship I'd seen on the beach so long ago. I knew my ship would never be as beautiful as the others, so maybe if I made an intentional shipwreck, I would have a chance. I breathed out and opened my eyes.

Then I began to make shallow passes over the white wood, peeling off slices so thin, they were nearly transparent. As I envisioned the broken-down ship, a calm, meditative state washed over me. I imagined that day on the beach, the waves and fog. The strong man and the rider who'd been so full of life. The webbing of light around the ship ... soon I felt relaxed and freed of all my anxiety as I remembered how alive I had felt that day. I began to enjoy making the ship come to life.

Only the thinnest spirals of wood fell to the floor from our workbenches. As the official and Mr. Mallon walked around, their feet crunched over the wood shavings. After a while, I was able to block even that sound out. I was pulled deep into concentration, more so than I had ever been. I knew, as everyone else did, that one tiny mistake would ruin my block.

Time became irrelevant. I wasn't sure how long we had been working. While I focused on cutting out the little sails, making sure that they fit within the height requirement, I was distracted by a glint of light.

I looked up. Mr. Mallon and the official were talking in a corner, but their backs were toward me. I quickly glanced over at York. He was leaned back in his chair and his ship was at the edge of his desk. But I didn't understand what I was seeing.

Curious, I leaned back further in my chair so I could see into his workstation better. Parts of his ship were strangely catching the light. But York didn't seem to notice. He brushed the fresh pile of white wood shavings off his desk onto the floor.

Then he shook his hands out, just like he had when he said they were tingling. He continued to work ... But I couldn't look away.

There was light around his ship, just like the dust in my father's journal.

And around the broken ship.

And around Cora.

I set down my tool and rubbed my eyes. I was seeing things again, but this time, it was because of York.

I looked again.

York's carving didn't look like wood anymore. I squinted—how could his white wood look like *that*?

York wiped his face but didn't seem to notice anything different. He kept working. It seemed to me that the harder he worked and the more he concentrated, the brighter the ship shone.

As York moved to carve a last detail on his ship, his knife wouldn't cut into the ship the same way. The material had changed.

York finally seemed to notice. He sat back slowly, confused.

His ship now shone a muted golden color. And it was translucent.

A firm hand clamped down on my shoulder, but before I could cry out in surprise, Mr. Mallon leaned down and whispered, "Ivy, you have broken the rules of the Tournament. Remove the cuff and leave through the door you came in." He pointed to the side door. "Someone will show you where to wait for me. We will talk later."

My stomach twisted. He must have thought I was cheating because I was watching York. "But—"

"Do not argue. You *will* leave now," Mr. Mallon whispered, his voice sharp as a steel blade.

His large hand squeezed my shoulder; I could feel his heat through the thin fabric of my shirt. I stood quickly, my heart hammering as I untied my cuff and left it on the table.

I turned toward the door but stopped when I saw Mr. Mallon

walk over to York. He threw a small black cloth over York's ship before whisking it off the desk and slipping it into his pocket.

York looked up, ready to protest—until he saw it was Mr. Mallon. He swallowed, his face ashen. He looked like he'd been drained of every ounce of energy and was too exhausted to think clearly.

"Stand and leave without a scene. Don't make me repeat myself."

York looked to where I stood and his brow furrowed in confusion. But he stood too, like he wasn't sure what had just happened.

The door was only steps from our desks, and we were concealed by the wood panels. While this felt like the biggest ordeal to me, one that lasted forever, it took place in seconds and without anyone noticing. Everyone kept their heads down as we walked to the door. It opened noiselessly. No one looked up. And no one saw Mr. Mallon pocket York's ship.

With a sinking feeling, I exited through the side door with York following me.

Together, we left the Count's Woodworking Tournament behind.

THIRTY-FOUR
THE COUNT

Flickering candles and the glow from the stone fireplace were all that lit the dim room.

Heavy drapes hung over the windows, shielding the sunlight. A thin layer of dust covered bookcases that lined the walls.

An older man with a striking but worn face sat in a leather chair. An abundance of black hair, now peppered with white, covered his head, and his bushy eyebrows were drawn together in contemplation. A chime from an old clock hidden somewhere in a bookshelf stirred him from his thoughts.

His long fingers caressed the bone-white queen as he debated using her in his next move. Finally, he plunked down the chess piece and captured a black knight.

"Checkmate." The Count's voice remained emotionless and flat.

"You win again," the man sitting opposite of him said, sounding cheerful despite just losing.

The Count inspected the younger man's face, noting the absence of tension in his eyes and mouth. Jack always appeared unruffled, despite losing week after week. The Count congratulated himself on finding such a malleable young man.

"Your skills are improving. However, if you practiced more, you might occasionally win."

Jack smiled. "I doubt I would ever surpass your skills, but I appreciate your vote of confidence."

The Count didn't respond, although he was pleased with the answer. He prided himself on his excellent control over his emotions. He revealed them to no one. He was also of the opinion that other men were lesser than him. If *he* was pleased by Jack, he knew that Jack's personality could flatter and win over anyone. That also irked the Count, admitting that Jack naturally possessed a skill he did not.

He studied Jack's younger, stronger body, full head of dark hair, and blue eyes that always seemed too bright, too positive. He'd selected Jack as his heir because of his natural ability to move through the world with ease but found himself always slightly irritated by it too. This ability highlighted the Count's own weakness with people. But he consoled himself knowing he wielded Jack's gifts as his own, and that counted for something.

He would always be the Master, Jack the puppet.

The Count settled back into his chair now that the game was done. "Has the Stygian ship arrived?"

Jack nodded. "Two days ago. It took the usual route to avoid Windermere, but veered slightly off course due to thick fog and some delays. I inspected the ship myself and everything should be unloaded later this afternoon. They'll take the back road through the hills into the castle, as always."

A knock on the door startled them.

They were not startled by the sound of the knock itself but by which door the knocking came from. It was a door that only a select few knew of, being that it was hidden inside the bookshelf next to the stone fireplace.

The door creaked open and a tall man dressed in a black suit stepped inside the room. His usually coifed hair was now limp against his head and his face seemed flushed from hurrying.

"Mr. Mallon," the Count said slowly. "This is a most unusual time to visit."

Mr. Mallon nodded and walked over to a table that held several glass decanters. He set down his hat and picked up the largest glass bottle, which held a dark, glittering liquid, and began to pour himself a drink.

"I hope you don't mind," he murmured, as the liquid drained into the crystal glass. "It's been a long day."

"Not at all." The Count masked his annoyance that Mr. Mallon was helping himself to his rarest and most expensive drink —a drink only made on the Count's family's legendary island and rumored to include drops of starlight. Mr. Mallon knew this. The Count considered what this action implied; Mr. Mallon had never helped himself to the best drink before. He watched the man more carefully.

Mr. Mallon sat down, took a small sip, and smiled in pure pleasure.

"How was the Tournament?" Jack asked.

"Excellent, excellent. Both this drink and the Tournament."

Silence descended over the room.

Jack and the Count waited for Mr. Mallon to continue, but he appeared to be enamored with the fine quality of his drink. He sipped it very, very slowly.

The Count cleared his throat and glanced pointedly at the clock.

Mr. Mallon looked up and glanced pointedly toward Jack.

"Speak freely. As my heir, Jack is now privy to our talks. He will also be working with Dr. Ply," the Count responded.

"Ah. Well, then. It seems as though we have another gifted Transposer in town." Mr. Mallon swirled his drink casually as he waited for a reaction.

As usual, the Count's face remained blank, but inside he felt a flash of surprise. Dr. Ply had not foreseen this.

Jack spoke so the Count would not have to. "That's very unusual," he said, leaning forward.

"And unexpected," the Count replied slowly. He hated being ambushed with unknown information. Again, he wondered how Dr. Ply had missed this. "Our current transposer is becoming, shall we say, rather difficult. I believe we will soon require another."

"It's still Carl, isn't it? Perhaps I can be of some service there. This new Transposer is young, possibly too inexperienced right now for the usual task," Mr. Mallon said, laying out his terms. "You will have to be patient while he is prepared. Then you may have him."

The Count's eyes narrowed. "How inexperienced?"

Mr. Mallon hesitated. "As you know, I won't divulge details until the transposer is delivered. It's much easier for me to do my job if I don't have to worry about your people spying." He smiled as if to show he meant no offense.

The Count did not smile back.

Mr. Mallon shifted uncomfortably in the dark leather chair but continued to lock eyes with the Count. He would not budge on his terms.

"Very well. You must have your reasons." A threatening edge crept into the Count's voice. "And up till now, I have had no reason to doubt you. But exactly how long will this take? I have a right to know when I can expect him."

"Yes, I can see no harm in that." Mr. Mallon thought hard for a moment. "His talent is advanced, but certain skills are lacking. In fact, he may be more talented than any other Transposer you have acquired. I believe one month will be sufficient . . . then he will be stronger and ready to handle life at the castle."

"Any attachments we need to be aware of?" the Count asked casually.

"I don't believe so. The family is not held in the highest regard in town, so I don't think it's anything I can't handle. His story will be similar to Carl's—people will believe it happily because they would like to think this young man finally escaped a rough life."

The Count picked up his glass and took a long sip. After a moment, he spoke. "I trust you will let us know if anything goes wrong or needs to be managed."

"Of course."

"Then we will wait. Thirty days *only*." The Count's voice sounded ominous. A warning.

Jack spoke quickly as if to settle the Count's temper. "Send word when I can bring the new transposer to the castle."

"Very good." Mr. Mallon finished his drink and looked inside the empty glass, disappointed. He set the glass back on the tray but made no move to leave.

The Count cleared his throat deliberately. "Something else you'd like to discuss, Mr. Mallon?"

Mr. Mallon nodded. "Yes, and I think you're going to be very interested. I will require your fetching services much earlier, Jack. Today, actually."

Jack looked to the Count, who brought his long, thin fingertips together and rested his jaw on them. "I'm listening."

"It has to do with a name you haven't heard in a while."

The Count simply inclined his head in a silent invitation for Mr. Mallon to continue.

"It concerns Mr. Rune. Specifically, his daughter, Ivy."

THIRTY-FIVE

When we stepped into the narrow hallway, we found that same woman there, waiting.

She turned on her heel. "Follow me."

York and I walked side by side in silence down the dim hallway. I peeked over at him, startled to find a dazed look on his face as he looked down at his hands. I didn't think he even noticed what was happening to us, or maybe he didn't realize he should be worried about it. He was still thinking about what he had just done with the wood.

The woman stopped and opened a door. She stepped to the side and gestured for me to go in. I swallowed and stepped inside a small office. There was only room for one desk and chair. The wooden walls were blank and empty. It smelled musty, like it wasn't used often.

"Do not leave until someone comes for you," she said sternly.

She only meant me. I whirled around to protest and found the door shut in my face. I pulled on the knob—it was locked. Panic ballooned in my chest. I hadn't even asked York if he was OK. Where were they taking him?

And why had they locked me inside here, alone? Even if they thought I cheated, why did I need to be kept here?

I took a few deep breaths, trying to calm myself before I collapsed into a full-blown panic. Maybe they were just making sure I didn't interrupt the rest of the Tournament. Mr. Mallon clearly didn't trust me to listen, especially with how much I argued with him. They would come get me as soon as the Tournament was over. It wouldn't be long.

I took a step back from the door. If they thought York and I had cheated, they probably didn't want us together before they questioned us. My stomach sank. I didn't think my life could get worse, but this was really bad for York. Being disqualified from Carving . . . it was unthinkable. It had never happened before.

I turned and sat in the chair, wondering how long it would be before someone came back. Would it be the woman, or Mr. Mallon? Or the Taylors? They would be so disappointed in me. They would learn all at once that I'd failed as an Arborist, gotten eliminated from the Count's Tournament, and had no job or place to live.

I buried my head in my hands. How had everything turned upside down? I should never have gotten the extra ticket. My life was over.

How could I explain that I hadn't cheated, that I'd been staring at York's ship because his wood had changed into light— or had it been gold? I wasn't completely sure what York had made, but it was something new. What did it *mean* for us? That he could make light, and I could see it?

I wasn't sure how long I sat, waiting, going over and over solutions to fix this. The Tournament must have ended by now. Where was Mr. Mallon, and where was York? I wondered if his parents had been asked to come get him. Why weren't the Taylors here to get me? The longer I sat alone, the less today made any sense.

There were voices in the hallway. My heart lifted, hopeful, as I went to the door and pressed my ear against it. Another door creaked open down the hall, and I heard a deep voice. It sounded similar to Mr. Pembroke's, but I wasn't certain. It could have been Mr. Mallon. But if it was York's parents, was that good or bad?

I heard more footsteps, heading closer to my door. I jumped back just as the door opened. The woman stepped inside. She held a tray with tea and a sandwich. My stomach growled.

"Mr. Mallon wanted to make sure you ate."

I rubbed my arm. "Is he coming soon?"

"He's talking with York's family right now."

"Oh."

"You sound worried."

I stared at her. "We were just kicked out of the Tournament. Of course I am."

"Oh, about that. Mr. Mallon wanted me to tell you he may have acted in haste. York's ship was simply the most detailed he'd seen in years and he wanted to inspect it further, as he was sure it would be the winner. And, after inspecting your ship, it was clear to him that you were not copying York's at all. There was nothing in the least bit comparable."

I cringed at the insult, imagining what my ship had looked like compared to his. But I knew York's ship hadn't looked like anyone else's in the room, either.

"So York is not in trouble?" I asked, carefully.

"Not if you consider winning the Tournament as trouble."

I sat, shocked. "He won?"

The woman frowned. "I've said too much. Forget that last part. Nothing's been announced yet."

I frowned back. I knew nothing about her, but I found it hard to believe she would let something slip that she wasn't supposed to.

"Mr. Mallon also wanted me to ask why you were staring at York's ship? If you were not cheating, he would like to know what you were looking at?"

Her tone was casual and she set down the tray in front of me and busied herself with pouring tea into the cup, as if her question was just friendly conversation.

Alarm bells sounded in my head. I swallowed and said carefully, "I didn't mean to stare. As Mr. Mallon said, it was the most impressive ship I'd ever seen."

"There was no other reason you looked away from your work?"

"No," I said, firmly. "And I wasn't cheating. I swear it."

She nodded. "Mr. Mallon will be glad to hear that."

She moved back to the door and I panicked at the thought of being locked in again.

"Can I leave? If I'm not in trouble?"

"That is Mr. Mallon's decision. It shouldn't be much longer now."

The door clicked shut. I sank back down in front of the tea and sandwich. My hunger overtook my thoughts—the sandwich was from Wilder's Bakery. Just French bread with turkey and cheese, but it was delicious. After that, I drank the black tea, wishing for cream, but it was warm and had a bite to it.

Once my hunger was satisfied, I thought about what the woman said. Was it possible I didn't have to worry about York anymore, and he had won? How much longer would I have to wait to see him? I hadn't heard any more noise from the hallway.

The relief I felt that York was going to be a Carver—not just that, a *Master Carver*—filled me. If it was true, he was OK, and I was, too. I could work with him, help him. And I could still follow my father's clues, even though I'd hit a dead end.

I leaned my head on the table. This had been the longest day of my life. I was ready for it to be over. If they didn't think I had cheated, why was I still here? Maybe Mr. Mallon was busy announcing the winner. That meant the list would be up for the trades, including whoever inherited Forest and Fern—and everyone would know it wasn't me.

Time slipped by and the next thing I knew, the door opened again.

I jerked awake at the sound, realizing I'd dozed off. I rubbed my eyes and smoothed my hair back from my face, then jumped to my feet as a stranger walked into the room.

Except he wasn't a stranger—he was the rider from the beach.

THIRTY-SIX

He didn't look real, and he certainly didn't look like he belonged in Windermere.

He was taller than I remembered. His broad shoulders stretched under his dark shirt, the color again reminding me of black sand, his tousled dark hair curled slightly above his collar. His eyes were the color of the sea and when they found mine, he flashed a friendly smile.

I stood, too shocked to smile back. I was suddenly aware of how awful I must look.

That same energy I felt from the beach radiated from him and made my heart skip. It was new, full of life and places I had never been but wanted to experience. Instead of shrinking away from the unfamiliar feeling, I wanted to lean in.

"Hello, Ivy." He walked toward me and extended his hand. "I'm Jack."

My hand disappeared in his and I swallowed, my mouth suddenly dry. "Do I know you?"

He seemed surprised by the question. "No, why?"

"You seem like you already know me."

"No." His smile returned as he released my hand. "But I do know of you."

Given the circumstances, I wasn't sure if that was good or not. "Where is Mr. Mallon?" I asked, looking behind him.

"At the moment, occupied."

Jack reached back to close the door and his eyes swept the room. A frown creased his face.

"You were left here overnight. I'm sorry. You should have been moved to a more comfortable room."

No wonder I was so stiff. Things were not as fine as the woman made them out to be. Maybe they hadn't believed me about not seeing anything different about York's ship. But how could they know?

I rubbed the tightness from my neck, irritated about being left in here. "The Tournament is obviously over."

"Yes."

"And why are you here, exactly?"

Jack looked surprised by my bluntness. "Because I am the one who takes care of these matters."

I narrowed my eyes at that vague answer. It reminded me of the way he'd handled the strong man by the ship. He was used to being unchallenged. Maybe people listened because of how he spoke; his words were delivered polished and crisp, equal parts authority and charm.

I realized again that I couldn't identify him by his clothes. They were a similar dark color to the carefree ones he wore that day on the beach, but today the cut was more elegant and refined.

I tucked a loose strand of hair back behind my ear. Next to him, I felt disheveled. "What matters?"

"Matters that concern the Count, as I am his heir."

My eyes widened, and now I studied him more closely. "I didn't know the Count had a son."

Jack shrugged. "He doesn't."

"Then—"

"I didn't say anything about being family. Only that I am his prospective heir."

"What does that mean, prospective?"

His eyes twinkled as if amused by my questions. "I'll explain another time. Right now, I am here to discuss you."

"Why? Am I in trouble?"

"This was poorly handled and you must be feeling uneasy. Please sit and I'll explain everything."

I sank back down in the hard chair I'd slept in. Jack leaned against the desk and folded his arms. His voice took a more serious tone. "Ivy, I also work for Dr. Ply."

I felt the smallest flicker of recognition at the name, but I couldn't place where I'd heard it before. "Who is Dr. Ply?"

"He works for the Count."

"How interesting," I said casually as if all this new information didn't have my heart racing.

Jack smiled and crossed his long legs. "Dr. Ply requires an assistant for his work at the castle. We understand that you have skills as an Arborist."

I grimaced. "I failed my test. And I've been stuck in this room because Mr. Mallon thought I cheated at the Count's Woodworking Tournament. I don't think you want me."

Jack nodded. "We know all that. But there are many things you don't know. Like your family history. Dr. Ply thought you would like to know now."

A chill crept through my veins. I fought to keep my voice calm. "My family history?"

"You know that your father was both a Professor and an Arborist?"

I nodded. The mention of my father suddenly had me feeling like I was falling. This was not what I'd expected and I wasn't sure I was ready for it.

"Well, what you do not know is that your father also worked at the castle. For the Count and Dr. Ply."

I felt like the ground was rushing up to swallow me, but I managed to keep my face blank. My father had drawn the Count's crest, but I thought ... I'd thought he had been researching the Count. My breath felt too shallow, like I couldn't take in air fully.

I had gotten it wrong, again.

My father had been working for him.

My mind raced through every clue, trying to connect them quickly and stay ahead of whatever Jack might reveal next.

The carving tool. The Count's crest. The secret compartment. Carl at the castle. Light around the broken ship, the strong man. Cora. The Tree Garden. And now, light from York. The light I'd seen because of my father's journal.

Did all his clues lead to the castle? To the Count?

"Of course, it was a closely guarded secret," Jack said, watching me carefully. "Dr. Ply is very protective of his work. No one from Windermere was allowed to know your father helped. You discovered that he was in charge of the Tree Garden, but what you don't know was that he also worked at the castle."

"How did you know I discovered the Tree Garden?" I asked, raising my eyes to meet his.

His expression gave away nothing. "The Tree Garden is under the Count's protection."

In other words, they had been watching me. "Why? It's nowhere near his land."

Jack shrugged. "You may learn the answer to that in the future."

"How long did my father work at the castle?" I asked.

"Many years."

"How many exactly?"

"At least a few, but Dr. Ply would know for sure."

I stared down at my hands in my lap, feeling like my whole life was slowly unraveling, thread by thread. If he'd worked at the castle for two years, then I would have been about five years old when he'd started. My mother would have been gone one year or less. Had that pushed him to work for the Count in secret? Or had he worked there for longer? Had my mother found out and left?

This was unbelievable.

No one was allowed to know about the castle, or visit, or talk about it. But my father had. And now I was being invited there?

When Jack spoke again, his voice was softer. "As you know, the castle doesn't normally employ people from Windermere. There are a few rare exceptions. Because of your father, Dr. Ply sees potential in you and thinks that you'll be a good candidate for this work. If you agree, you will come to live at the castle. Permanently."

I shook my head, feeling numb. "Permanently? As in, my entire life?"

He nodded, and I thought some of the light in his eyes dimmed. "Yes."

I wondered if he liked living in the castle. At that moment, I didn't think so, but then again, he was the Count's heir. He must. If my father had created this position, I doubted I was smart enough to fill it. This would only be another failure.

"Does Dr. Ply work as an Arborist?" I asked.

"No. Dr. Ply is a very distinguished and respected scientist in lands beyond Windermere. He can explain his work better than I can. But I will tell you that he is extremely demanding. He's not a man who forgives mistakes easily. This position requires a certain amount of decorum. You'll need to control your emotions and remain impartial."

I frowned, unsure what that meant.

"And there is a condition to this offer," he added.

I stared at him in disbelief. "Besides giving up my whole life?"

Jack's lips pressed together as if smothering a smile. The light was back in his blue eyes. "Yes. You're not allowed to tell anyone that you work at the castle. You won't be allowed to visit Windermere again. The castle must maintain its privacy. It won't be compromised for your sake."

"I can't ever come back?" My heart sank at the thought of never seeing York again. Or Mr. Gable. Or tasting another sweet roll, or smelling the scent of fresh wood being carved. Or walking by Forest and Fern. Even though it wasn't mine, it had always been there, like an anchor. Could I leave Windermere? It was all I'd ever known.

"Unfortunately not."

"But what will people be told when they realize I'm gone?"

"Mr. Mallon didn't announce you as the winner of the ticket; they won't even know you were in or left the competition. A story will circulate that a distant relative across the sea was made aware of your situation and claimed you. We'll give Mr. Taylor as few details as possible. He'll be instructed to imply, to those who ask, that it's only for a short time. Eventually, people in Windermere will accept that you liked your visit so much that you chose to stay."

Something about this explanation bothered me. Mr. Taylor wouldn't like lying. And York would never believe this. "But everyone knows I don't have relatives anywhere else."

"Your mother did."

I drew in a breath and a full moment passed before my voice was under control. "What do you know of her?"

Now Jack looked surprised. For a moment, his guard slipped and he seemed younger. "Your mother was not from Windermere. Surely you knew that?"

I hated the pity on his face. It was unfair that he knew more about my life than I did. I forced any weakness from my voice. "Where was she from?"

Jack's expression changed as if he remembered his position. "You should speak with Dr. Ply. When you get to the castle, you can ask him."

"You're assuming I decide to come."

"Won't you? I must say, I hope you do." He smiled again, his easy charm back.

"Why?" I asked, my heart thumping unevenly.

Jack shrugged. "Because sometimes, it's rather dull, and you talk more than anyone else there does."

I frowned, not sure if that was a compliment or not. But it did make me think. My father had been very reserved, and Jack said this scientist needed an assistant with restraint. Did they think I was like my father?

They couldn't be more wrong.

"Why did my father choose to work at the castle?" I asked, ignoring his last comment.

"I would assume he was enticed by working on important matters with a distinguished scientist."

I chewed my lip, considering. Nothing drew my father's attention more than his own work.

But what if he'd discovered something more important than that? Something more important than the entire Arborist trade? That was interesting.

Maybe I had to go to the castle to solve his clues. Maybe his clues were not for an Arborist after all. Maybe they were for someone who knew about his work at the castle?

If I went, I could uncover what had happened to York and me. Light had changed for me because of my father's journal, but York was changed in the Tree Garden. I had to figure out what that meant, what it was.

Cora lived there; she had the light around her too. Maybe she would be able to tell me what it meant. Once I figured it out, I'd come back and help York. I knew I could come back; I'd seen Cora and Carl in town. So I'd figure out a way. They didn't need to know.

Just like they didn't need to know about the dust in my father's journal or the light. I would keep that a secret, just like my father had kept his secrets.

I was done with self-doubt and crippling worry about my future. This could be my chance to become someone new, someone worth something on my own.

Jack was analyzing me as if he was reading the thoughts rushing across my face. He seemed satisfied that he had me, and somehow, that didn't bother me. Jack was ... interesting. He was the Count's heir. I wanted to know more about him. I found myself noticing everything he did, in ways I never had with anyone else.

A realization struck and suddenly, I felt like a fool. "I don't have a choice, do I?"

Jack shook his head, almost apologetic. "I'm afraid not."

I glared at him. "Then why not just drag me out of here? Why present it to me as a choice?"

His voice was soft when he answered. "Because I wanted you to feel like you had one. I would have."

That startled me. It sounded ominous. Jack must have seen my reaction because his face cleared of all emotion and he smiled again, easily. As if he was joking.

But I was not fooled this time. I cleared my throat, wondering what I was getting myself into. "Then I have no choice but to accept."

"Dr. Ply will be glad to hear it. If you're ready, you can leave the vest on the desk. You won't need it at the castle."

"Now?" I jumped up; this was happening too fast. "Don't I at least get to say goodbye to anyone? How will I know who took over Forest and Fern? And my horse, Loon. She has to come with me!"

"You have a horse?" Jack looked at me, curiously. Was he thinking about his beautiful black horse?

I nodded. "She's the only family I have left."

A single knock rapped on the door.

As if he had been waiting for it, Jack stood. He looked down at me, his blue eyes soft. "I am sorry, Ivy. But it's time for us to leave. I promise I'll speak to both Mr. Taylor and Dr. Ply about your horse. But as for goodbyes, the answer is no."

"Promise you won't forget about Loon," I said, knowing I had no right to demand anything. "I can't leave her behind."

Jack nodded. "I understand. I promise."

I swallowed, my knees suddenly weak. This was what I wanted, but now I was suddenly unsure. With shaking fingers, I unbuttoned the black vest and folded it neatly, leaving it on the desk.

Jack opened the door and gestured for me to go first. I took a deep, steadying breath and walked through the doorway.

I was leaving everything I'd ever known and cared about behind. I was leaving Windermere.

And I was going to live at the Count's castle.

Forever.

Acknowledgments

This book has truly been a labor of love. It has gone through countless transformations to become a series I'm really proud of. It would not have been possible without the support I received from my amazing family and friends.

To each person who read the earliest drafts of this book, thank you so much for your time and for letting me share work that was far from ready to be published.

To my editor, Megan McCullough, thank you for making this book better. To my cover designer, Krafigs Designs, thank you for creating such a magical cover! I love it so much. To Kim Churchill, thank you for bringing the audiobook to life!

To my beta readers, Laura Tiffany, Raina Bray, Holly Schacht, Lauren Terry, Toshia Wagner, Josh Schacht, and Anika Watkins, thank you for your excellent feedback!

To my parents. Thank you for childhood surrounded by nature, woodworking in the garage, pursuing art, and pushing us to make our own way.

To Laura Tiffany, thank you for reading (and remembering) every draft! Thank you for always being available and encouraging. Again, sorry about all the name changes.

To my readers, thank you! I hope you found a place to escape into for a little while. I hope you were entertained and intrigued. Books really are magic and I'm looking forward to sharing the rest of this world with you!

To my little family, Aaron, Kennedy, and London. You guys

are my everything. My light, my loves, and my joy. Thank you for supporting me and giving me time to write. Aaron, I couldn't have done this without you and your support. Thank you.

Most importantly, thank you, God. For leveling mountains, and always watching over me.

About the Author

Sara Knightly is a recovering nomad who lives in Boise, ID with her husband and two daughters. She spends her days dreaming up the next story idea, searching for the perfect coffee shop, and planning another trip to the Redwood Forest.

TURN THE PAGE FOR
MORE . . .

CASTLE EVER DARK

CHAPTER ONE

The carriage rolled down the dirt path, stopping by the Count's marble gates.

Jack left his seat next to mine and jumped down to push the heavy gates open. I took a moment to examine his broad shoulders, blue eyes, and tousled black hair. A stranger who had shown up moments ago and was taking me from Windermere, the only home I'd ever known. My eyes moved to the two sea serpents that stood sentinel on either side of the gate. Their writhing bodies and claws stretched out, ready to maul anyone who passed beneath them and dared to enter the Count's land.

Instead of fear, a lump formed in my throat. The first time I'd seen these serpents, I'd been with York. Now I was going into the castle without him. I felt more alone than ever.

Jack and I had left Windermere without seeing a soul. I'd whispered goodbye to the empty town, wondering if it really was the last time I would see it. Next to me was my bag, containing my father's final journal, the wooden cube, and my mother's owl: The objects that had started me down this road; the clues that had opened my eyes to the strange things happening just outside of my small town.

I shivered and pulled my jacket around me. At my feet was my late father's leather satchel, packed by Mrs. Taylor—the woman who had taken me in when I'd had no one, and who I would never see again. When I'd seen it inside the carriage, I'd known it was the only goodbye I'd get. No one was coming to save me.

Everyone in Windermere would be told I had a new life across the sea and that I was happy to go. They would never know I was just down the road inside the Count's castle.

I took a deep breath, reminding myself that not everything was lost. Somehow, York had won the Count's Woodworking Tournament. My best friend had succeeded in getting away from his angry father and would open his own Carving shop. York's future was secure in Windermere. *I* was the one with no reason left to stay.

I had ruined my chance at my trade, lost my childhood home, and been disqualified from the Count's Woodworking Tournament.

Again, I puzzled over why they wanted me at the castle. Was it really to be a scientist's assistant, as Jack had told me? No one at the castle knew about the items in my bag, or that I had a burgeoning ability to perceive light differently than the average person—I didn't think.

But I did know that my father's clues had led me to this gate and I had to uncover why.

I had to know why I saw light around certain people from the castle, and what that light meant. And how York had transformed his wood to gold in the Tournament.

And I needed to pass between these sea serpents to get my answers.

The carriage shook as Jack climbed back in and whistled at the horses to continue. I held my breath as we crossed the threshold into the Count's land.

The property inside the gates was nothing like I'd imagined. The woods felt hollow, not bursting with life like the forests around Windermere. I looked around, seeing nothing but thin trees and silver dew drops clinging to blades of grass. Mist seeped through the trees like cold fingers. It was eerily still. I shivered again.

We followed the path as it wound through the forest, the only sound was wheels rolling over packed dirt. Jack hadn't spoken much during our journey here, but the silence was not uncomfortable. I guessed he was giving me space to be upset, or to prepare myself for what was ahead of me.

But I didn't know how to prepare for any of this. All my life I had been told to stay away from the Count's castle, that the Count was a recluse and had no interest in our town beyond the Carving trade. But now I knew that wasn't true. Things were happening out here.

Somewhere high above, a raven shrieked. I jumped, the hair on my neck rising.

"Alright?" Jack asked. I could feel that he wanted to laugh, but didn't.

"It's colder here," I remarked, ignoring the part of me that wanted to tell him to turn back. The part that was sure I'd made a big mistake coming here. But I had no choice. I had nowhere else to go. Mr. Mallon, the Count's Regent, would never let me set foot in town again.

"I should warn you, the castle is always cold," Jack remarked.

My stomach sank as glimpses of stone grew more frequent through the trees. As we followed the path out of the tree line, the castle loomed in front of us.

It was enormous. Formidable. I felt like an ant, squinting up to the highest points that stretched into the grey sky. It was an ancient fortress made of stone towers, aged balconies, and countless windows. I wondered which window was the Count's.

Chills rolled through me as we passed through the vast, unkept lawn. The path split around a large stone fountain that reminded me of the fountain in Windermere's town square, except this one was dried up and cracked. Two stone knights on horses guarded the entrance by the door, but it looked as though their arms sagged under the weight of their swords.

Just as I wondered if the castle was truly abandoned and everyone I'd seen going into it that fated day with York was all in my head, a person stepped out of the tall wooden door.

It was a girl dressed in dark clothes similar to Jack's. Her black hair was woven tightly into a braid that laid over one shoulder. She watched us approach, but her thin lips never lifted in greeting. The solemn expression on her small, round face did not waver. She almost looked like a child. However, when we stopped before the door and her grey eyes found mine, I took that thought back immediately. There was an emptiness in her eyes and I had to look away. It was too unsettling.

Jack turned to me, his warm blue eyes a welcome relief from this girl's cold grey ones. "I'm afraid this is where we part. You need to get settled, and I need to take the horses to the stable."

The mention of the stables was like a knife to my heart. I already missed my own horse, Loon, and wished she was with us right now. But Jack had promised he would see about bringing her.

"You're not coming inside too?" I asked. Even though I'd just met him, I felt reluctant to leave his side.

His lips lifted. "Not just yet."

I stood, not wanting to seem afraid to go inside alone. Jack held my arm steady as I climbed down from the carriage. But as soon as my feet touched the ground, uncertainty overwhelmed me. I looked up at Jack, panicking. He handed down my bags and smiled as if he sensed how I felt.

"Chin up, Ivy. I'll see you around."

Then the carriage moved forward, drowning out my attempt at a parting reply. As it pulled away, the strange, silent girl and I stared at each other. I shifted uneasily, wishing I could look anywhere but her.

"Name?" The flatness of her tone matched her blank expression.

"Ivy Rune."

I searched her face for any indication that she recognized my name, or my father's, but her face remained stoic.

I swallowed. "I've come to work for Dr. Ply."

The girl nodded and turned back to the ancient wooden door. Only now I could see it was carved with strange symbols and patterns.

"Follow me." She disappeared inside without waiting for a response.

I grabbed my bags and hurried after her into the dark, narrow passage. We continued silently until the hallway opened into a stone courtyard with more dead grass. Every muscle in my body was tense and wary. I tried to brush the unease away, but it clung to me. I wanted to turn around.

"What's your name?" I asked.

"Anna."

"And what do you do here, Anna?"

She didn't respond.

We walked deeper and deeper into the castle, my apprehension and confusion growing with each step. The castle was bigger than it looked, but it felt like a ruin. The air was stiff and heavy. And even though we were the only ones walking through the hallways, I couldn't shake the feeling that we weren't alone.

It was still unbelievable to me that my father had walked under these chipped stone archways. Why had he worked here? What had his role been?

What would mine be?

It had to be different, that much I was sure of. Because my father had been allowed to live in town, and I was not. I felt another wave of longing for Windermere and York.

As we entered yet another silent courtyard, I finally saw another person, but my skin prickled at the wrongness of her.

A woman stood looking out of an arched window at a view hidden by fog.

There was an elegance to her like she had once been magnificent, but now she'd fallen into ruin like the stone around her. A crumbled velvet shawl hung from her thin shoulders, and the hem of her faded black dress was covered with dust.

She slowly turned to watch us pass. Her eyes and lips were lined with years and her hair was high on her head, encased in a black net.

My heart thudded as we passed by, but she did not smile or acknowledge us at all. I avoided her eyes, but not before I noticed one was blue. The other, violet.

I let out a breath when we turned the corner. I didn't have the courage to turn around and see if she was still watching. I wasn't even sure if she was real or a ghost, because Anna didn't slow or acknowledge the woman.

I couldn't stand the silence pressing in on me any longer.

"How long have you lived here, Anna?"

Anna stopped and turned to face me. "That's personal."

I stepped back, surprised. "It is? It's a common question to ask someone you've just met."

Her grey eyes studied me. Then she shrugged. "I'm not accustomed to conversation anymore. I've been here longer than I can remember not being here."

"What do you do?"

Anna sighed. "I was in training, but that ended. Now I'm on task."

"What does 'on task' mean?"

Anna turned on her heel. "Come. Dr. Ply doesn't appreciate being kept waiting."

My stomach dipped. The man my father had worked for, and who I would now work for. We continued on and finally arrived at two doors covered in the same strange carvings and symbols as the front door.

"This wing is called the Center. The first floor is offices, where you will work. The second is living quarters, where you will stay. You are not allowed anywhere else in the castle without permission or an escort."

"Is the castle always this empty?" Where were the people on

the ship, or Cora and Carl? Anyone would be a welcome addition to Anna's indifference.

She didn't respond.

I tried again. "That woman we passed . . . Does she work here too?"

"Stop with all the questions!" Anna snapped, revealing her frustration before she concealed it. "They will not make you a single friend here."

I bit down a response and followed her quietly, feeling the somberness in the air press into me again. After another flight of stairs, Anna stopped at a door and opened it, gesturing me inside.

"This is your room."

I walked inside, and my stomach dropped.

There were two rows of ten beds, each with a small dresser beside them. The only light came from two small windows on the far back wall, but their thick glass was covered with dust. The old wooden floors and bare walls made the room feel abandoned and cold. A crumbling fireplace sat in the center of the room, but there was no fire. A stack of chopped logs was piled beside it.

"Who else stays in here?" I asked, taking in the long room.

"Just you. Take your pick of the beds," Anna said as if that somehow made this situation better.

I walked to the bed closest to the fireplace and sat down, cringing at the thin and lumpy mattress. The blanket and pillow were even thinner. I stood back up on instinct as if I could leave, but then I realized I was really going to have to stay here. *Sleep* here. I didn't know if I could. Anna; the ghost woman; and now this horrid, cold room.

I couldn't live like this.

Panic built, making my shoulders tense. I took a deep breath. I couldn't lose it in front of this strange, emotionless girl.

"Before you meet Dr. Ply, he would like you to familiarize yourself with some of his research." Anna pointed to a large stack of papers sitting on a dresser.

The pile was nearly the size of my hand. "You want me to read *all* of that?"

"Dr. Ply thought an hour would suffice."

Without another word, she walked out of the room, leaving me all alone.